Whisper

by Cheryl Twaddle

Prologue

Edric paced back and forth along the path of stars that make up the Milky Way. Everything was complete yet he still felt restless. He should be feeling exhilarated; it all looked so beautiful. The stars, the planets, the galaxies; everything made to perfection but something was not quite right.

"I'm just not happy," he sighed and sat down. "How can something so beautiful make me feel so…so uncontrollably angry?"

He reached down and grabbed the planet he just finished creating. It shone a coppery brown and when he held it in his hands he could feel its warmth. He looked at it with fascination and then a great turmoil within started to rumble to the surface and his face dropped in dismay. His hands started to tighten around the planet and, before he could stop himself, he squeezed it until all that was left was dust. He opened his hands and watched as the dust floated through the stars and the blackness. A smile appeared on his face and a surge of excitement rose from the pit of his stomach.

"If I have the power to create, I must also have the power to destroy!" This gave him an invigorating feeling as he rose and started pulling things out of the sky, crumbling them within his mighty hands and then throwing them away. It started a frenzy that he couldn't seem to control as he wandered the Universe searching for things he could destroy.

Then, just as quickly as it started, it stopped. He was reaching for a planet when a star shot past his eyes, lighting it up. It was beautiful. It was blue and purple with parcels of green and brown. This shouldn't be destroyed, it should be nurtured and given time to grow and prosper. He stood up and looked around at what he did. There were dust and rocks flying everywhere and black holes had been created where stars should have been. What had he done? This was not the wondrous Universe he so meticulously planned out. This was wrong. He fell down to his knees in a fit of deep despair and wept. He wept for the loss of beauty and he wept for his joy in bringing it all down.

He stayed in this state for what seemed an eternity, tossing and turning, trying to figure out who he was. What part of him was better? What part of him should reign over everything? There was no way to solve the problem and he deteriorated as the battle within continued until all that was left was an empty shell that was barely able to lift its head.

"I can't go on this way!" he gasped, then screamed in agony as his body started to thrash about, tortured by his inner battle. The Universe shook with his convulsing body until it seemed everything would come crumbling down.

Edric stood up, holding his head and crying with the pain. Just when he felt he could stand no more, something happened. He began to split in half, light pouring out of him. Something was ripping him apart, destroying him.

When he thought he could stand no more, blackness overcame him and he fell down again. Everything went quiet; nothing moved for a long time. Then, out of the darkness two beings arose; one dressed completely in white and glowing like the stars, the other as black as the Universe itself.

"Who are you?" asked the one in white.

"What do you mean? I am you."

"How can that be? How can I look at myself?" The one in white held out his hands and saw how they glowed. "You don't glow like me. What is your name?"

"How silly you are. Don't you know what has happened?" The one in black smiled at the ignorance of his brother. It would be easy to rule over such an incompetent counterpart. The one in white looked around and saw the beauty that surrounded him. He let the peace of the stars and planets fill him up and he closed his eyes and took in a deep breath.

"I am Gwynn, ruler of the Universe," he stated as he looked at the one in black, "and you are Dougall, my brother, and you will help me in my reign." Dougall threw back his head and laughed so the Universe shook again. Gwynn looked at him, puzzled.

"Oh, I'm Dougall all right, but it is I who will rule. You're not fit to rule anything." A sinister look came over his face. "You must be destroyed." Gwynn sank with the realization of what his brother planned to do.

"No, brother, we must rule together in peace," he tried to explain.

"Prepare to die, brother!" Dougall lifted his hand and a force greater than the wind and more powerful than the stars flew out at Gwynn, sending him flying through the Universe. This was not good; he must hide and find a way to fight back.

Chapter 1

Chrystalline is her home. It is now and, hopefully, it will always be. She has lived there for thousands of years, yet, she doesn't look like she's aged beyond her youth, a mere child in the depths of her adolescence. Her name is Whisper and her life is about to change. There is a force calling to her for something very important, but what is it? She's nobody special so why would anyone want her? But the gnawing in the pit of her stomach is getting harder to ignore.

In Whisper's family, it is her father who is important. He works for the governors and, although Whisper doesn't know exactly what he does, she knows that it's vital to maintaining their life in Chrystalline. Her mother stays at home and takes care of the house. She cleans and cooks and makes sure Whisper gets up in the morning to go to school. She's always there and Whisper loves her very much.

She has three really good friends and they do everything together. They hang out at the mall, go to the theater, share fries at the food court and check out all the guys. During the week they go to school all day which is very boring but, if they're lucky and have no homework, they can go to the coffee shop at the end of the day, drink lattes and gossip about everybody they

5

knew. Whisper loves her life and doesn't want it to ever change.

Chrystalline is one of the most beautiful worlds on the planet. Snow covered mountains lie in the west, vast oceans of deep blue holding many wonderful creatures separate one land from another. There are meadows sprinkled with flowers and fruit trees, forests that are dark and mysterious and deserts dotted with every shade of brown imaginable. Among all of the beauty lie cities of varying sizes. Whisper lives in Paragon, a city of about thirty thousand. It's a good city and Whisper and her friends go to the only school there, Chrystalline Academy.

The people from the Earth dimension have no idea Chrystalline exists. The two worlds are parallel to each other; occupying the same space but existing in different dimensions. They imprint on themselves and sometimes appear in various states of existence to each other. When the people from the Earth dimension catch a glimpse of anyone from the Chrystalline dimension they think they've seen a ghost because they have no other explanation for what they are seeing.

The Chrystallinians have accepted their many-layered planet and have acquired great knowledge and understanding. They are far more advanced than other worlds and use their minds for many different things. In fact they can transport themselves from one place to another just by using their minds. It's called mind-porting and Chrystalline is the only dimension where this is done.

Whisper has a good life and she is happy or, at least she

was happy. Now, she's restless. Something big is about to happen, but what? Earth is calling to her and she doesn't know why.

#

"Whisper?!" Gypsum, Whisper's mother, called. "Whisper, get up! You have to get ready for school." She heard something but couldn't quite make out what it was. She knows she was in a forest and it was raining. She saw a chipmunk on a log hiding underneath...

"Whisper!!"

'Holy crap, that chipmunk can talk!' Whisper said to herself, 'That can't be.' She leaned over to get a better look. WHAM!!

"What the...?" She turned over in her bed and saw her mother standing over her with a pillow in her hand.

"Get up Whisper. I'm sick of trying to wake you up every morning. You should really go to bed earlier. You're young and you need your sleep." Blah, blah, blah... It was the same speech every morning. Whisper wished, just once, she'd let her sleep in.

"Okay, Mom, I'm getting up see? I'll be downstairs soon." She sat up and tried to wipe the sleep from her eyes. She didn't even want to know what her hair looked like; better for her to just get in the shower.

"Well, if you hurry you can have your breakfast with your father and me. If not you'll have to fix your own."

7

'I think I'll take my chances and fix my own,' she said to herself. 'Seeing my father right now is not on the top of my list.'

Whisper's father is the epitome of righteousness. He's not religious or a preacher or anything like that. In fact, in Whisper's house, they rarely ever talk about religion. It's just that her father is *so* good. He works for the governors and he loves it. He's a real by-the-rules kind of guy and expects his daughter to be the same way and Whisper's usually pretty good at following rules except for yesterday. Yesterday was a bad day. Yesterday Whisper broke the rules.

It was nothing real serious, just one of those little rules that her school has. She was supposed to be taking a test and started to daydream, she did that a lot lately, and when she looked up at the clock there were only fifteen minutes left. She panicked and didn't know what to do, so she cheated. Well, not cheated in the literal sense. She knew the answers; she just didn't have time to write them down. So, she empowered her pen to write faster, but not just faster, super fast. The people of Chrystalline can do that, command inanimate objects to do what they want. Whisper can move small things like a pen but she's not that good yet. They learn it at school but they're not supposed to use it until they graduate, unless it's for a real emergency and writing a test is not an emergency. Miss Foster did not appreciate Whisper's need for this empowerment and grabbed her test. She got a zero and was sent to the office and, worst of all, they phoned her father.

8

When her father got to the school, the look in his eyes tore Whisper's heart apart. He was so disappointed in his daughter. He apologized to the principal and took Whisper home and let her have it.

"What were you thinking? How could you do this?" It seemed like such a silly little rule, but not to Whisper's father. To him there's no such thing as a silly rule. So, now Whisper is grounded. No mall, no friends, no nothing. Her friends are not that easy to avoid either. She knew they were going to be angry when they found out about her grounding; they were supposed to go to the mall on the weekend.

Whisper dragged herself out of the shower and started to comb out the knots from her hair. Sometimes she wants to cut her hair short. It would be so much easier to comb and dry, but she just can't do it. She *needs* her long hair which seems totally ridiculous but she has her reasons. She uses her hair as a curtain. When she doesn't want to face certain things she just closes the curtain and hides. That way no one can see her face or see how upset or embarrassed she is. She just pulls her hair in front of her face and voila, she disappears.

Blowing her hair dry was taking way too long so she decided to just leave it damp. It would dry eventually. She brushed her teeth, made sure her eyes were clear, no make-up, she hated it, and headed to her room to pick out clothes.

Today she felt blah so she wore all black. Black jeans, black t-shirt, black hoodie, even black socks. Whisper liked to dress how she felt. It let everyone know her mood without saying a word. Not too many people ask how you are when you're wearing your emotions. They just know by looking at you. Thinking that she'd spent enough time upstairs getting ready and that her father had gone to work already, Whisper headed downstairs.

The house that Whisper and her parents lived in was quite modest considering the high position her father had with the governors. It was a small two story house with three bedrooms on the second floor; one for her parents, one for Whisper and one for company. The main floor had a small living room with a bay window looking out onto the neighbourhood and a fireplace that rarely got used. The kitchen and dining room were right next to each other, separated by a breakfast bar. There was a tiny basement full of boxes and a small yard that was just big enough for her dog, Regal, a small, fluffy, white dog that looked like a stuffed animal. He was so cute and usually happy to see Whisper, but not this morning. This morning he was hiding in his bed under the sideboard. He could sense the tension between father and daughter. Her father was still sitting at the dining room table.

'Oh great,' she thought as she stepped timidly from the stairs and headed for the sink. 'I'll just get a drink and head out the door.'

"Whisper? Come, sit down with me. I want to talk to you." It was not a request it was an order, not a strong military order, but an order nonetheless. Whisper sat down opposite him. She pulled her hair in front of her face, better to close the curtain for this one. He saw her move and reached over and pushed her hair back behind her ears.

"Look at me, Whisper."

"Yes?" She looked up and tried hard to avoid his eyes.

"Whisper, you know the rules. Even breaking the smallest one is wrong. We have them for a reason and we trust in you and in ourselves that we can abide by them. It's not a hard thing to follow; it's nothing we don't ask even of ourselves." It was a statement of such disappointment in her that she was consumed with guilt. "Why did you cheat?"

"I-I-I don't know. I was writing the test and then I looked out the window. The next thing I knew time was almost up and I still had half my test to write. I panicked. I didn't know how I was ever going to finish. It seemed so easy to tell my pen to write. I didn't even think I was doing something wrong. I'm sorry Daddy really I am." She tried to use big sad eyes to convince him of her repentance but she knew it wouldn't work with him, he could see right through her tricks.

"Whisper, Whisper, Whisper. Don't try to fool me. You knew you were breaking the rules. If you do something wrong, *admit* it!" His voice was rising. "Right now you need to think about this; your powers of the mind are to be used when you are ready, when you understand their purpose. If you use them before that, you will only delay them."

11

'What the heck is he talking about?' she asked herself.

"By the look on your face I've confused you. Good, this only means that I'm right and your punishment is just. I want you to walk today and leave your mind free to think and I want you to learn to control your anxieties." That was it, the talk was over. He got up from the table and put on his suit jacket. "One last thing, I love you and will always be here for you." Whisper stared at him as he disappeared, teleporting himself to work.

'Great, now I have to walk,' she thought to herself. 'I hope its nice out, yesterday was a little chilly.' She grabbed her book bag, tied up her runners and headed out.

The sun was bright in the sky and it felt warm outside. A smile came to Whisper's face despite her punishment as she realized it wouldn't be too bad to walk. She enjoyed the quiet and listened to the birds sing. The birds in Chrystalline are the same birds in all the dimensions. They have the ability to cross from dimension to dimension. No one knows how they do it and, despite the fact that Chrystallinians can speak to animals, they won't tell anyone either. Speaking to animals was something the people of Chrystalline learned to do thousands of years ago. Today the birds were singing a song to the sun thanking him for warming things up. Birds are the only animals from the Earth dimension that can cross over worlds and fly between dimensions. Cats and dogs, like other animals, can see and hear other dimensions but they can't cross over to any.

It wasn't long before Whisper was on Willow Street, one

more block and she'd be at the school. She turned her attention towards the day's lessons. Universal History was her first class; a hard class to stay awake in. The Universe is old and filled with so much information that it's hard to remember it all. Sometimes her eyes glazed over and she drifted off; the voice of her teacher going on and on and on. There was no way she could do that today though, that was what got her into trouble in the first place.

She got to the school a few minutes later and started up the steps towards the front doors. A familiar voice rang out behind her.

"Whisper, wait up!" Nascha, one of Whisper's best friends, raced towards her. She stopped and waited for her to catch up.

"Hey!" said Whisper as Nascha linked her arm through hers and stared into her face.

"Well? What happened? How bad is it? Did your father go ballistic?"

"Whoa! Slow down." She started to fill her in on all the details.

"You're grounded? For how long?" Nascha asked.

"I don't know. Dad didn't say and I was too afraid to ask." They walked arm in arm as they made their way to their lockers. The halls were full of students talking loudly and getting ready for class. Thankfully, Nascha's locker was right next to Whisper's.

"Well, I hope it's not for too long," Nascha pouted. "We

have to get together with Elsie and Odella before Summer Dreams or we'll never figure out what to wear to the Enchantment."

The Enchantment was a dance that was accompanied by a huge festival as well. The school had at least two of them every year. It was a fun event that the whole town got involved in. Booths were set up in the school field selling all kinds of food, enticing people with games of chance that offered prizes that ranged from teddy bears to free shopping cards at the mall; a prize that Whisper always tried to win. There were rides and contests that rated pies, cakes and all sorts of goodies. A huge picnic filled the hours in the afternoon and everyone got the chance to visit and talk with friends and neighbours. After all the festivities, people made their way home to relax from the day's events. The students, however, were not done yet. They, along with the teachers and some chosen chaperones got changed into fancy dresses and suits and returned to the school at night for a dance that was beyond belief. This was where the real 'Enchantment' began. The teachers used their mind powers to transform the school into some mystical realm that when you walked through the doors it was as if you entered a whole new world.

The Winter Ice was a great example of true enchantment. The school became an ice castle with snowflakes slowly drifting to the floor. The walls looked like they were made of ice, yet, still felt warm to the touch. When you stepped into the building, you were surrounded by white and crystal and soft furry arctic animals; it was amazing. Whisper let her mind wander over all the different Enchantments she had attended.

"Whisper, are you listening?"

"Huh? Yeah. What did you say?" she tried to clear her mind of the memories.

"You've got to stop daydreaming. Seriously, will you grow up already?" She knew Nascha was kidding but it still hurt a little to hear her friend talk to her that way. "I said do you think your grounding will be over before Summer Dreams?"

"Man, I hope so!" But she wasn't so sure. Her father seemed really angry with her. "He can't keep me locked up forever, can he?"

"With your dad, anything's possible." The bell rang, making them both jump. "Oooh, yuck, Universal History. Did you study?"

"Study?" Whisper panicked.

'What? What was she talking about? We have a test?'

"You know, for the test on the Hedra Galaxy. You didn't study did you?" She could tell from the look on Whisper's face that she hadn't. "Whisper! Okay just keep your mind clear and your pencil in your hand."

"Very funny," she said as they entered the classroom. Suddenly her stomach didn't feel so well.

#

As the final bell of the day rang Whisper felt exhausted,

15

relieved, but exhausted. The test in Universal History was not that bad. Luckily she seemed to remember quite a bit about the lesson on the Hedra Galaxy and she thought that, maybe, she got a passing grade. The next class was Biological Substances and all they did was watch a movie about the properties of a raindrop. After that was lunch, which Whisper chose to spend on her own in the library catching up on some homework. It might have made Nascha mad but she couldn't stand to listen to her, Elsie and Odella all talk about how tragic it would be if she couldn't make Summer Dreams and begging her to appeal to her father to let her go to the dance. They didn't understand that an appeal to her father would only make things worse and she didn't want to blow any chance of going to the enchantment. The afternoon only had two classes to get through; Choral and Spiritual Geometry, both favourites of Whisper's. Even so, she just couldn't seem to get into them.

When the bell rang Whisper remembered her father's order to walk in the morning and wondered if it included walking home too. She wasn't sure, so decided that it was probably better if she did.

After she went to her locker and packed up her book bag, she started home. It was still warm outside and Whisper started to relax and enjoy herself. Maybe this was something she could do more often, maybe even tomorrow. She hated to admit it, but her father was right, walking really seemed to clear the mind. It gave her time to unwind and think about nothing in particular.

16

WHAM!!

"What the…? What was that?" She looked around for the source of the noise. Nothing seemed out of place. The trees were still standing, the birds were still singing, the houses still stood quietly on their street. She was a few blocks from school, so there were no students around. They had all mind-ported home anyway. Whisper was the only one on the street.

WHAM!!

"There it is again," Whisper looked around, searching for the noise. "Where is it coming from?" She clutched the strap of her book bag tighter, more than a little concerned about the strange noise.

"WHY DAMN IT? WHY!?!"

"Okay, that was loud. Like right beside me loud!" She didn't get it. What could be making all the noise? There was no one around for blocks? Then she realized what was happening.

"Of course!" she exclaimed. Some other world had just overlapped into Chrystalline. That happened sometimes; different worlds would cross over each other. It could be a little weird but it did happen. It started to come in from all sides now and completely surrounded Whisper. She held her head to try to stop it, to try to cut it off but it wasn't working. Everything started to shift until it felt like *Whisper* had crossed over to another world. She panicked, feeling she had to get back to Chrystalline.

"Of all the God damned things! You son of a bitch.

WHY?" There was so much emotion in the voice, so much anger and despair. She looked around and tried to get her bearings. She was standing inside a building, a very clean smelling building. There seemed to be a lot of chaos around, people walked hurriedly up and down the wide hallway. Orders were being yelled out and voices were coming from hidden speakers somewhere. There were a few people in long, white coats signing pages clipped to boards or studying them intently. She continued down the hall, knowing that nobody could see her. To her right was a large room filled with chairs where dozens of people were sitting. They looked hurt and sick and impatient and tired. She understood where she was now; a hospital somewhere in the Earth dimension. There were wheelchairs piled in a corner and stretchers were pushed up against the wall. She tried to adjust to her surroundings because now she was curious. She started to feel the surge of emotion that brought her there in the first place. Its pull was so strong. It was the strongest emotion Whisper had ever felt in her life. She scanned the halls and tried to find the source of the despair.

"God, God what did you do?" There, away to the side, in a separate room she heard the voice. She started for the door; she needed to see what was behind it. She got there and hesitated.

How was she going to get to the other side? She couldn't mind-port here and she couldn't walk through doors either. She debated for a minute or two and then, without having to do anything, the door opened and a sober looking man, probably a

18

doctor, came out. She saw her chance and slipped through the open door before it had a chance to shut.

The room was small. There were three chairs, a small table with a couple of magazines and a telephone on it. The floor was white and speckled with grey flecks, probably so no one would see the dirt scattered across it. The walls were a pale yellow and looked very aged with the paint starting to peel.

'Yeah, this is a real cheery place!' she thought to herself.

In the corner was a small, black cabinet with a sink and standing above the sink was the figure of a man. He had his back to Whisper and was washing his face in the running water. He was wearing dark jeans and a worn out black jacket. He turned off the water and leaned on the counter, shaking as if he were sobbing.

'I've gotta find a way out of here,' she said to herself, 'get back to my world.' If her father found out she was there without permission she could kiss Summer Dreams goodbye. She was pretty sure travelling to different worlds was not part of her grounding. Anyway, what could she do to help this guy? He couldn't even see her. He didn't even know she existed.

WHAM!! The man clenched his fist and slammed it into the counter.

"OH!!" she exclaimed out loud, startled by the loud bang. "Who's there?"

'What? Did he hear me? No way!'

He whipped around to search the empty room and

Whisper felt her heart fall. He was beautiful, if beautiful was a word that could be used to describe a man. He was so perfect that, surely, he had been carved out of marble. His face was thin and strong. His jaw was square and sturdy like he could command a legion of men, even at his young age which was probably around twenty. His brow furrowed, as he questioned his own sanity at hearing a voice when, obviously, there was no one there. Black, wavy hair rested just above his shoulders. Whisper unconsciously let her eyes wander over his entire body and felt a rush of warmth rise up inside her. She started to blush.

'No, don't be stupid,' she thought as an embarrassed smile formed at the corners of her mouth and she forced herself to avert her eyes. He reached up to put his hand through his hair and Whisper looked into his eyes. They were an icy blue, almost clear like crystal and they were filled with deep sorrow and anguish. That he had been crying was evident by the redness and puffiness around his eyes but, why was he so angry?

He looked like he had the weight of his world on his shoulders. What could be making him so unhappy? Whisper felt compelled to do something. She had to know what happened to him. She had to get into his mind and find a way to help him. She knew the risk but couldn't help it. He looked so lost, so helpless.

She closed her eyes and started to concentrate on his thoughts. Mind reading was easy here because the people had not yet learned how to use their subconscious. They left their minds wide open for others to read. She started to close in on his thoughts. Almost immediately a barrier as strong as a steel wall went up.

'What? Is he blocking me?' she asked herself. 'No one from the Earth dimension has ever done this before. How?' She opened her eyes and stared at him. He stared right back; at least it looked like he was staring back. It threw her off guard and she wondered if he really could see her.

"Is there anyone in here?" he asked the room. A feeling of relief washed over Whisper as she realized that he couldn't really see her, he could only sense her. She figured he must be one of those people who could sense other worlds, they hovered on the edge of knowing but not quite there. There were a few people like that in this dimension, unaware that their minds were capable of so much until something drastic happened to them. Whisper wondered if that was what happened to this guy. Had something terrible happened to him to make him more conscious of what was really around him? Or was he always aware? Whisper wanted to talk to him. He intrigued her. She tried again to enter his mind, meeting the same barrier. He grabbed his head and squeezed his eyes shut, obviously trying to shut out the foreign presence in his mind. Whisper was fascinated.

All of a sudden something grabbed her arm, startling Whisper. The pressure grew stronger and started to hurt. She felt herself being pulled quickly through space.

'Oh no! This can't be happening. But how did he know?'

"WHISPER!!! What are you trying to do?" Her father's voice was loud in her ear. It ripped her out of the Earth dimension and, once again, she found herself standing on the street just a few blocks from school. She looked at her father's face and knew at once that she was in trouble.

Chapter 2

Cael stood in the small, dingy room with the heel of his hands pressed hard against his eyes, trying to get the tingling out of his head. He was standing by the sink, washing his face when he heard something. It almost sounded like a voice but not quite loud enough to tell. He thought it came from right behind him but when he turned around, no one was there. It must have come from outside the room. Then he started to have this feeling in his head like something was trying to get inside. It felt like little tiny shock waves running through his brain. Right away he knew the feeling wasn't right and he shook his head to try to get it out. It stopped for a minute then it came back. That's when he squeezed his eyes shut and held his head. Something was in this room. He knew it.

It wasn't like this had never happened to him before. He had many encounters with what people would call the supernatural; although, he would never admit it out loud. Admit that and people would think you were crazy. Lock you up and throw away the key. Sure it was becoming more and more main stream to talk about life after death and ghosts and things like that but not for him.

Once, when he was five, he was sure he had seen a ghost.

He was in his basement playing hide and seek with his best friend, Scott. He had found the best place to hide, right between the furnace and the hot water tank, when he felt someone watching him. He squeezed his eyes shut then too, not wanting to turn around. He was very much afraid of the bogeyman at the time. Finally, his curiosity got the better of him and he slowly turned his head around to sneak a quick peek. What he saw would stay with him for the rest of his life. Standing just two feet behind him and staring down at him was a woman all dressed in white. She looked very kind and she smiled at him. Then she raised her arm and pointed out towards the stairs. Cael was confused, what did she want him to do? The woman made a gesture to shoo Cael away from his hiding spot but he refused, knowing that Scott would never find him there. All of a sudden, the woman got angry and her face turned mean and nasty which scared Cael to the point that he ran from his hiding spot crying and screaming for his mother to come and make the scary lady go away. Scott thought this was funny and went home laughing and making fun of Cael.

For the rest of grade one he spent most of his time trying to defend himself from other kids who teased him, calling him a scaredy cat and beating him up. His teachers didn't know there was any bullying going on and so notes would get sent home warning his mother that if he didn't stop acting up in class she would have to find a new school for him. Cael, however, believed the woman had saved his life. Three days after she

24

chased him out of his hiding spot the hot water tank almost blew up. Thankfully, his parents noticed something was wrong with it before anything bad happened but Cael knew that the woman had tried to warn him to stay away from it.

After that day Cael vowed never to mention to anyone, not even his mom or dad, anything about ghosts or spirits or anything else he believed in. He would not be made fun of again. So, he went through life trying to make up for that first year of school. When he was old enough, he joined every tough sport he could; wrestling, football, hockey and judo, anything that would prove he was not a coward. It was during his training in judo that he met Mr. Yamanaka. All martial arts require dedication and discipline and Mr. Yamanaka was the perfect teacher to provide this for him.

Cael was twelve the first day he entered Mr. Yamanaka's dojo. The sensei was a small man, not very tall and not very heavy. He had a black belt in judo and karate and was in the process of learning Kung Fu when he met Cael. He seemed so smart and was willing, right from the start, to take the boy under his wing. He could see the built up frustration in him and vowed that he would help him to overcome it. He taught him everything he needed to know to deal with the pressures of school and home and friends. He showed him how insignificant each person was when they let their minds be crushed by outside influences. This kept Cael away from the usual temptations of youth. He didn't smoke or drink or try any drugs at all while he was growing up.

Mr. Yamanaka took him through the paces of breathing and meditating and learning how to control the mind. It was all a matter of self-discipline and Cael was an eager student.

When he experienced any more sightings of ghosts or feelings of psychic phenomena he went to his teacher and talked about it. Mr. Yamanaka taught him about the spirit world and showed him how to work his mind to become more accepting of this world. As time went on, Cael became more and more comfortable with the way he could see things others could not. Sometimes he could even anticipate things that were going to happen in the future. Just little things, like who would win the next big game. Mr. Yamanaka scolded him for this and told him there were a lot more things to concentrate his talents on. He shouldn't use his abilities for such silly things. Instead, he should try to see things that would bring fulfillment to his life, make him a better person. This was how Cael tried to live and everything was going good until today.

Cael had just received his black belt in judo and Mr. Yamanaka wanted to take him out for lunch to celebrate this hard earned accomplishment. This was rare because he seldom saw his teacher outside the dojo so he was really looking forward to this lunch. He had many things he wanted to talk to him about.

They planned to meet at the restaurant at around one o'clock. Cael tried to look suitable for his teacher. Mr. Yamanaka was very strict about how one should carry themselves. They should always be clean and present themselves

26

with dignity and honour. This included your clothes, your room and even your car. This last part was the hardest for Cael to keep up. He drove a black, 1995 Jeep YJ and he loved it. Many weekends were spent out in the woods 4x4ing, getting the Jeep covered in mud and dirt, loving every minute of it. But, come Sunday, everything had to be washed and wiped clean because Monday morning was judo and Mr. Yamanaka could see the Jeep from the upstairs window of the dojo and if it wasn't clean it meant extra push ups for Cael.

Cael thought of this as he parked his sparkling Jeep in front of the restaurant. It was an Italian restaurant. They both agreed that pizza should be the main food on the menu today. Cael opened the front door and there was his old friend, sitting on a bench by the hostess's stand. He looked to Cael as if he had been waiting a lifetime. Cael looked at his watch, thinking that maybe he was late. Five minutes to one, right on time. So why did he look so impatient?

"Cael, I am so glad to see you!" He stood up and clapped the boy on the shoulder. "Come, they have our table ready for us." Cael followed him to the back of the restaurant where it seemed so dark, not a very joyous setting. Oh well, if this was where his sensei wanted to sit, then this was where they would sit.

"You look like you've been waiting for me a while. Am I late?" Cael knew he wasn't but he wanted to find out why Mr. Yamanaka had such an anxious look on his face.

27

"No, no. Of course you are not late. On time just as you always are. I am so proud that you take your training seriously and that you apply it to every aspect of your life. No, I was deep in thought about something else when you came in. I didn't even realize you were there." He dismissed Cael's look of concern with a nervous smile. The waitress came with menus and asked them what they would like to drink. Cael asked for a Coke while his teacher wanted tea.

"So, what do you want? Ham and pineapple, pepperoni, all vegetable?" The man was staring at the front doors, lost again in his own thoughts. "Mr. Yamanaka?"

"Yes, Cael?" He turned his head back to Cael, eyebrows raised, wondering what he had missed.

"I asked what kind of pizza you wanted."

"Anything will do. You pick." He turned his attention back to the door.

"Okay, that's it. What's wrong? You haven't taken your eyes off that door since we sat down. Is everything all right?" Cael set the menu down and tried to search for some kind of answer in the old man's eyes. Mr. Yamanaka turned to Cael and looked in the boy's face, his hands tightly squeezing the edges of the table.

"How long have I known you, Cael?" he asked. His demeanour was starting to worry Cael.

"Almost eight years, exactly. It was one week after my twelfth birthday when I walked into your dojo and I just turned twenty." Mr. Yamanaka nodded impatiently.

"Cael, in all the years I've known you, have I ever lied to you or tried to get you to do something you didn't want to do?"

"Well, no, sir." Cael was starting to feel a bit of panic at his behaviour. "What's this all about? Mr. Yamanaka, what's wrong…?"

"Cael, I have things I must tell you, things that cannot wait another minute. I'm afraid my time is growing short." He turned his attention away from the door so he could read Cael's expression and know that he was paying close attention to him.

"What do you mean? Your time is growing short? What are you talking about?" Cael was growing more and more confused, this was supposed to be a celebration lunch, wasn't it?

"Cael, LISTEN!!" The tone in his voice made Cael sit up and take notice. "When I met you it was not by accident. I was sent here to teach you."

'What was he talking about, sent to teach me?' thought Cael.

"You are a very special boy and there are people out there that want you because of this. I was sent here to show you the ways of the ancients. To teach you everything I know." The waitress was back with their drinks and to take their orders. Mr. Yamanaka looked very impatient as Cael told her that they'd have a large ham and pineapple pizza. She took their menus and left. Mr. Yamanaka took a sip of his tea before continuing.

"Many centuries ago there was a man named…"

BAM, BAM, BAM.

Cael jumped out of his chair at the sound of the gunfire. He swung around, looking for the source of the eruption. There was nothing to be seen, no gun, no gunman, no nothing. He thought that, maybe, he was the only one who heard it but then a scream came from the front of the restaurant, then another followed by many more. Something bad just happened, of that he was sure.

"Sir, did you hear that? Sounded like gunfire, don't you think?" He turned to his teacher and felt bile gather at the back of his throat. Mr. Yamanaka was slumped down in his chair, blood running down the front of his shirt.

"Mr. Yamanaka? Oh, God! Mr. Yamanaka?" He started for his friend's chair. "Someone call 911!" he yelled to the front of the restaurant. "I need help back here, a man's been shot. Hurry! Please, someone help me!" He was desperate in his pleas to get help for his friend.

#

He followed the ambulance to the hospital in his Jeep. It was hard for him to concentrate on the road, thinking about who could have shot Mr. Yamanaka. It was as if his wise old teacher had known something was going to happen. It must have been why he chose to sit in the back of the restaurant and why he was so desperately trying to tell him something. But what was he trying to tell him? What did he mean he was put here to teach him? Cael didn't get it. He tried to remember if there was

30

something special about what drew him to Mr. Yamanaka in the first place.

He had been twelve years old and deep into judo. All the other sports he tried didn't seem to grasp him the way that judo did. He loved the way the sensei made them work, push ups, sit ups, break falls, grabs, rolls. The strength that it took to do judo was amazing and yet it seemed so effortless to an outsider. He also liked the respect it demanded. You had to bow to enter the mat, bow to your sensei, and bow to your opponent. Cael learned a great deal about himself in those first few months of training. When sensei Jiro suggested that he take special instruction from Mr. Yamanaka he didn't ask any questions. His parents were easily convinced that this was the best road for him to take and so sent him to his new dojo.

Cael and Mr. Yamanaka struck up an immediate friendship and his new teacher didn't seem to mind that he was young and inexperienced; in fact, he welcomed the idea of teaching him everything he knew. From the very first day, Mr. Yamanaka taught Cael about ancient breathing techniques and meditation practices. Cael loved it and never asked why Mr. Yamanaka never wanted to be called sensei nor did he ever know his first name.

In all his years of training there, he never saw another student. He always assumed that Mr. Yamanaka gave private lessons and other students just trained at different times. Nothing was ever questioned and everything seemed so easy to accept for himself and for his parents. Mr. Yamanaka was the kindest man he ever met. He understood all about his ability to connect with the supernatural and explained many of the ancient beliefs in the paranormal. It was like getting his life back, no longer embarrassed about what he saw and felt. He still never talked about it outside of the dojo but at least someone didn't think he was totally crazy.

He arrived at the hospital not long after leaving the restaurant. The ambulance pulled into an underground garage where it would be met by doctors and nurses racing to try and save Mr. Yamanaka's life. He searched for a place to park and found one not too far from the main doors of the emergency room. After filling the meter with as much change as he could find in his glove box and pockets, he grabbed his old ragged black leather jacket out of the back seat and headed in.

He ran up to the head desk, cutting to the front of the line and making a lot of people very angry. His shirt was still covered in blood from his teacher and his face showed all the strain of the past twenty minutes.

"Please, a man just came in here in an ambulance. He was shot. Please, where is he?" He was leaning on the desk looking desperately at the woman standing there.

"Sir, calm down. The doctors are working on him now. Are you family?"

"No, he's my teacher...my friend. We were having lunch when someone shot him," he tried to get everything out. All he wanted was to see Mr. Yamanaka.

"Sir, I have to tell you again to calm down. Do you know his family? Or how we can get in touch with them?"

'A family? Did Mr. Yamanaka have a family?' In all the years he had known him, he never mentioned a family and Cael never thought to ask. 'Isn't that weird? How could I never ask him about his family? Because Mr. Yamanaka never brought it up and you only talked about things he brought up himself. That's just the way he was.'

"No, I don't know if he has a family." The woman looked at him suspiciously.

"Well, I have forms to fill out. Maybe you can help me with some information."

'Forms? What is this woman talking about, forms? I have no time to fill out forms. I have to see Mr. Yamanaka.' Cael was screaming inside.

"I don't think I can help you very much. My friend doesn't like to share information about himself." The woman could see the stress on his face and finally showed some compassion for him.

"Can I get *your* name, then?"

"Sure, sure, it's Cael, Cael Fraser."

"All right, Mr. Fraser, I'll tell you what; there's a room at the end of the hall." She pointed towards the waiting room. "You can go in there. It's small and it's very private. There's a phone in there if you need to call someone and there's a sink if you need to wash up." She finished this sentence with a look at Cael's shirt. He looked down and noticed the blood on his shirt for the first time.

"Thank you." He put his jacket on to cover his shirt and started toward the room.

"Oh and sir, don't go anywhere. The police will probably want to talk to you about what happened."

'Sure they will and what can I tell them? Nothing, not a single thing. I didn't see anyone or hear anyone until the bullets sank into his chest.' He suddenly felt very heavy and knew he would have to sit down before he collapsed.

When he got in the room the first thing he did was call his mother. He wanted to tell her what happened and ask if she knew of any relative that Mr. Yamanaka might have. After all, she was the one who made all the arrangements for his special tutoring. For the first five or six years in his new dojo, she was the one who made out the cheques to him. Since Cael had gotten a job and moved out of his house, he paid for his judo with cash and it wasn't always the same amount. It was whatever he could afford and Mr. Yamanaka always seemed to know exactly what that amount was.

There was no answer at his mother's and no answering machine either. That seemed a little strange. His mother always put on the answering machine when she left the house. He thought nothing more of it and tried to reach his father's cell phone instead. Maybe he knew where his mother was. No answer. He was rattling around in his head who he should call next when there was a soft knock on the door.

"Mr. Fraser? It's Dr. Michaels, may I come in?" Cael's heart raced. That was quick, too quick, this couldn't be good news.

"Y-yes, come in." He tried to stand up and fix his jacket but when he saw the look on the doctor's face he knew he would have to sit right back down.

"Mr. Fraser I'm afraid I have some bad news…"

#

His friend was dead. That's all that kept running through his mind as he drove his black Jeep home. Mr. Yamanaka never regained consciousness at the hospital. They tried everything they could but there was no use, he was dead. He tried to wash up in the tiny sink but then that strange feeling that someone else was in the room came over him and he tried to pull himself together. The police came after that and asked him all sorts of questions. Some questions he could answer and some he couldn't possibly know. Did he see any gunman? Did he hear anything besides the bullets? What were they doing at that restaurant? Did Mr. Yamanaka have any enemies or was he into anything illegal? This last question really upset Cael. He knew what they were getting at. There had been a slew of gang shootings over the past few months in the city and he had the feeling they were trying to link Mr. Yamanaka's shooting to one of those.

"NO!!" he shouted. "Mr. Yamanaka was the most decent

man I know. He never did anything wrong, let alone illegal."
When the officer looked at him with disbelief, he wanted to
punch him. He had to remind himself to calm down. The police
finished with their questioning, told him not to leave town and
took his blood stained shirt as evidence.

He couldn't wait to get back to his apartment, take off his
clothes and have a long hot shower. He wanted to wash the blood
off of him and clear some of the confusion out of his head. He
wanted to be alone so he could be angry and start to grieve the
loss of his mentor. Yes, that was what Mr. Yamanaka was, his
mentor. He wanted so much to be like him right now. He wanted
to take the high road and accept his death as a part of life. To not
act on the searing vengeance he felt bubbling up inside of him.
He wanted to be able to calm the anger and soothe the hatred he
was starting to feel towards everything simply because he
couldn't put a face to the killer or figure out a reason for it.

He parked his Jeep in the underground parking lot of his
apartment building and headed towards the stairwell. He lived on
the third floor of an old converted warehouse. It looked pretty
rough on the outside and it wasn't in the best part of town but it
came with secure parking and a great view of the mountains.
Cael loved the view so much, he didn't bother to complain about
all the noise the pipes made or that sometimes his heat never
worked. He would just sit on his old brown leather sofa, stretch
out his legs and stare out the window, coffee in hand, wondering
about life and where he was going. Today there was no interest

in the view or the sofa. He opened his door, walked right by his kitchen with no thought of food. He unplugged his phone, not wanting to talk to anyone and then he went to his bedroom, grabbed the first pair of sweat pants he could see and headed for the bathroom. He turned on the shower, and stripped off what he had left of his clothes and tossed them into a pile. He wanted to throw them in the garbage when he was done. He waited until the shower was good and hot and climbed in. After about five minutes of holding his face in the path of the hard spray of the water, he felt the day come down on him. He leaned his arms on the wall, put his head down and felt a heavy sob seize his body. He started to cry then, not a baby cry like he did when he ran from the basement so many years ago but a man cry. A cry that came from the sorrow of losing someone you loved; someone who had become such a part of you that you didn't know if you could go on. Cael stayed like that for a long time, until the water ran cold and he couldn't stand it anymore. He got out, put on his sweat pants, not even bothering to dry himself and headed for his bedroom. He threw himself onto to the bed with a heavy thud and fell almost immediately into a deep sleep.

Chapter 3

Even though her father's grip on her arm tightened, Whisper didn't say a word. She knew how much trouble she was in now. She wouldn't find any sympathy saying "Ow". She wondered, though, how he could have known to find her wandering the Earth dimension when she didn't even know she'd be there.

"Whisper, I asked you a question. What were you trying to do?" He searched her face, waiting for her to answer.

"N-n-nothing, Daddy!" She tried to look as innocent as possible. He wasn't buying it.

"I don't believe that for a moment. I saw the dazed look on your face. You've been standing there for a few minutes now."

'Wait a minute!' What he said stirred something in her mind. 'He saw me standing here and he saw my face? If he saw me that must mean that only my mind went over to the other world. My body must have stayed here. Or, maybe, I imagined the whole thing. Either way, he doesn't seem to know what really happened.'

"Well, I'm waiting."

"I wasn't really doing anything, just daydreaming a little.

H-how did you find me?" She tried not to sound too nervous.

"Well, I know how much you hate walking, so I came to pick you up and you were nowhere to be seen. I assumed you hadn't mind-ported because I trusted you remembered our conversation this morning about walking. So, when I didn't find you at school, I came to look for you," he paused to let go of her arm. He was sure his daughter would not try run away. "That's when I saw you standing here. I called your name but you didn't answer and when I got closer I saw the blank look on your face. I figured you were trying to mind-port. Am I right?"

'Trying to mind-port?' Whisper couldn't believe her good luck. He really didn't know what had just happened to her. 'I can handle this.' She averted her eyes from his face and tried to look guilty. It wasn't hard, after all, she was guilty of far more than just trying to mind-port.

"You're right, Daddy," she said quietly, "I was trying to mind-port. I hate walking and I didn't think you'd get mad if I just did it home. I walked to school this morning, though." Her father actually smiled when he heard this.

"Oh, Whisper, what am I going to do with you?" He grabbed her in his arms and gave her a warm hug. "You have to stop daydreaming and quit being so lazy. It's time you start taking responsibility for yourself."

"I'm sorry, Daddy." Her heart started to settle inside her chest.

"Come on, we'll walk home together. It's been awhile

since I've enjoyed the great outdoors."

#

The walk home was not that bad. Father and daughter actually got along pretty good. They talked about school and Whisper told him about her test in Universal History and how easy she thought it was. He was glad she was doing well. They stopped a couple of times to try and pick out the different songs the birds were singing. He told her how busy it was getting at work, being that the summer solstice was coming.

At every equinox or solstice there were celebrations throughout Chrystalline and throughout many other dimensions as well. A change of seasons was felt by everyone no matter what dimension they were in. It was the one constant. To make sure the change goes smoothly, the Chrystallinian government works out a strategy for quiet and peaceful celebrations but there was one time where this didn't work out.

#

About a thousand years ago, at Winter Solstice, a terrible tragedy happened. A portal was accidently opened between Chrystalline and the Abyss. The Abyss was a very dark and evil world that had been banned to its own dimension, its inhabitants forbidden to cross over into any other world. That didn't stop them, however, from opening portals and wreaking havoc whenever they could.

The government of Chrystalline scrambled to close the

40

portal before anything horrible could happen. They tried everything within their powers but nothing worked. They set up guards just outside the opening in the hopes of catching anything that might try to come through. It was a tragic mistake. The men were no match against the nightmarish creatures that came through that portal. This was how the Crogans came to live in Chrystalline.

Crogans were dark, vicious creatures that could rip a person apart in a matter of seconds, tearing flesh from bone like peeling an apple. They were massive beasts, the size of an elephant and weighing twice as much. They were covered with short, black, bristly hair and reeked of rotting flesh. They had four muscular legs and long, claws that had incision-like sharpness. Their body was thick and sturdy and their tail was long and pointed. But it was their head that was the most disturbing. It resembled an insect, like an ant with pincers that could crush a man instantly and long antennae that twitched and flicked looking for prey.

When the Crogans got through the portal there was pandemonium everywhere. The guards that were posted were killed immediately and without mercy. It was a brutal scene. The Crogans went on a rampage, killing farmers in their fields, travelers on the roads and worst of all children on their way to school. The Chrystallinians could find nothing that could kill them as the governors stood by, helplessly.

While these beasts wandered the land, a man came

through the portal. He was short and fat with long, tangled grey hair and a beard that matched. He looked rough with his dirty face and his tattered old clothes. His eyes crinkled up almost painfully when he smiled and a wooden pipe hung out of the corner of his mouth. He had a huge bell tied to the belt loop of his pants.

"Anyone seen me babies?" He said in a loud, gravelly voice.

"Come on ye twitter brains! You ain't seen me babies? I know'd they come through here." Everyone stared at him in silence.

"Bunch of no-brain, in-bred idiots. I know'd they'd be here, I can see they'd be playing with you no good, sour faced morons." No one knew what to say, so he walked by them and followed the path of death looking for his 'babies'. When he got to one particular village, he knew he was close because he could hear screaming and he could smell the aroma of rotting flesh and blood. He walked towards the stench until, finally, he could see them.

"Aaah, there you'd be! I been lookin' fer ya'." He took the huge bell from his belt loop and started to ring it with a metal rod he had pulled out of his shirt. The bell made a loud clanking sound that echoed throughout the land. Almost at once, the beasts lifted their heads and twitched their antennae back and forth trying to find their master.

"That's right ye sweeties, come to me now and we can go

back home. We've both had enough of this wretched place."

With amazing precision, the Crogans, five in all, lined up and started marching towards the man like they were under some magnetic spell. As they began moving through the streets and out of town, the villagers started to appear at their doors and windows to watch the strange procession. Then, running from the direction of the open portal, one of the governors arrived. He was excited and started shouting out the news that was both a blessing and a curse.

"The portal's been closed! The portal's been closed! All is well!" He could hardly control his joy and then his eyes fell upon the little death parade of man and beasts and he fell silent.

"WHAT!!!??'" The man stopped and yelled his question at the governor. The governor tried to swallow down the lump that had formed in his throat as he realized what this would mean.

"Say again you insolent wretch of a man!" The man was livid.

"I said the portal's been closed." It was barely a whisper that came out of the governor's mouth. What was he to do now? With the portal being closed, there was no way these creatures could get back. They were stuck in Chrystalline

"Of all the blasted, stupid, idiotic things to do! Ya couldn't wait 'till I got back could ya. No, you pea-brained twits had to go and close the door. Now what do you propose I do? Huh? Shall I just turn me babies on ya all??!!" The man was turning red with fury now.

"N-NO! Don't do that! I-I think we can work something out. L-let me talk to the other governors. I'm sure something can be worked out."

After long negotiations the governors agreed to give the man, Mistle was his name, anything he wanted for having to stay in Chrystalline; food, a huge house, gold, jewels and much, much more. In return, Mistle agreed to keep the Crogans penned up and out of everyone's way. The beasts didn't mind really, they had a big field to play in, fresh meat fed to them every day and a warm barn in the winter. Every once in a while one would sneak out of its pen but Mistle would catch it and bring it back before any harm could be done. They slowly adjusted to life outside of the Abyss. They are still there in their pen with Mistle by their side.

#

Whisper found it nice to spend time with her dad. She liked having him all to herself, but all too soon, their walk was over and they were home. With a heavy sigh, her father reached out and opened the door for her. As she passed him their eyes met and a smile came to her face.

"Thanks Dad," she said.

"For what?" He looked back at her and tried to hold his smile in.

"For the walk, it was nice."

"No problem, like I told you this morning I really do love

44

you."

"I know, but sometimes I just get the feeling you don't *like* me very much." He rolled his eyes and stepped through the door.

"Oh, Whisper, of course I don't *like* you. I'm your father I'm not supposed to *like* you." Whisper started to laugh and punched him in the shoulder. He laughed too as he rubbed his shoulder, pretending to be hurt.

"Gypsum? We're home," he called to his wife, who was more than likely in the kitchen getting supper ready.

"Hey guys! What took so long?" Gypsum answered as she came down the hall from the kitchen. She had her sleeves rolled up and an apron tied around her waist. She held a half peeled potato in one hand and a paring knife in the other. She gave her daughter a smile and then turned to her husband, stood on her tip toes and gave him a kiss on his cheek.

"We decided to walk today," he said as he swooped her up and gave her a big hug. Whisper could never get over how much her parents re
ally loved each other and weren't afraid to show it but sometimes it got annoying.

"That's nice. Whisper, go put your books away and then come help me cut the carrots. You're so much better at it than I am."

"Sure Mom. You know you don't have to flatter me to get me to help." Whisper could hear her mom laugh as she headed up the stairs to put her stuff away.

#

After supper, Whisper helped her mom with the dishes and then headed up to her room to do homework. She didn't have a lot but she wanted to get it out of the way before she got distracted with other things.

'My room is starting to look a little messy,' she thought to herself. 'I should really clean it. Maybe after my homework.'

She cleared her desk as best she could and then reached for her book bag. She had no homework for Universal History, which was a relief, she had to read two chapters and take notes for Spiritual Geometry and then a bit of vocabulary for Biological Substances. It wasn't much and shouldn't take too long. She pulled out her textbook from her book bag and an envelope fell out from in between the pages.

"That's odd. Where'd that come from?" she asked herself. She picked it up and turned it over in her hands. It was a small, white envelope like the kind you put a small invitation in. The flap was sealed just on the tip so it was easy for Whisper to run her thumb under and flip it open. Inside, was a small sheet of paper with fancy handwriting on it.

Whisper,

*Please come to my office tomorrow
at lunch. We need to discuss your
Universal History mark. I would
like to talk to you to see what can
be done about it. We will involve*

*your parents if it becomes
necessary.*

*Thank you,
Principal Greene*

'Principal Greene wants to see me? What did I do now?' Whisper couldn't imagine her principal wanting to see her for something good. She thought about what she could have done to get a personal note from Ms. Green. She did have that test in History she didn't study for; maybe she totally blew it. But the envelope had fallen from her Geometry textbook not her History one. Besides, she didn't remember even seeing Principal Greene today so how could she even get a note into her bag. Thinking about it, made concentrating on her homework almost impossible. She kept looking down at her book bag, knowing the tiny envelope was inside. There was no way she wanted her mom or her dad to see that note. Not after she seemed to have patched things up with her father. No, it was better to talk to the principal first.

What should have taken her half an hour to do, took Whisper over two hours. When she finally closed her books and turned off the desk lamp, she couldn't believe how dark it was. She looked around at her messy room and felt a yawn coming on.

"Oh well, guess I'll tackle you another time," she said out loud to her dishevelled room. She went downstairs to watch a little TV with her dad before she went to bed; the thought of the note from the principal still playing tricks on her mind.

Chapter 4

After Whisper crawled under the covers to go to sleep, all she could think about was what Principal Greene could possibly want. It kept her tossing and turning for what seemed like hours. But when she finally drifted off, it wasn't the principal that filled her thoughts. It was the man she saw in the hospital room earlier that day.

She dreamed they knew each other and were in love and happy together. They held hands and walked down a country lane in the sunshine. The smell of the green fields filled her senses and she felt safe and comfortable in his presence. He was laughing and she was smiling, the two of them together with not a care in the world. Then she thought it would be funny to run away and have him chase her, so she let go of his hand and bolted away. She turned as if in slow motion and yelled *"Catch me!"* He started to run after her. She ran to a group of trees and hid behind a majestic old oak, trying not to giggle and give herself away. They were young and in love.

Then the sun went away and the dark clouds gathered above. It started to rain and she wondered what was taking him so long, why he hadn't come to look for her. She decided to come out from behind the tree and discovered the world had changed dramatically. She was now surrounded by a burned out forest and the mighty oak she had hidden behind was gone. There was smoke smouldering up from the ground and the rain was starting to pour down. It was dark and empty and she felt panic start to take hold of her.

Where was the man? Where did he go? Then she saw him, on the top of the hill where the beautiful country lane had once been. He was reaching his arms out to her and she started to run to him. As she got closer she could see his face. The rain had soaked his hair and she saw how it stuck to his neck and face. He was looking at her with a strange look in his eyes. She couldn't tell if he was upset or happy, but he seemed to be pleading with her. Suddenly she stopped and realized he wasn't reaching his arms out to her at all but, rather, he was waving her away, telling her to run. It was then that she saw the dark figure standing behind him. There was a man dressed in a black cloak with a hood pulled low over his face. He had an axe in his hand that he raised above his head, ready to strike. She screamed and the hooded figure looked up, an evil smile peeking out from beneath the hood. He quickly started to swing down the axe...

She sat up with a jolt. Sweat was starting to cover her face and she was out of breath. Her heart was pumping fast. She was terrified. She looked around her dark room and tried to get her bearings. The dream had seemed so real and it took her a few minutes to calm down. She got up and went to the bathroom. She had a drink and washed her face and tried to clear her head. She climbed back into bed and tried to go back to sleep and eventually she did. Before she knew it, her mom was at the foot of her bed, yelling at her to wake up. Life was back to normal.

#

She walked to school again in the morning; her dad had not lifted the grounding yet. Although their time together was nice it had done nothing to change his mind. He wanted his daughter to still think about what she had done. She tried hard to concentrate on what was going on outside but it was hard. She had too many things racing around in her head. The nightmare from the previous night still weighed heavy in her thoughts and the upcoming meeting with Principal Greene was tying knots in her stomach. She hoped she could keep it together through the morning classes.

Nascha was at the top of the school steps again, waiting for her. She was dressed in a short denim skirt, a long white shirt with a black vest and black leggings. A pair of flats on her feet completed the outfit. Whisper looked at her friend's ensemble and smiled.

"Kinda cold for a skirt isn't it?" she teased. She could tell that Nascha was cold.

"N-no, I'm fine," she said, not willing to let the cold interfere with her fashion. "Now, would you hurry your butt up here so we can go inside?"

"Not cold eh?" Whisper laughed.

"Shut up." She glared back at her.

"Hey, I didn't tell you to wear that," she protested. "How long have you been waiting anyway?"

"Too long! I forgot you still had to walk." She opened the front doors and they both hurried inside. "Anything from your Dad yet, about how long you're grounded?"

"Nope, not yet," Whisper tried to sound casual.

"Nothing? How long is he going to keep you waiting? Elsie wants to go shopping on the weekend and we really need you to come with us." They ran into Elsie and Odella just then.

"Elsie wants what?" Elsie asked. She had obviously overheard their conversation.

"…me to go shopping on Saturday," Whisper finished Nascha's sentence as they headed towards their lockers.

"Yes, you have to come!" exclaimed Odella. "We're going to look for dresses for Summer Dreams and you have to be there so we can coordinate our colors." Whisper rolled her eyes.

"Honestly, Odella, we really don't have to match. We *can* look different. There's no law against it," she said as she opened her locker.

"Oh, you don't know the half of it," said Nascha. "'Della would just die if we went to the Enchantment looking mismatched. She's been planning this in her head now for weeks." Everyone laughed at Nascha's comment. Odella looked away, embarrassed but not ashamed, by her friend's comment.

"No, all kidding aside, do you think you'll be able to come?" Elsie asked as Whisper closed her locker, her books in her hand.

"I don't know," she answered, "but I wouldn't count on it. I just can't see my dad letting me go anywhere by the weekend. Besides, we still have almost two months before the Enchantment." Elsie put her head down, clearly disappointed.

"Okay," she said, "but you could at least have lunch with us today. You kind of ditched us yesterday."

"What? I didn't ditch you," she lied. "I had lots of homework to do."

"Okay, that was yesterday, what about today?"

"Sorry, I can't eat lunch with you today either," she stated.

"Why not?" asked Nascha, looking a little ticked off.

"I have an appointment at lunch that I don't think I can miss."

"With who?" Suddenly Whisper was not so sure she should tell anyone. The way the letter had been tucked into her text book was so mysterious and Principal Greene had mentioned not to even tell her parents. Maybe she was supposed to keep their meeting to herself.

"With the Study Hall, I have to go there at lunch and retake an exam I screwed up the other day." It was a stupid excuse. They were sure to see right through it and it would be so easy for them to check the story out.

Brrrrrrrrrring! The bell!

"See ya later," Whisper said and quickly turned around to

go to class before anyone could ask any questions.

By the time lunch came, Whisper was literally shaking she was so nervous. Getting called to the Principal's office was one thing but doing it under all the secrecy was taking a toll on her nerves. She kept thinking about the test she had taken the previous day. Did she really screw it up that badly? Was that what this was all about? Was Principal Greene trying to find a way to improve Whisper's test score before her dad found out? She didn't know why she would do that but maybe she knew how much trouble she'd gotten into for cheating and felt sorry for her? Although it was a little weird for the principal to interfere in family business. With all these thoughts running through her head Whisper headed to the main office, preparing herself for a lecture.

There was no one there, the office was empty. Miss Tuttle, the school secretary, wasn't at her desk. The vice principal's door was open but he was nowhere to be seen and the photocopier, which always had a teacher standing at it, stood silent for once. This was weird. Where was everyone? Was she just supposed to go to Principal Greene's office and let *herself* in? She looked around for a note or something telling her what to do but hoping that she wouldn't find any and could just go.

"Ah, Whisper, right on time I see." Whisper jumped as Principal Greene came out of her office.

Principal Greene was really quite pretty. She had long, black hair, green eyes and high cheek bones that set off her rosy, pink complexion perfectly. She looked young too; not much older than twenty. She definitely did not look old enough to be the principal. She had on her coat and was carrying her purse.

"Principal Greene? Are you going somewhere?" Whispered asked as she saw Miss Greene with her coat on. Maybe she had to cancel the meeting and take care of something else.

"Please, drop the 'Principal'. Miss Greene will do and I thought we'd go out for lunch. It can get so stuffy in my office." Whisper looked at her blankly. She wanted to go out for lunch? Her lunch break wasn't that long and what about her grounding. If she left the school her dad would be furious and besides, going out for lunch with the principal just sounded strange.

"Actually," Whisper tried to explain, "I'm not supposed to mind-port anywhere. My dad sort of grounded me from doing that."

"Don't worry; I'll do all the mind-porting. You just grab my hand. Your father will never know."

Whisper didn't know if she should go. What if her dad did find out? But, then again, Miss Greene was the principal and she should be able to trust that she could explain it all rationally to her father and if she could help Whisper with her Universal History mark , it was worth it.

"Is something wrong, Whisper?"

"No, I was just thinking, we don't have a lot of time before we have to get back."

"Don't worry; we'll be back on time," she smiled at Whisper and then reached out for her hand. Whisper took her hand hesitantly and in an instant they were gone.

They arrived a few seconds later in what looked like a very unique restaurant. Miss Greene explained that the owners loved the Earth dimension, especially the land of Japan and that the restaurant was modeled after some of the traditional eateries there. They were led down a long corridor and given their own private room to dine in. They entered the room and took off their shoes, another Japanese thing, to sit on the floor. There was a low, black table surrounded by big pillows to sit on. Their food was already spread out on the table waiting for them. The room was enclosed by paper walls and there was a sliding door which the hostess closed on her way out. Miss Greene smiled at Whisper and motioned for her to sit down.

"Hope you like sushi." Whisper gave her a confused look. She had no idea what sushi was. "It's another thing the owners took from Japan. Sushi, it's raw fish, seaweed, rice...it's actually really good."

"I don't know." Whisper was not sure she wanted to try raw fish. It didn't sound very appetizing and she really wasn't very hungry. She was too nervous to eat. Miss Greene took off her coat and put it on a coat rack in the corner. She came over to the table and sat on a pillow opposite Whisper and noticed the apprehension in her eyes.

"First, we eat, and then we talk," she said, as she started

passing Whisper food.

#

Whisper thought the meal was delicious. Once she started eating and discovered how good it was, she soon forgot her nerves and gorged herself. She felt so full afterwards that she could hardly move. She leaned over and poured herself some more tea. The server came to take away their empty plates and Miss Greene wiped her mouth delicately with a napkin. She thanked the server and waited for her to leave before she spoke.

"Now, let's talk."

'Okay here it comes,' thought Whisper. 'She's buttered me up with all this food, now she's going to let me have it.'

"I know, I know I didn't study for that test yesterday but I still thought I did all right," Whisper started. "I mean I finished all the questions and…" A look of confusion came over Miss Greene's face.

"Test, what test?"

"In Universal History, isn't that why you wanted to see me?" Now Whisper was confused.

"Universal History? Oh, yes," she started to laugh, "that *is* what I put in the note isn't it?"

"Y-yeah, that's not why I'm here?" Whisper asked.

"No, no, I have far more important things to discuss with you." Whisper stared at Miss Greene, not knowing what to say, waiting to hear her explanation. "Whisper, do you know why I didn't want to stay at the school to have this meeting?"

57

"No," Whisper stated.

"I didn't want to stay at the school because I didn't want anyone else to listen in on our conversation, it wouldn't be safe."

'*Safe*. What is she talking about, safe?' Whisper didn't like the way that Miss Greene said that.

"I've been coming to this particular restaurant for many years now. The owners are old friends and I know that I can trust them with my life. You see, I'm not really a school principal. In fact, I have never even *taught* school before I got this assignment."

"Assignment?" asked Whisper, still not understanding what was going on.

"Yes, that's right, my assignment. I was sent to watch over you," she stopped, waiting for a response.

"Watch over me? I don't get it. Who told you to do that? My father?" Whisper was starting to get angry. Was this his way of keeping an eye on her? She couldn't believe he would do that. Would he really go to such lengths? Miss Greene could see that the girl was getting worked up.

"Calm down, no it was not your father." She reached over and put her hand on Whisper's arm and tried to reassure her. "Let me tell you who I am and what my purpose is." She settled herself so she was sitting more comfortably. Obviously it was going to be a long story, so Whisper readjusted the cushions around her to do the same.

"I am a Soul-healer and so are you," she stated. Whisper

looked at her, stunned. She didn't know what she was talking about.

"I'm a what?" she asked.

"A Soul-healer." Miss Greene repeated. Whisper started to ask a question but Miss Greene held up her hand to stop her. "Let me explain everything before you ask any questions, okay?"

"Okay," Whisper said reluctantly. It was really hard for her to keep quiet.

"A Soul-healer is someone who heals the souls of those who are suffering. It's why we're so sensitive to the emotions of others. We often sense the emotions of beings from many worlds but, sometimes, one soul in particular stands out and calls for our help. We are actually *pulled* towards them. This *attraction* enables us to try to heal them. With our help their soul can be saved," she looked at Whisper hoping that she was following along, "or it can be lost forever but that's not our fault. We are only there as guidance. We can't determine their fate.

"As you know, there are many dimensional worlds within this planet." Whisper nodded. This was something everyone was taught in their early years of school. "Every dimension has their own civilization with their own rules and laws but there is only *one* power that oversees it all. Although it has many names and forms, we know it is the same power for everyone.

"You already know that some of us can cross over dimensions and, although we can go to many different ones, the Earth dimension is one of our favourites. We're fascinated by their many emotions and complexities. They have made their life more difficult than it should be. So, it's no surprise that, among all the different worlds, it is the souls from Earth that call for the most Soul-healers.

"After a Soul-healer heals the soul, they are sent to the Forest of Dreams to recuperate. The memories of what they have just done are erased so that they're not tortured by the suffering they may have had to endure during the healing process. The task of healing a soul can become very complicated. To do the job right, we must become so intertwined with the other soul that we become one with them. We feel their pain, their joy and their anger. We become so attached that it's hard to let go. We form a bond that is almost impossible to break. It's so strong that it interferes when we are pulled to save another soul. Therefor, our memories must be erased.

"When we return from the Forest, we have no memory of anything. We only know our names. We're given a new life and a new family. We start school and learn quickly about our world and all the other worlds around us. Every day we learn more and more about ourselves until we're pulled by the emotions of another soul that's in need of our help. Then someone like me, who has been watching over your growth, can take you aside and explain everything to you." She looked at Whisper, waiting for her to respond. Whisper didn't know what to say. What could she say? Was this real? She started to pull apart the napkin in her hands, concentrating deeply on the task. Then she dropped her hands into her lap and rolled her eyes, blinking back disbelief. She looked around the room then brought her focus back on the woman in front of her.

"Okay," she started, "what???"

"I know this all sounds a little bizarre but, trust me, it's the truth." Again she leaned over and touched Whisper's arm.

"I don't get it. *I'm* a Soul-healer? How the hell can I not know that??" She straightened her back and ran her fingers through her hair.

"Because when you were in the Forest of Dreams your memory was completely erased. They're very good there," she smiled as she spoke, as if she was proud of these memory erasers.

"But wouldn't I have some inkling of what I am? Some clue?" It was starting to freak the girl out. "Maybe a screwed up dream every once in a while? Something?"

"Nope, this is the way it works and, by the way, this isn't the first time I've had to explain this to you." She took a sip of her tea.

"What do you mean?" asked Whisper.

"I've had you under my charge before. A few times, actually, and you always have that same look on your face," she laughed. Whisper didn't find any of this amusing. "If I could, I would take a picture of you right now so I can show you the next time I have to do this soul awakening."

"But I don't understand, if everyone in Chrystalline is a

Soul-healer then why all the secrecy with this meeting?" This part confused her more than any other. Why all the secrecy?

"Did I say everyone in Chrystalline is a Soul-healer? I didn't." She had anticipated this question. "Only some of the people here are Soul-healers. Most of them attend your school. Some, like me, are now teachers and guides for those about to awaken."

"But what about everyone else? What about my parents?" She needed to know about her family. It was hard to believe they hadn't always been there.

"Some of the people that live here are souls from other worlds that could neither be healed nor lost. They have no idea of their former lives and can't seem to move on. So, they come here and learn to nurture their own soul. They can stay here for centuries going through the same life pattern over and over, comfortable in their destiny.

"The healing of your mother's soul was the mission of your friend Nascha while Odella looked after your father. The people you know as your parents were once a king and queen of a land in which their greed got the better of them. They ended up selling their children to people that exploited them just to keep their wealth. They were brought here so they could learn how to love themselves and slowly regain the capability of being responsible for their actions. They needed to learn how to feel love for others. If they had truly loved their children and had compassion for them, they would never have given them away.

Their progress has been good and they like it here. So, when you're gone they, too, will get their memories erased and they'll take charge of another Soul-healer. They'll nurture them and take care of them. They will never remember you or the Soul-healer before you."

"Nascha…" Could this be true?

"Don't worry, like you, she has no memories of them."

"I still don't understand the secrecy," Whisper was still suspicious.

"Ah, well, that's because it's not as simple as I make it out to be," she said. "Since time began there have always been two sides to this Universe. Where there is good there will always be bad, for without one you would not have the other. This is still true even to this day. Where we try to go in and heal a soul there are others who try to go in and take the soul for their very own. These creatures are called Soul-*stealers* and they have spies everywhere. They don't always know who are the Soul-healers and who are the teachers but they don't care, they'll go in to steal a weak soul regardless. They can do *us* no harm but they can wreak havoc with those around us. We always have to be ready for them." This all seemed unbelievable.

"Why should I believe you?" asked Whisper.

"Because you know I'm right." She put her hand on Whisper's arm once again, this time holding it tightly as she stared into her eyes. A warm feeling started to come from Miss Greene's hand and slowly spread up Whisper's arm and through her body. It was as if someone had turned on a light inside Whisper's mind. Suddenly, there was a burst of energy and she could see the Universe as she had never seen it before. She was breathless. She saw the sun, the stars, the planets and more suns and more planets and hundreds of thousands of galaxies! She closed her eyes and felt the truth of her being and knew that Miss Greene was right. She didn't have the memories of her former soul-healing missions but she knew she was someone special and she knew why she had been called back to duty.

"Thank you, Miss Greene," she said, with a look of peace in her eyes.

"Call me Aria," she said with a smile. "Now, let's get started."

Chapter 5

Cael lay on his bed still in a deep sleep. He had been that way since coming home from the hospital the previous day. He was dreaming and in his dreams the long forgotten woman who had once scared him out of his hiding place in the basement had come to him. She didn't seem scary at all now, in fact, he was happy to see her. She came to comfort him and it made him feel safe and warm. He was lost in a blanket of security when he started to hear a whining sound. He turned onto his back and the whining grew louder. Slowly he opened his eyes and started to come back to reality. The whining continued and he realized what it was; his intercom by the front door was going off. Someone was trying to buzz up. He rubbed his eyes and turned to look at the clock on his nightstand.

6:00 P.M.

'Oh God, I slept for over twenty-four hours!?!' he thought as he jumped out of bed and threw a t-shirt on and headed for the intercom. When he got there, he pressed the button.

"Hello?"

"Cael? Cael is that you? Could you please let us in, we've been standing here forever." He should have known. It was his mother, probably accompanied by his father. He buzzed them in and then hurried to the bathroom. He wanted to go to the bathroom before they came up. He had barely finished washing his hands and wetting down his hair when the doorbell rang. He went to the door, took a deep breath and opened it.

"Hi Mom. Dad."

"Oh, Cael, we've been trying to phone you. We saw the news and came as soon as we heard." She barely got in the door when she grabbed her son in her arms and squeezed him tight.

"Mom, Mom, it's okay." He wasn't quite sure he was ready for his mother's overzealousness.

"Gladys, give the boy some space. We just got here for crying out loud, let him breathe." Thank God his father was a little more reserved. That was more of what he needed, calm and stableness.

"Thanks, Dad. Can I get you guys anything?" He took their coats and started to hang them up in the tiny closet by the door.

"Let me do that! You go sit with your father." She grabbed the coats from him, relieved to have something to do. It made her feel useful. "Hal, take Cael to the living room and I'll go make coffee. You do have coffee, right, Cael?"

"Yeah, Mom, in the cupboard above the stove." She put the coats away and made her way to the kitchen. Cael's apartment was not very big. The living room and the kitchen were really one big room, separated only by a counter and a few cupboards. He led his dad to the old brown couch and sat down.

"Trust me, she feels better if she's puttering," his dad

66

said. "Tell me son, how are you?"

"To be honest, Dad, I don't know. I was actually sound asleep when I heard the buzzer. That's why it took me so long to answer it," he said. "I came home from the hospital yesterday, had a shower and went to bed. I've been asleep ever since."

"Since yesterday?! Oh, you poor dear," his mother chimed in from the kitchen.

"Your mother and I were out of town yesterday, you know how Gladys likes the country markets. Well we didn't get back 'til late and had no idea any of this had even happened. Then, when we did get home, we heard your messages..." his father was trying to explain.

"...you sounded so upset. We tried phoning you last night and then again today but there was no answer. Finally, we decided we'd better come over here and see you for ourselves," his mother finished.

"Yeah, I unplugged the phone when I got home. I didn't really feel like talking to anyone." He leaned back on the couch and stretched out his legs.

"Do you feel like talking about it today?" asked his dad tentatively.

"I don't know," said Cael, "there's not much to tell. We were just sitting there, then bang, all hell broke loose."

"Poor Mr. Yamanaka, to die in such violence," his mother said, shaking her head and making a t-t-t sound between her teeth. "I wonder how long he had been involved in such..."

"Gladys!!!" his father quickly interrupted her.

"Involved in what?" Cael sat up, suddenly very interested in what his mother was saying.

"Well, it's just that…" stammered his mom. She looked down at the counter, not wanting to upset her son.

"Just that WHAT Mom?" His voice had gotten louder. His mother looked desperately at her husband for help.

"What your mother is trying to tell you," continued his father, "is that the news has not been very kind to your friend."

"What do you mean?" asked Cael.

"Well, they're saying that Mr. Yamanaka was a hit by a gang that he was most likely a member of," his mom blurted out.

"Jesus Christ!!" Cael got up from the couch and started to pace back and forth. "I *told* them he wasn't involved in anything like that. I *told* them he was a good man. How can they say such lies about him?!! I need to talk to them, make them understand. They can't just ruin his name like this!!"

"Do you think that'd be wise?" asked his father. "I mean they've already tagged Mr. Yamanaka as a criminal what makes you think they won't do the same to you. After all you *were* there."

"Come on Dad, you know they can't prove any of it." He was starting to shout now.

"It doesn't matter. They just have to suggest it and your life may be ruined," he stated. Cael glared at him but he knew he was right. The city had been deeply embroiled in gang wars for a few years now and there was no sympathy for anyone associated with their members. Even if they came out right now and said Mr. Yamanaka was innocent, his name would still be linked to gangs.

"But he was my friend," he looked at them with so much pain in his eyes. "He was everything to me." His parents looked uncomfortably at each other, and then his mother came to him and held him close.

"Oh, sweetie, I know, I know," she said, soothingly. "You were very important to him too. He told me how much he enjoyed teaching you. If there's anything we can do…"

"Actually," he pulled back from his mother's embrace, "you could tell me if you know of any family he might have had."

"Family?" asked Gladys. "Why would I know about his family?"

"I just thought that, you know; since you enrolled me in his class that maybe you talked to him, got to know him a little. I don't know, I just thought I'd take a chance." He could see that his parents knew as little about Mr. Yamanaka as he did.

"I'm sorry Cael, I can't help you," she said as she started opening cupboard doors, looking for coffee cups. "I still can't believe you were there and didn't see anything."

"He knew, you know," Cael said quietly. He was standing and leaning his forehead on his window looking down into the street below.

"What was that?" asked his dad.

"Mr. Yamanaka; I think he knew something was going to happen," he turned to look at his father. "He had us sit at the back of the restaurant. I wondered why he wanted to sit way in the back; I just assumed it was the only table he could get. Then he started acting all weird, like he was scared or something." He came to sit beside his father again. "He kept looking at the door. I had a hard time getting his attention long enough to order a pizza. Then he seemed to get real serious. He looked straight at me and said 'Cael, I need to tell you something.'"

"And..." prodded his mother, who was now standing in the living room, holding two cups of steaming coffee in her hands. Cael reached for his cup.

"Thanks, Mom," he said. "...and nothing. That was when they shot him."

"They? There was more than one?" asked his father.

"I don't know. I just assumed there was. It seemed like there were so many shots coming from everywhere." He took a tentative sip of his coffee, testing how hot it was.

"So you saw no one?" his mother asked again. She had returned to the kitchen to get her own cup of coffee.

"No, it was like they were invisible."

"What now? Did the police say anything to you?" asked his father.

"Yeah; *'don't leave town.'*" he laughed.

"You don't think they believe that you had something to

do with it?" gasped his mother.

"No, I think they're just happy acting tough and telling people what to do." He remembered his conversation with the officer and how frustrated it had made him.

"Is there anything else you want us to do?" his father asked. Cael sat back and thought about this. What could they do?

"You could help me arrange a memorial service for him." It was all he could think of.

"Dear, do you really think you should do that? I mean he must have some family somewhere?" his mother said.

"That's just it, Mom; I don't think he had anyone. I don't even remember seeing any other student at the dojo in all the years I went there, let alone friends or family. It was like he was only here for me. I have to do something." With that, his composure failed him and he started to feel his sorrow take hold of him. He got up and walked off to the bathroom. He didn't want his parents to see him like this. When he returned a few minutes later they were getting their coats on.

"You're leaving already?"

"Your father and I talked about what you said and thought we'd go home and make some phone calls, try to help get this memorial thing going." His mom sure had a way with words. "You get some rest. Take it easy and don't try to stress yourself. I mean it."

"Yes, Mom," he rolled his eyes as he hugged her.

"And, if the police start giving you a hard time, let me

71

know," his father said. "I have a very good friend with the city I could phone. He owes me a few favours. In fact, maybe I'll give him a call anyway."

"Oh, Hal, do you really think you'll need his help?"

"It couldn't hurt to put some feelers out there," he said, "just in case." His mother did her head shake and the t-t-t between her teeth again.

"I think I'm going to call Sensei Jiro," Cael said.

"Sensei Jiro? Why him?" asked his mom.

"It's the only other person I can think of that might know something about him. Besides, I think the people at Jiro's dojo should know the truth about him and that all the stuff they're saying in the news is lies."

"Of course, you're right," she kissed her son on the cheek. "Call me if you want to talk."

"Thanks Mom." And with that they left. Cael returned to the living room, slumped down on the couch and finished his coffee. Tomorrow he would go to his old Sensei and talk to him about Mr. Yamanaka.

#

Gladys and Hal Fraser took the stairs down to the main level which led out onto the street where their silver Range Rover was parked. They hated parking it out here but there was nothing they could do about it, besides it was insured. They had tried to convince Cael to get a nicer apartment closer to where they lived, even offered to pay for it for him, but he would have none of it. He wanted to do things on his own, be independent. Well let him, if that's what he wanted. Hal pressed the button on his key chain, heard the familiar beep, beep, and walked to the passenger side to open the door for his wife. They never said a word until he was safely in his seat and the engine was running. Gladys took out a cigarette and lit it. She slowly inhaled and let the smoke drift from her mouth as she stared straight ahead out the window.

"Do you think he knows anything?" she asked candidly.

"Not yet."

"What can we do?" she asked again.

"He must never talk to Jiro," he stated.

"Do you think that will help?"

"Yes."

"Are you sure?"

"Yes."

"You'd better be. It is not only your life this time but mine as well."

"I know dear, I know."

The Range Rover slowly pulled away from the curb and drove down the street, leaving the old rundown warehouse apartment behind.

Chapter 6

Cael got up early the next morning to get ready to go and see Sensei Jiro. He was actually looking forward to seeing him and hopefully finding out some information about Mr. Yamanaka. It had been a few years since he had been to his old dojo and he hoped Jiro remembered him. After coming under the tutelage of Mr. Yamanaka, there had been no reason to continue his training there and as time went on Cael seemed to forget all about Sensei Jiro and the place where he used to go almost every day. Now, his time had been consumed with his new teacher and learning different methods of training from what he had known before.

Cael also had another reason to get up early; he had to attend to his job. Despite his young age, he was fast gaining a reputation as a pretty good web designer and was compiling a long list of clients. It was another reason he loved this apartment. With the wide open warehouse layout of his living room and kitchen, it gave him many options as to where he could set up his computer and files. Right now he had everything set up at the far end of his living room, just off his bedroom. It was out of the glare of the huge window but it was not too far away that he couldn't push his chair back and look at the view as he brainstormed another idea. He worked for himself, which allowed him the luxury of choosing his own hours. Sometimes he would work for twenty hours straight, eating and drinking right at his computer, and sometimes he wouldn't work for a few days at a time. As long as he met his deadlines, his clients were happy and as long as they paid him on time, he was happy.

Today he needed to finish a job that he was in danger of completing late, something he never did. He prided himself in doing everything on time. He also needed to invoice a couple of clients and he needed to answer a whole lot of e-mail that had piled up over the last couple of days. Doing nothing since the whole incident with Mr. Yamanaka had put him behind. He got out the coffee and filled the coffee pot. By the time he was out of the shower, the coffee would be freshly brewed and ready for him to drink. He rarely ever ate breakfast but this morning he thought he'd have a bagel with his coffee. He headed for the shower, thinking it would be good to get his mind off Mr. Yamanaka for a while.

#

After his shower and breakfast, Cael walked over to his computer and turned it on. While it warmed up he got out the file of the client whose web site he had almost completed. Just a few more tweaks and it would be done. By now he could almost do this job blindfolded it had become so easy. It was good he was a computer geek in school; it provided him with a comfortable living. Having a father who was a banker was helpful too. In fact, it was his dad who had suggested he set up his own business. He even helped him with all the legalities of it and assured him that working for himself was the only way to go. He had been right of course and Cael wouldn't have it any other way now.

He looked at his watch. It was just coming up on eight o'clock. He figured he could finish this file and invoice his customers but going through all those emails right now did not appeal to him. No, he'd do that after he got back from his visit with Sensei Jiro. He took one last drink of coffee and set to work.

#

It was nearly eleven o'clock by the time Cael finished up his work. He shut off his computer, rinsed out his coffee cup and grabbed his jacket and left. It was a little chilly out; the icy cold weather still hung in the air, not wanting to let spring have its chance, even though it was already May. Out on the roads, the rain that had fallen the day before was now frozen for another day in time. You could tell by watching the pedestrians that the sidewalks were icy and very slick. They were stepping cautiously around all the frozen puddles. Their breath could be seen as a fine mist reminding one of the biting cold that was still in the air.

It was that time of year when every weekend people would flood all the garden centers, buying up the flowers and the bedding plants. Then they would try and make the perfect garden in a matter of a few hours and hope it would last until the fall. Cael was glad he was in an apartment now. He had hated spring

76

when he lived at home. His mother was one of those people panicking at the Garden Depot. She always wanted to have the best garden with the biggest variety of flowers even though she really had no idea what she was doing. Every year it was the same; rototill the dirt all around the house, in the backyard, all along the back fence, and, oh yeah, the big garden plot in the front yard too. It was *this* garden plot that was the biggest pain. Some years it was a rock garden, some years it was all flowers, and some years it was a variety of many different things. One year, his mother had even tried to plant all ferns there, which had turned out to be a disaster. Nevertheless, she wanted this garden to be the focal point of the yard. The one thing that she was sure would put the neighbours to shame and lift her yard to the prettiest on the block. That's the way it was in a lake community; everyone competed against everyone else to have the best yard. After the rototilling, came the endless hours of planting, then the daily upkeep of watering and weeding, not to mention that the lawn needed to be meticulously manicured as well. And who got to do all this labour intensive work? It was Cael, of course, under the strict supervision of his dear old mother. He hated it and now that he was on his own, he always made sure he had extra work at home when the dreaded spring planting season came. Last year he had even taken a camping trip just to get away from town for awhile.

He was thinking of this as he pulled into a parking stall in front of his old dojo. He got out of the Jeep and looked at the familiar old building. Hanging over the door was a huge white sign with the words 'Mountain Judo Club' written in black across it. He looked at the sign and smiled; this used to mean so much to him. Before he even got to the door he could hear the guttural yelling coming from the judokas as they threw each other and practiced their break falls. When he opened the door the familiar smell of sweat and gym mats flooded his nose. He looked around and was impressed by the size of the class. There must have been about twenty people working out, guys and girls, ranging in ages from eight to fifty-eight. It was good to see such a variety of people interested in judo. When he trained there, the biggest class he had ever been in had only about ten students in it. He could see the gym had changed a bit too. There were now three huge mats instead of the two ragged ones that were there before and they had padded the walls around the entire workout area. There were five ropes hanging from the roof to test their strength at climbing and a small area where one could lift weights if they wanted. They had also added a small reception area where parents or friends of students could sit and relax while they watched the workouts. It looked really nice with a couple of couches, a few chairs and a table with magazines spread out on it.

Cael stood with his hands in his jacket pockets. He was contemplating going and sitting on the big black sofa and waiting for the class to end. It would be kind of fun to observe a full class of judokas, he had trained on his own for so long now. He looked to see who was teaching the class and was surprised to see that it wasn't Sensei Jiro. As he made his way to the reception area he looked around, trying to spot the man he had come to see.

'Great, the one day I come in eight years,' he thought as he sat down on the sofa, 'and the man has the day off; just my luck.' Feeling dejected, he tried to figure out who was teaching the class. It was a young guy, about the same age as Cael, with blonde hair, kind of a big guy. Cael thought he had seen him before then opened his eyes wide as he recognized him.

'Rob! Rob Patterson! He was teaching?!' he thought as he gave a soft chuckle to himself. The last time he saw Rob, he had just turned twelve and Rob was still eleven, one month younger than himself. They were best friends and the biggest rivals when trained here. He and Rob joined judo around the same time and for the same reasons. They had hit it off instantly, both skinny little runts who had a habit of getting beat up at their respective schools. Rob went to a private school and Cael went to public school. Rob would get beat up just because he was small and cried a lot. He couldn't help it; he never could keep his emotions in check. Someone would say something mean to him and the tears would flow, not something you wanted to be known for when you went to an all boy's school. So the two of them wanted to learn to fight and stand up for themselves.

When they first met they would talk about how hard it was for them at school and how much they hated their classmates. They vowed that things would be different once they learned how to fight and that they would get back at those kids who had made their lives miserable. Funny thing was, though, once Cael started to learn more about martial arts, the more he became at peace with himself and the things people said to him didn't seem to bother him anymore. Rob, however, never seemed to quite get this part of it.

When it came to competing there was a distinct difference between the two, Rob loved it and Cael hated it. Rob was so involved in the tournaments and winning that it started to eat away at their friendship. Because they were the same age and the same size, they would always end up fighting each other at some point. Cael didn't care whether he won or not, which sometimes he did and sometimes he didn't, but Rob would take it way too far. If he lost it was the refereeing or Cael had somehow cheated and if he won he was even worse. He would laugh at Cael and say it was an *easy match* and he would brag about how much better he was. Cael would never say anything because, despite everything, Rob was still his friend. Eventually it got harder and harder for him to separate Rob, his friend, from Rob, the competitor. When the opportunity of training with Mr. Yamanaka and the promise of no more competitions came, it was no surprise that Cael took it. It meant not seeing his friend but by then he didn't seem to mind. And, now, after all this time he had almost completely forgotten about Rob.

He sat back and watched the class continue for another ten minutes then the door opened. He looked over to see who it was. A young couple walked in and were waving at one of the little girls in the class, obviously their daughter. They made their way over to the reception area and took a seat on a couple of chairs facing the mat. They watched the little girl with pride and talked about how much progress she seemed to be making. The door opened again and a man walked in by himself. He stayed by the door and kept checking his watch; it must be almost time for the class to end. Sure enough, five minutes later, Rob had all the students line up and do their final bow out and let them leave the mat, most senior judokas first. The little girl ran to her parents with a big grin on her face.

"Did you see me!? Did you see me!?" she asked.

"Yes, we saw you," said her mother, as she held out her daughter's shoes for her to put on.

"I threw Sensei!!" she sounded so excited.

"Did you?" asked her father. He picked her up and the three of them headed for the door. The rest of the students were hastily putting on their coats and shoes, chatting about the class and getting ready to head outside. Slowly, the gym started to empty. Rob was kicking the mats back in place; they always got a little out of line after any workout. He was so busy doing this that he didn't notice Cael approaching.

"Make sure you do that right, we wouldn't want anyone getting hurt now," Cael said, teasingly.

"I always make sure everything…" Rob started to reply as he looked up to see who he was speaking to. His mouth

81

dropped and his eyes popped open wide, then a huge smile came across his face. "Cael!! What the hell are you doing here?" Rob came off the mat, forgetting to bow and grabbed Cael's hand and pulled him into a friendly hug. "I haven't seen you in what…?"

"Eight years," said Cael, shaking his friend's hand.

"I see you've moved up in the dojo," Cael said, pointing at the black belt tied around his friend's gi.

"This old thing," Rob laughed, as if this achievement didn't mean anything, "just something I like to wear every once in a while." The two laughed at Rob's nonchalance.

"You look good," said Cael, "and big!"

"Yeah, I filled in," Rob flexed his muscles with his arms in the air, laughing. He put his arms down and looked at Cael. "No, seriously, what brings you here after all these years?"

"I came to see Sensei Jiro, is he here?" Cael asked. Rob's smile faded, he looked around and watched the last of the judokas leave. They were the only two left in the building.

"Let's talk," he said as he put his arm around his friend and led him to the reception area. He sat in one of the chairs and encouraged Cael to sit on the sofa, which he did. "Cael, Sensei Jiro is not here."

"Well, I can see that. Is it his day off?" Cael asked, suddenly feeling that he didn't want to hear the answer.

"No, it's not his day off. He's gone," said Rob.

"Gone? What do you mean gone?" Cael asked, not understanding what Rob meant.

"I mean gone. About three weeks ago I got this weird phone call from the Sensei asking if I wanted to teach for awhile. It seems he had to leave town real quick and needed someone to run his classes. He said he would pay me cash and that he would send me the money by mail. Then he emailed me the schedule and said he would be in touch. He told me to get Stephanie, that's the secretary he hired a few months ago, to handle any office matters without him. The next day, at around six o'clock in the morning, I got a knock on the door. When I opened it up there was no one there, just an envelope on the floor filled with twenty dollar bills and a note saying thank you and I'll be in touch," Rob was speaking like he still had a hard time believing it. "Pretty weird, huh? When I came here later that day and told Steph everything, she was really great about it and the students didn't question anything. Even the other black belts were okay with it; some of them help me teach some of the classes. Strange, though, eh?"

"I don't get it, where did he go?" Cael asked, still stunned by what he was hearing.

"That's just it, no one knows," said Rob. "One minute he was here next minute he vanished. He's not here, he's not anywhere and no one knows anything. He didn't even leave a number where we could reach him at."

"He just disappeared? How does that happen? Doesn't this Stephanie know anything more?" This was starting to sound just a little suspicious.

"Nope, she's just as much in the dark as me. We both think he'll be back soon, though. He's only paid me for two months," said Rob, as he leaned back in the chair. "Weird, eh?"

"Yeah." Cael didn't know what to say. Where was Sensei Jiro? He really wanted to talk to him. Could this have something to do with Mr. Yamanaka? Cael now had more questions than when he first came here.

"Cael?" Rob was trying to ask him something.

"What?" He came out of his stunned trance.

"I was just asking why you wanted to talk to Sensei Jiro," he repeated.

"Oh, I just had some questions," Cael paused and decided he would ask his questions anyway. "I just wanted to know if he had heard about Mr. Yamanaka."

"*I* heard about it. What a mess and that poor guy that was with him, he must be feeling pretty damn lucky to be alive," Rob was shaking his head then he stopped short as he saw the look on Cael's face. "Wait a minute…that was you with him, wasn't it!? Holy sh…! I can't believe it! How are you man!? That must have been pretty harsh."

"Yeah, well," Cael didn't feel comfortable talking about it with Rob, "it's not true what they're saying, you know. He wasn't involved in any gang activity."

"Oh, definitely, I didn't believe that for a second," said Rob.

"I just thought I'd make sure that everyone knows that,"

Cael said. "I also wanted to ask Sensei Jiro if he knew of any family Mr. Yamanaka might have had, you know so I could let them know. I'm planning to have a memorial for him."

"You didn't know?" Rob looked at Cael as if he were joking.

"Know what?"

"Mr. Yamanaka, Sensei Jiro…?" Rob said.

"Yeah...?" Cael didn't know what he was getting at.

"They're brothers," stated Rob, amazed he knew something Cael did not.

"What?" Cael's question was almost inaudible. He sat there, feeling his stomach drop, staring at Rob. Sensei Jiro was Mr. Yamanaka's brother? Why had he not said anything to him? How could he not know this?

"Yeah, it's why Sensei Jiro sent you to him in the first place. He knew how good he was and that you would be getting the best," Rob said. "You know, I was kinda jealous when you were the one that got to go with Taro. I thought I should have got that privilege."

"Taro?"

"Mr. Yamanaka's name? Boy, you really don't know anything do you?" Rob felt a sense of superiority over his friend. Cael felt stupid. Why didn't he know any of this?

"No, I-I…Mr. Yamanaka never talked about his personal life and I never asked. It was just the way it was," Cael ran his hands over his face and drew in a deep breath. "His brother."

"Pretty cool, huh?" Rob said. "Actually, Sensei Jiro never talked about it either so don't feel too bad. I think only me and Steph know. Nobody else ever made the connection, besides; Mr. Yamanaka never really came here after you went with him."

"How did *you* know?" asked Cael.

"Steph told me. I guess Sensei Jiro told her after she started working here. I think Jiro and Taro kept in touch over the phone," Rob said. "Anything else?"

"No," Suddenly Cael wanted to get out of there, go home and try to figure out what the hell was going on. "I-I have to go."

"Already?" Rob sounded disappointed. "You just got here. We have so much catching up to do. We could go for lunch or something."

"I know but I have a lot of work to do at home. Can I take a rain check?" Cael stood up wanting to run for the door.

"Okay, I guess. Man it was good to see you." Rob walked his friend to the door. "Next time try to stay a little longer."

"I will." Cael grabbed for the handle.

"Hey!" Rob stopped him.

"What?"

"When is this memorial, I'd like to go and I'm sure some of the other guys would like to as well?" Rob asked.

"There's nothing set, yet. My mom is making most of the arrangements. As soon as I know I'll call you okay?"

"Thanks," said Rob, "and Cael?"

"Yeah?" Cael looked at his friend.

"Take care okay, you look like shit," Rob laughed as he said goodbye to Cael.

Chapter 7

Whisper sat back on the pillows and looked at Aria. Even though she was now aware of who she was, there was still so much for her to learn. She was at peace in her heart and she understood her purpose for being but she still felt unprepared with a long way to go before she was completely ready to save a soul. She knew whose soul she was supposed to save. It had to be the man she had seen in the hospital. It was *his* deep despair that had pulled her into his world. She knew that now. But there seemed to be a sense of urgency with him and she knew she was not ready to help him.

"You look confused," said Aria, who had been watching her closely.

"Is it that obvious?" Whisper asked.

"Yes," she said, "what is it that has you looking so baffled?"

"I don't get it," she started, "if I'm supposed to be able to save a soul when I get called why do I not feel ready?"

"Because you're not," she stated simply. "You need to take a sort of crash course before you're even remotely ready to save the soul that chooses you."

"The soul that chooses me?" asked Whisper. Did that

mean that the soul that she was supposed to save had not chosen her yet? Maybe she was wrong about the man in the hospital.

"Yes…" Aria started, and then it dawned on her. "You want to know whose soul it is you have to save, don't you."

"Well, yes, I thought that's why we had this meeting." She thought the meeting had been called because of her sudden pull to the Earth dimension the day before. "You know, when I…"

"We don't need to talk about it yet. What we really need to do is get started." She stood up and reached for Whisper's hand to help her up.

"Started?" Whisper asked as she slowly got up. "Are we going home now?"

"Oh, we're not going home, not now. There's way too much to do." Aria smiled, her green eyes sparkled with excitement.

"But, if I don't go home, people will get worried and wonder where I am," said Whisper, a little apprehensive. "My father is already on the war path over my cheating incident. If I don't go home he'll send a whole search party after me."

"That cheating incident was one of the reasons we knew it was time for you to come with us," she said, concerned. "Don't worry, no one will become suspicious and no one will come looking for you."

"How can you be so sure?" asked Whisper.

"Because, right now you're visiting your sick

grandmother. Her illness came on suddenly and you had to leave straight from school. Your parents came to the school and picked you up during lunch. No one saw you leave, you were so upset so I made sure you got out of the school quickly and quietly. I, on the other hand, am at a conference in Hydritch."

"What? My grandmother?" This woman was just full of surprises. Whisper had never met her grandmother before. In fact, grandparents were never discussed before and Whisper had never really thought of them before. That suddenly felt strange to her.

"Your very sweet, very old grandmother," she said. "She will be sick for awhile so we don't know when you'll be back. It's been very upsetting for you, I just may drop by to see how you're doing while I'm at my conference."

"And everyone believed you?" asked Whisper.

"Why wouldn't they, after all, your family is very close," said Aria with a smile.

"I don't know…"

"Why? I'm really quite convincing, you know," Aria finished, looking quite proud of herself. "Now, come on, I have so much to show you." They put their shoes on and Aria grabbed her coat, and headed out through the sliding paper door. Whisper followed right behind, so many questions racing through her mind.

Aria lead the way down the long corridor that lead to the kitchen. They didn't see anyone until they opened the big double

90

doors. It was a flurry of activity in there. There were at least ten people, chopping, cutting, stirring and cooking. They were speaking in a chorus of cooking chatter and were working like a well choreographed dance, preparing meals for their customers. Whisper was fascinated by their remarkable precision and found herself standing still, staring at them in awe. Aria pulled her hand and she came back to life and followed her once again.

At the back of the kitchen was another door that lead to a narrow staircase going down. They went down the stairs until they came to the basement. Three giant walk-in freezers stood before them. Whisper looked around and saw nothing else. She wondered why Aria would bring her down there. Then Aria went to one of the freezers and opened the door.

"Come on." She waved Whisper over to the freezer. "Shut the door behind you."

"What?" Whisper wasn't sure if she should do that. Wouldn't they be locked in? Aria noticed her hesitation.

"Trust me," she said and Whisper slowly closed the door, hoping Aria knew what she was doing. When the door shut, they were thrown into total darkness and for a moment Whisper felt panicked. Then she heard a sharp knock followed by a high pitched whistle. The room filled with a bright light that was coming from an opening at the back of the freezer.

'Well, I'll be damned!' thought Whisper. She moved toward the back of the freezer and saw Aria walking through to the other side.

It was like walking into another world when Whisper passed through the door. They came out into a long hallway that was wide enough to drive a car down. Its walls were made of old grey stone and lit by bright torches that were placed in holders attached to the walls. The floor was made of cobblestone and stretched a few hundred feet in either direction. There was a man standing there, dressed in black from head to toe, even his face was covered. He appeared to be guarding the door.

"Hello, Kisho," Aria nodded to him.

"Aria, good to see you again," the man nodded back. She turned left and started down the hallway. They walked almost to the end and stopped at the last door on the right. She opened the door and was greeted by a woman who seemed to be expecting them.

"Aria! We've been waiting for the two of you!" The woman said, looking relieved that they had finally gotten there. She was a tall woman with long, flowing white hair. She looked very wise and kind with grey blue eyes and softly wrinkled skin. She wore a long white gown that hung effortlessly over her body with long wide sleeves that came almost to the ground. After she embraced Aria she turned to look at Whisper and smiled. Whisper felt comfortable in her gaze.

"Whisper, it's so good to have you back." She grabbed the girl up in her arms and hugged her. Although Whisper did not know this woman something about her felt familiar. She laughed when she saw Whisper's face. "Don't worry, in time you

92

will remember us all. I am Alannis and I come from the world of Atlantis."

"Oh! Hi," Whisper said timidly as she realized the woman came from one of the more highly intellectual worlds. Alannis stepped aside to let them enter the room.

It was a huge room reminiscent of a castle ballroom. The walls, like the hallway, were made of stone with the same kind of torches mounted in metal brackets to provide light. There were long blue velvet draperies hanging on one wall that, when opened like they were, displayed an array of paintings, each depicting a variety of beautiful landscapes. Along another wall were bookshelves filled with books from different worlds and different times. There were a few tables scattered about, surrounded by mismatched chairs. In the corner stood a table pushed up against the wall and on top was an urn filled with coffee on one side and hot water on the other. There was a pitcher of water with cups and glasses stacked up beside it and off to the side were sugar packets, little creamers and a box of stir sticks. There were a few people in the room and Whisper quietly looked them over.

Three men were gathered at one table and appeared to be deep in conversation. They didn't seem to notice Whisper and her friends. One of the men looked elegantly dressed with a neatly trimmed beard and fine features. He wore a velvet, burgundy suit and sat with his legs crossed, a cup of tea in his hand. The other two men didn't look quite so elegant and

93

Whisper could tell they weren't from Chrystalline. They were short and had long beards and long shaggy hair. They wore brightly coloured clothes and instantly Whisper knew who they were. Gnomes from the Lorynth dimension and she wondered what they were doing there. It wasn't unusual to see gnomes, goblins, brownies or many other mystical creatures in Chrystalline because they had the ability to physically enter any world without a portal. In fact they were known to go back and forth from one world to the next, trading goods, stealing goods, and sometimes causing chaos.

Aside from these three men was a woman looking at the books on the shelves, and another woman reading quietly in the corner. At a table off to the right sat two very distinguished, official looking men. It was this table that Aria and Alannis were headed towards. Whisper had seen men like this before. Her father worked for them and she knew how serious men like this could be. They both had short, neatly cut black hair, dark eyebrows and dark eyes. They had the kind of face that looked angry even when they were happy. They sat very straight, as if a pole had been shoved up their spine. They wore dark grey suits, that were perfectly tailored with no wrinkles, no seam out of place and they sat perfectly still, each holding a cup of coffee. Aria headed straight for them. Whisper reluctantly followed and as she got closer, she noticed the two men looked identical. They were twins.

"Miles, Marcus, how good to see you." The two men

stood up and smiled, or as close to a smile as they could get. Their faces didn't move as their mouths showed gleaming white teeth. It looked disturbing. They embraced Aria in a cold looking hug and pulled out a chair for her to sit down. Alannis took the chair she had obviously occupied before Whisper and Aria had arrived. "Thank you. I believe you know Whisper?"

'What? I knew these two cronies? On what planet?' Whisper asked herself, thinking there was no way she could know these two men.

"Yes, we've been watching her for some time now."

"I'm sorry, but do I know you?" asked Whisper, thinking how creepy it sounded that they had been 'watching' her.

"No, no," the man on the left laughed which sounded more like he was clearing his throat. "What Miles meant was that we have been following your progress very closely. You have become very important to all of us here."

"I have? Why?" she asked.

"All in due time, Whisper," said Alannis. "Gentlemen, if you please, let's not overwhelm Whisper on her first day. Remember, she came through her awakening way too early and has only had her memory partially restored."

"I have?" Aria never told Whisper this but it explained why people seemed to know her but she didn't know them.

"We know and we apologize. We were just a little excited that's all," said Marcus, looking ashamed.

"Whisper, would you like anything to drink? Coffee or

tea maybe?" Alannis tried to set the girl at ease.

"No, I couldn't possibly put anything else in my stomach after that huge lunch." She was still feeling very full.

"Well, in that case," started Aria, "Marcus, will you come and open the dorms? I'd like to show Whisper to her room."

"My room? I'm staying here in this restaurant?" Whisper was surprised by this.

"This is far more than a restaurant," said Aria. "It's a sanctuary for people like us when we're in transition and right now it's the safest place for you."

"Oh." Whisper sobered; again the implication that her life was in danger. She was starting to believe it.

"You have to understand, Whisper, there are people out there that don't want you to heal anyone. There is fierce competition over souls and they will kill to get one on their side and we can't let that happen," Marcus looked at her so intensely as he spoke that it kind of made her feel more protected to have this strange, serious man on her side. "Let's go." He got up from his chair and headed for the door. Whisper waited to see who else would get up. Only Aria; Alannis had started a deep discussion with Miles and didn't seem to notice them leaving.

They went back out through the door they had come in and then down the hall. The man in black was still standing there, guarding the door to the freezer, he nodded as they passed. They continued down to the very end of the hall where they came to a wooden door that looked thick and heavy. Marcus took out a black key from his pocket, unlocked the door and pulled it slowly open. Again there was a staircase leading further down into the ground. Whisper wondered how far underground this sanctuary went. Marcus held the door open for them as they passed through.

"I'll go back to the lounge. If you need me just call," he said as he smiled his blank smile at Aria.

"Thank you, Marcus and I'll see you later," Aria said as she looped her arm in Whisper's and started to lead her down the stairs. "This place is really quite remarkable. It was built a couple of thousand years ago by a group of Cross-overs, you'll learn more about those tomorrow. Down these stairs are a few rooms that we like to call 'the dorms'. There aren't a lot of them, ten in all, but it's enough. They're all really nice, sort of like hotel rooms. You'll have all the privacy you'll need and you'll be able to get a good night's sleep."

"But I have no clothes, no toothbrush, no hairbrush, nothing." Whisper was starting to feel like she was being kidnapped.

"I've put a suitcase in there for you. It has all your personal stuff in it and we've supplied the room with a few other things that we thought you might need." They got to the bottom of the stairs and made their way to the third door on the left. This time Aria pulled out a key and opened the door. She hurried into the room before Whisper and fiddled with something. When she finished, the whole room lit up and Whisper could see that she had manipulated a translucent crystal to emit a strong bright light.

"How'd you do that?" asked Whisper.

"Come here and I'll show you. You'll need to know anyway because when I go you'll have to work this thing on your own." Whisper went over to the small white table the crystal sat on. Aria showed her how to hold her hands just inches from it. "Now, concentrate your inner mind on the light within the crystal. Once you can feel it, you can tell it to turn on or off." She demonstrated and almost as soon as she put her hands near the crystal it went out, throwing them into total darkness; Whisper couldn't even see her anymore. The light went back on, very dim, and Aria took her hands away.

"Now, you try." Whisper was not so sure she could do this but she put her hands out toward the crystal anyway. She held them just as Aria had shown her, closed her eyes and concentrated. Minutes passed and she felt doubt in her ability to do this seemingly easy task. She was not ready for this. She should return home and continue studying and wait for another soul to require her assistance. She felt tears come to her eyes as her humiliation grew with each passing moment.

"Whisper, you have to release the doubt in your mind. We wouldn't have gone through the trouble of bringing you here if we didn't believe you could do this." Whisper was amazed at how Aria always knew what to say. Her words put Whisper at ease. Slowly she felt her doubts going away and her mind started to refocus on the crystal in front of her. She started to feel the energy of the crystal flow through her hands and up through her body. Her mind started to become aware of the power held within the rock and she softly told it to turn brighter.

BAM!! The room filled with a blinding light and neither Aria nor Whisper could see anything.

"WHOA! Turn it down or we'll both go blind!" Aria yelled as she shielded her eyes with her arms. Whisper refocused on the crystal and instantly the light subsided to a much more comfortable level.

"I did it!" She was proud of herself for this small accomplishment.

"Yes, you did," said Aria with a smile on her face, "and much more powerfully than any of us did when we first tried."

"Really?" Whisper found this hard to believe.

"Seriously, it took me half a day to get that thing to light up just a little bit," said Aria. "Crystals are something that Alannis brought with her from Atlantis. They're quite fascinating and hold a lot of power that we had no idea of."

"Cool!" exclaimed Whisper. "Will I get to see more of them?"

"Maybe. For now, though, I think you should settle in. Have a good look around your room and maybe have a rest. If you need anything, I'm in the next room on the right, just come and knock," she said as she started for the door to leave.

"You mean I'm not locked in here?" she asked.

"Good gracious, no! Why would I do that?" Aria seemed surprised by this question.

"I don't know, I just sort of feel like I've been kidnapped or something. I mean when you did that thing to me upstairs and I remembered who I was, it's kind of like not everything came back to me," Whisper tried to explain. "I mean I know who I am in my heart, but there's still so much I don't remember. It's all so confusing to me right now and I'm starting to feel frustrated and lost."

"We had to bring you to your awakening way earlier than was planned. I can't explain why right now but soon it will become clearer. You just have to trust us. I know that's a lot to ask
but you have to try," Aria pleaded with her. Whisper looked at her and nodded, she really had no other choice. "As for locking you in your room, we wouldn't do that. You can lock the door, yourself, if you want but other than that you can leave your room whenever you want. I'll leave the key right here on the table. Like I said, I'm right next door and there are others that are staying here that you'll meet later. There's a telecommunicator over on the desk. If you get hungry or want to go upstairs, you'll have to call Marcus; it's button four. He's the only one with a key to the door at the top of the stairs. Even I have to call him for that. You can't mind-port down here, none of us can. It's the way this place was built. No one can mind-port out and no one can mind-port in. If you want to go in the restaurant or outside please

don't do it alone. Until you learn everything you need to know it's safer if you don't go anywhere alone."

"What do you mean, safer?" Aria looked away and took in a deep breath. It was obvious she didn't want to say more. "Okay, okay, I won't ask any more questions. I'll just look around my room and go to sleep."

"Don't sound so depressed, it will get better, I promise." She took Whisper's hands and gave them a little shake. "Okay?"

"Okay," Whisper said, with a slight grin. She didn't want Aria to see how sad this whole thing made her feel. She missed her home, her parents, her friends and even her dog and knowing she might be there for awhile made her feel even worse.

"Okay, there's food in the fridge and cupboards, shampoo and soap in the bathroom, lots of movies and books stacked on the shelves and remember, if you need anything…"

"…you're right next door," Whisper finished for her.

"Right," she said as she let go of Whisper's hands and looked around. "You know, this really is a beautiful room. I think it's even better than mine. I'll see you tomorrow morning as soon as you're ready to come upstairs." She turned and left.

She was alone. She was scared and not so sure she could do this. She felt tears start to come to her eyes and tried hard to push them away. She decided to explore the room; that might keep her mind occupied. She didn't even look around when her and Aria had come in; she had been so fascinated with the crystal. Now that she was alone, Whisper began to explore and realized Aria was right, it was a beautiful room. It wasn't like a hotel room at all though. It was actually more like an apartment. Past the door and the little white table the crystal sat on, was a nice sized living room with a big billowy white sofa and a chair. Red cushions were placed neatly in the corners of both. The floor was covered with a rich dark hardwood and an oriental rug lay neatly beneath the sofa and chair. There was a brown coffee table with a vase full of beautiful red roses sitting on top of it. A mahogany bookshelf filled one wall, loaded with books and movies. Mounted on the other wall, facing the sofa was a huge screen for viewing the movies.

'Wow!! I'll have to try that out later,' she thought to herself. To the right of the living room was an entry to what appeared to be a kitchen. In between the two rooms was a small hallway that lead, Whisper presumed, to the bathroom and the bedroom. She decided to check out the kitchen first.

The kitchen seemed to have everything. There was a small sink with a drying rack to the side. The cupboards were lightly coloured which brightened the room despite the lack of any natural light. There was a white fridge in the corner and a small two burner stove stood beside it. A small table against the wall with another vase full of red roses sitting on top completed the room. Whisper walked over to the fridge and pulled open the door to have a look. It was full. There was milk, eggs, butter, juice, apples and lots more. Impulsively she grabbed an apple and headed out of the kitchen.

She peeked into the bathroom and saw a huge tub in the corner. It was surrounded by beautiful white and grey marble that reflected the shadows off the dim light the crystal's luminescence provided this far down the hall. There was a separate shower to the left surrounded by the same marble. Whisper had never seen a bathroom so beautiful.

"Man, I'm definitely taking a bath later," she said out loud.

She went back into the hallway and approached the last room. She opened the door to darkness; the crystal didn't reach this room. She stepped inside and let her eyes adjust. There was another small white table with a crystal on top. She walked over, put the apple down, placed her hands above the crystal and closed her eyes. It only took a couple of seconds for the light to come on this time. She was getting better at this.

She looked around the room and her jaw dropped. It was amazing. The light the crystal gave off was different in here. It was a soft blue and it illuminated the room making it look like it was outside in the dusk. The big double bed sat up so high that there were little steps beside it to climb up. A thick white comforter stretched over the entire mattress, overflowing on either side. It was a four poster canopy bed with a soft white veil that fell from the canopy and surrounded the entire bed. There were a dozen pillows of all sizes spread out at the head, inviting Whisper to go bury herself among them and fall asleep. She was very tempted. There was a nightstand beside the bed with more red roses set in the vase on top and, beyond that, a door.

She went over and opened it and gasped. It was a huge walk-in closet full of clothes and shoes. She saw her suitcase sitting in the middle of the floor just like Aria had said it would be. There was a built-in dresser and Whisper pulled the drawers open and found t-shirts, pyjamas and sweaters and all sorts of jeans, hoodies and skirts hanging neatly on hangers. Odella would have been in heaven. She went back into the room and looked longingly at the bed again.

'I should try it out, see how comfortable it is,' she said to herself. She walked around to the steps, slipped off her shoes and climbed up. It was like slipping onto a cloud. She buried herself beneath the pillows and felt her whole body relax. 'Oh, this is nice,' she smiled and closed her eyes. Within ten minutes Whisper was fast asleep.

Chapter 8

Whisper woke up the next morning feeling more rested than she had ever felt before. The bed was amazing and she felt like she could lie there forever but knew that could never happen. Sooner or later someone would come looking for her. She turned over onto her back and realized the light in the room had changed. Instead of the soft blue it illuminated the room with when she had fallen asleep, it was now bright like a sunny day. It was hard to believe that she was several feet underground.

"Cool!" she said out loud. She figured the crystal must mimic the sky outside. She wondered if it would get dark in there if it started to rain outside.

She contemplated the crystal and all the different types of light it could display, delaying actually getting up. Finally, she decided it was time to move. She sat up and swung her legs over the side. She couldn't believe she had fallen asleep in her clothes; she must have been pretty tired. She went to the closet and grabbed her suitcase to see what had been packed for her. She put it on the bed and opened it up. She was relieved to see her toothbrush and hairbrush. She didn't care how many fancy things these people brought her, it was nice to have something that was hers.

She figured it was probably too late for her to have a long bath, so, she would save it for later. She grabbed some clothes, found some towels in a cupboard in the short hallway and jumped in the shower.

It felt so good to be washed and dressed. Now, she could tackle anything. She went to the kitchen and made a small breakfast, just some fruit and a glass of milk. While she was washing the couple of dishes she used, she debated whether or not to call Marcus or go next door to get Aria. She decided the latter was probably better. Marcus made her feel uneasy.

#

Aria answered the door on the second knock, probably waiting for her Whisper guessed. She smiled as she saw how refreshed Whisper looked. It seemed funny but, now that Whisper had been 'awakened', Aria seemed more like a friend than the school principal. She was happier, too, not having to pretend to be something she obviously wasn't.

"Whisper! You look great. Come in!" she exclaimed as she opened the door wide for her to enter. "Did you have anything to eat yet?"

"Yeah, some fruit," she answered, looking around Aria's apartment. She was right, Whisper's apartment did look better. This one was great, too, just a little too dark.

"Good. Did you sleep okay?" she asked as they made their way to the couch in the living room. It was a green leather couch that felt kind of stiff when Whisper sat on it.

"Yeah, I slept like a rock. The bed in there is *so* comfortable," Whisper answered.

"I know mine's great too. I think they have the same kind of bed in all these rooms." Aria spoke with a casual familiarity and, again, Whisper wondered if they had been friends before. "Are you ready for today?"

"I guess." She wanted to ask about their friendship. It would be nice to know if she had an ally in there. "Aria, did we used to be friends?" Aria looked a little apprehensive with the question.

"Why do you ask?"

"Because, us, here together, feels so familiar to me and you seem really happy to have me here," she stated. "You don't act like the 'principal' at all anymore. It's like, when we were at school, you were all stiff and in charge and now you're, like, relaxed and way more friendlier." Aria looked relieved to be able to drop the facade and show her real self.

"I hated being 'the principal'," she stated. "It was so boring but I had to do it, it was part of my mission."

"I know, you told me that before. I just get the feeling that maybe we were close before, you know, like friends or something." Aria looked nervously down at her hands.

"I guess it wouldn't hurt to tell you," she started. "Whisper, you were…you *are* my best friend. We've been through so much together and it's so hard to see you this way. Usually, after you've come through your awakening, you

107

remember me and everyone else. But this time is so different. This time you don't remember anything. I thought that if it was me that brought you here, you'd remember something but you don't do you?"

"No," Whisper felt awful. Clearly this woman wanted Whisper to remember their friendship but she couldn't seem to grasp the memory of it. "I'm sorry I don't, but believe me, it's very frustrating for me too."

"I can just imagine."

"But, it's good to know I have a friend here," she tried to reassure Aria as well as herself. "You don't know how lonely I felt last night. This whole thing is kind of scary to me."

"Whisper, you have no idea how much everyone is counting on you." She sat on the edge of the couch and spoke very quietly, as if she didn't want anyone else to hear. "This soul you're going to save is very important. There can't be failure."

"It's that serious?" Whisper asked and Aria nodded. "Then, maybe, I'm not the right one to do this."

"Don't say that! You'll push everyone over the edge." She laughed nervously. "You're the right one, believe me."

"But, I feel so useless." Whisper felt she could be more honest now.

"I told them you'd feel like this," Aria said, angrily. "But they assured me they'd bring you along slowly and that you'd be able to adapt."

"Adapt?" she asked.

"Well, yeah, it's virtually impossible to bring your memories back now. You came into this way too soon."

"I see."

'I would never get my memories back? I would always be stuck in this sort of limbo state?' These thoughts made Whisper want to scream with frustration.

"But, don't worry, after this you'll go to the Forest of Dreams and start all over again. All this will be forgotten and you'll remember your friends again."

"The Forest of Dreams? I forgot about that." Suddenly she felt encouraged. "Doesn't that wipe out everyone's memories? So the way I feel is normal. Nobody remembers things after being there right?"

"Well, not really," Aria said then continued. "The Forest wipes out your memories, yes, but only the ones of the soul you just healed are permanently gone. The rest start to come back gradually over time. You go to school for awhile and start to relearn about the way the Universe works. Soon you learn about the different beings that occupy our planet and how we got here. You could spend years relearning all of this. Then, when you go through your awakening, you remember your fellow Soul-healers and you know the different techniques used to heal a soul and your defence training comes back to you. Right now, it's like you were in your first year of school and we pulled you out so you could perform brain surgery on someone; almost impossible."

"Almost? How about *absolutely* impossible?"

"You're right, it does feel that way," Aria said as she thought about it. "But it's possible with the proper teaching. You should be fine."

"Okay," Whisper didn't feel quite as confident, "what do you teach me?"

"Nothing, I'm here for moral support." She saw the panic in Whisper's eyes and tried to soothe her. "Don't worry; your teachers are the best."

"Is Alannis one?" Whisper hoped she was, she felt comfortable around her.

"Yeah, she'll be your main teacher and she's really good too. Atlanteans are so smart." Relief washed over Whisper's face. "Then there are the twins, Miles and Marcus, they'll be teaching you about the different life forms that are around."

"*They're* going to teach me?" She didn't know if she liked that.

"You don't like them either?" Aria laughed. "I think they're so weird, but Alannis insists they know what they're doing and they seem very smart. Still, though, I think they seem more like robots than people." They both laughed at that.

"Is there anyone else?" asked Whisper.

"Yeah, there's a Cross-over from the Earth dimension who's going to teach you some fighting techniques. I know him quite well and, trust me, he's really good," she said. "Actually, we should probably get going. They'll all be wondering where

110

we are."

"Is it that late?" Whisper asked as they both stood up.

"No, but they've been so anxious to get started that I'm surprised they haven't been down here to get us already." She picked up her telecommunicator and called Marcus to come and open the door.

"Shall we?" she waved her hand, letting Whisper go first. When they got to the door Whisper stopped and turned to look at her friend.

"Aria, I want you to know how much I appreciate you being here," she started. "I'm sorry I can't remember you, but I do feel your love and concern and it makes me feel a whole lot better about this. I hope that we can become good friends again."

"Yes, I hope that too," Aria coughed, trying to clear the lump in her throat. Whisper reached out and gave her a hug. "I'm glad some parts of you will never change."

#

When they got upstairs Marcus was waiting with Miles by his side. He held the door open and greeted them with a fixed smile on his face.

"Ladies," he said, "good to see you this morning. Whisper, you will be coming with us and Aria you are free to do whatever you want. Alannis is in the lounge." Whisper swallowed hard and looked at Aria pleadingly. She didn't want to be left alone with those two. Aria understood and squeezed Whisper's hand.

"Right, then, I'll see you after, okay?" She looked at Whisper reassuringly who reluctantly nodded. Then she waited for the twins to turn their backs and whispered in her ear. "Don't worry, I'm told they're really quite harmless." Although they couldn't see him, Miles had a grin on his face when he heard Aria's comment.

Aria continued down the hall towards the lounge. Marcus and Miles took Whisper halfway down the hall and opened a door with a key that was on a ring filled with about two dozen more keys.

"You guys must be the official key keepers or something," said Whisper, as she looked at all the keys on the ring.

"Yes, we certainly do have a lot of them," Marcus said as he opened the door then put the ring of keys in his pant's pocket. They walked into the room and instantly Whisper noticed how different it was from the rest of the underground fortress. It was small and bare. There were a couple of tables and a few chairs and that was about it. It still had the familiar stone walls and Whisper could see that, like her apartment downstairs, it was lit by a crystal that sat on a table in the corner of the room. They all sat down around one of the tables. It felt more like they were in a boardroom rather than a classroom. There was no hesitation as Miles ploughed right into the lesson.

"In order for you to understand about who we all are, we need to explain how this planet works first. I know you have learned a bit about the Universe and the different galaxies that are out there but when it comes to this planet, you have only scratched the surface."

"Should I take notes or something?" She felt like she needed to do something with her hands. She didn't think she could just sit there and stare at the two of them as they talked.

"No, we need your full attention," said Marcus. "Now that your soul has been awakened, you should have no problem understanding the things we tell you. Besides, there will be no test at the end of these classes. Your test will come when you try to save the soul."

"Oh, okay." Like that made her feel any better. She sat back in her chair and tried to make herself as comfortable as she could.

"Okay," Miles continued, "to begin with, you know that this planet has many dimensions or worlds as we sometimes call them, but what you don't know is how these dimensions work. Picture a tree, if you will, and all the rings you can see when you cut that tree in half. Each ring represents another year of that tree's life. The most inner ring has been around the longest. It has seen the forest when it was just beginning and has watched the growth of each new ring year after year until the last, or outer, ring appears. The outer ring is new and has no tolerance for anything it cannot explain. It does not understand the depth of the tree because all it can see is the outside." Miles looked at Whisper to make sure she was understanding everything.

"This planet is like that tree. There are some dimensions that have built up an understanding of everything that happens here. The people that occupy these dimensions have gained knowledge and an acceptance of the other dimensions. For example, in Crystalline, the people have no problem sitting with a gnome from Lorynth or dining with a prince from Shy-ling or even building a pen for Crogans from the Abyss. Crystalline has been around for a very long time and has gained an appreciation for all other worlds.

"Some dimensions are like the outer ring, they can't see anything but what is in their own world. Even if they were shown the facts, they would still not believe. Like where your parents are from; their world can only see themselves and don't believe anything else exists.

"Another world like that is Earth, a fascinating dimension. The people that live there are in between two beliefs; they can feel that there must be something else out there and, yet, they still convince themselves that nothing else can exist beyond their world. What is truly remarkable about this world is the attraction it holds for every other being out there. From all over the Universe visitors have been coming to this world throughout time to study them and to even live with them and experience their life and yet, still, they remain oblivious. Even the people of Crystalline copy the way they dress and seem to be very fond of their TV. Unfortunately, this attraction has pulled the evil forces to them as well. These forces love that the people are so materialistic and find them easy to manipulate.

"We have tried, in our own ways, to let them know about the other worlds that exist but they refuse to accept it. They even go so far as to invent legends to explain away these worlds; some story made up by their ancestors. For example, Alannis and her people tried to teach them about Atlantis but it proved too much for them to grasp. Instead, they told of how it had become too intelligent, making the people there greedy and immoral. As punishment they were swept away under the sea. They would much rather believe there is a city lost under the ocean somewhere than accept the fact that there is another world that exists parallel to theirs. The Atlanteans even left portals for them to use so that they could come to Atlantis whenever they wanted to, but the people in the Earth dimension have never been able to find them."

"You mean a human from Earth can come into our world if they wanted?" Whisper was intrigued by this idea.

"If they possessed the knowledge to do so than, yes, they could," Marcus said. "But it can get far more complicated than that."

"Now that we have given you an understanding of the dimensions on this planet," Miles continued as he glared at Marcus. Whisper could tell he didn't like to be interrupted, "you are ready to learn about the different types of beings that exist here."

"Okay," She said as she realized that she was actually

interested in all of this.

"First, you have the Flatliners," Miles continued. "These are people that stay in their own world, never leaving and never wanting to. If they wanted to explore other dimensions, they would need to use a portal but they rarely ever do because they usually don't know that any other dimension exists. They live a relatively short life but their soul is eternal. When their body dies, their soul goes to a place similar to the Forest of Dreams where they are helped to choose a new body and a new life. They never remember their former lives and their goal is to allow their souls to grow until they can move on to become a Cross-over. Flatliners require Soul-healers more than anyone else. They can easily lose their way and call out for help continuously. Unfortunately, their calls are not only heard by the Soul-healers; Soul-stealers can come as well and many of them fall victim to these vicious creatures. It is up to the Soul-healers to show them a way of peace and enlightenment but they are easily tempted by physical pleasures and cling to wealth and power. The Soul-stealers know their weaknesses and use this knowledge to lure them away and then their soul is lost forever.

"Some Flatliners can't choose and are left confused, not knowing which way to turn. They are in a void and are sent somewhere to help them with their decision. Some come to Crystalline where they can live a seemingly normal life. They try to gain knowledge but usually their soul becomes stagnant, neither moving forward nor backward and most just stay where

116

they are for centuries, repeating the same life over and over again. Such is the case with your parents." He finished and asked Whisper if she wanted some water.

"Sure." She was starting to get thirsty. Miles explained that this was normal when opening the brain to let knowledge out. Marcus left to get the water and Miles continued.

"Next, there are the Cross-overs," he said. "Cross-overs are beings that have an understanding of everything. They have knowledge of all the worlds and they can 'cross over' into them anytime they want, provided they use a portal. They, like the Flatliners, have a physical body that can be damaged and even die but, if they're careful they can live for a very long time, hundreds of years even. Unlike the Flatliners, they are in charge of their own soul and very seldom call for help from a Soul-healer. This does not mean that they cannot be swayed by the evil this Universe possesses; even *they* are tempted by pleasures their bodies desire. If their body dies, they simply slip into a new life and continue on their path, still maintaining all their knowledge from before. These beings can be helpful to the Soul-healers but they can also help the Soul-stealers. They must be treated with caution because you never know which side they're on. Most of the creatures from the Lorynth dimension are Cross-overs and have been known to never stay in one place for very long." Marcus returned with a pitcher of water and three glasses. They each took a glass and filled it up. Miles drank his thirstily; all the talking he was doing must have made his mouth dry.

"Finally, we have the Soul-healers. As you have probably already guessed, these beings can visit other worlds, usually only in spirit, and don't need portals to do so. They try hard not to be seen but sometimes this can't be avoided. They have the ability to enter a Flatliner's mind and can make them feel their presence if they so choose. They rarely enter other worlds in their physical form but if they do they are at the mercy of that world and their bodies can be destroyed. If they stay where they are supposed to they can live for eternity, never aging and never having to worry about their souls. If they are destroyed, however, they are gone forever taking their soul with them with no chance of resurrection. Thankfully, this has never happened before." He finished and poured himself another glass of water. Whisper waited for him to continue.

"Do you have any questions?" asked Marcus.

"That's it?" Whisper asked. This couldn't be all they had to tell her. "What about the Soul-stealers, where do they come from?"

"Alannis will explain that to you, we were told to only tell you about the three beings that make up *this* planet," answered Marcus.

"This planet? You mean Soul-stealers are not from here?" She wanted to know more.

"It becomes complicated and is not for us to explain to you," Miles said. Whisper could see that she wasn't going to get anything else out of them.

"Okay, then, are we done?" She just wanted to go and find Aria now; get away from them. She still didn't feel comfortable around the twins.

"If you don't have any questions about the things we just discussed, then, yes we are finished," answered Marcus. "You may go to the lounge and meet up with Aria. I'm sure she is waiting for you there." Whisper didn't hesitate; she got up from her chair and headed for the door, then figured she'd better say something.

"Thanks, guys. You really helped me understand a lot. I appreciate it."

"You're welcome and, hopefully, next time you won't feel so anxious," said Miles, with a grin on his face. Whisper's face turned red with embarrassment, she probably shouldn't be so scared of them. They did seem nice.

Chapter 9

Whisper's lesson with Marcus and Miles didn't take as long as she thought it would so, she was happy to see Aria and Alannis still in the lounge when she got there. They were sitting at a table drinking coffee and looked to be deep in conversation. They didn't look up when Whisper opened the door so, she was able to walk right up to their table before they even noticed her.

"Hey guys! What's going on?" she asked casually. Aria snapped her head up to look at her; she was startled.

"Whisper, you're finished already?" she asked.

"Yep, I now know everything about dimensions, and Cross-overs, and Flatliners," she said. "Those two don't waste any time and get right down to business. I'm kind of glad they didn't teach at my school I would have tried everything to skip their classes."

"Oh, you have no idea," said Alannis with a smile on her face. "Seriously, though, you would be surprised at how smart they are; quite the little geniuses actually. Do you know they really come from the Earth dimension? They were Flatliners once but then progressed to Cross-overs in just two short lifetimes; virtually unheard of."

"Those two were Flatliners?" Whisper found it hard to believe that they had once been limited to one world. "But how did they manage to stay together? Were they always brothers?"

"Yes," said Alannis, "it is rare but every once in a while siblings that are born choose to stay together on their journey throughout eternity."

"Cool!" Whisper said as she pulled out a chair to sit down. She was starting to gain a whole new respect for the odd little twins. It seemed like quite a remarkable thing to achieve the status of Cross-over so early in their existence. She had to admire them for that.

"Well, what do you think Whisper, are you ready for another lesson?" Alannis asked. Whisper wasn't sure she wanted to know so much at once but there seemed to be such an urgency to teach her everything. She didn't want to disappoint anyone.

"Already? Shouldn't she rest or something? I thought we agreed we wouldn't tire her out so much." Aria jumped to her defence and Whisper looked at her and smiled appreciatively.

"It's all right, Aria, I'm really not that tired. I think I could handle another lesson," she said, not wanting to upset anyone.

"I'll tell you what," Alannis started, "I'll keep this lesson short, then we'll go upstairs and have a big dinner together okay?"

"Sure!!" Whisper was up for that! The food she ate in the restaurant yesterday was so delicious, she could go for some more.

"I guess," said Aria reluctantly. "I'll go check up on

everything at the school. How long do you think you'll be?"

"Not long, maybe an hour."

"Okay, I'll see you then." Aria excused herself from the table and left the room. Alannis waited for her to leave then turned her attention to Whisper.

"Are you ready?"

"Yeah," she started to stand up, "where're we going?"

"Right here," Alannis said. Whisper stopped halfway between sitting and standing and stared at her in disbelief. "Don't look so stunned. There's nothing wrong with this room. It's quiet and there's hardly anyone in here. We'll have all the privacy we need. Besides, it saves me the problem of trying to find an empty room."

"Whatever you say; you're the boss." Whisper started to sit back down.

"Wait, don't sit down yet," she put out her hand to stop me; "you might want to go get yourself a drink first, maybe some coffee?" She held up her empty cup.

"Do *you* want another cup of coffee, Alannis?" Whisper asked, seeing through her trick.

"If you don't mind," she said, smiling innocently.

"Aria was right, you Atlanteans really are smart." She laughed at this.

"Okay, all set," Whisper said when she came back to the table. She gave Alannis her coffee and sat down with her own.

"Thank you. Let us begin at the beginning," she said.

"When the Universe was created there was one ruler, we call him Edric. He created everything and was very proud of his accomplishments. After a while, though, Edric couldn't decide which creation he was more proud of and so an argument started within him. One part of him liked the gentle beauty and peacefulness the Universe contained while the other part relished in the force and power that he could command as ruler. This inner struggle continued for centuries and Edric got weaker and weaker as time went on. Finally, he could stand no more and split in two, each part of him wanting to rule over the other.

"They tried everything to gain some kind of advantage over the other. Eventually, they started to create soldiers for themselves. Each building an army that they hoped could eliminate the other. The peaceful side of Edric, known as Gwynn, created strong soldiers who could work with the innermost parts of their enemy. They wanted to convince them that there was a better way than fighting. A way where none would be destroyed and all could live together as one. The evil side, known as Dougall, would not hear of it. In his mind there could only be one ruler and he was going to be it.

"Once Dougall figured he had enough soldiers he made his move on Gwynn and soon a war broke out. It was to be the ultimate battle, one in which there could only be one winner. The fight that ensued was unimaginable and lots of soldiers died on both sides. Others fled in fear of their immortality. The Universe trembled in awe of the magnitude of the fight. Finally, Gwynn

123

could no longer bear the heavy losses on either side and he begged Dougall for a truce. He thought that, maybe, they could work a way to exist in harmony. Dougall laughed at this show of weakness and got ready to pounce but when he went in for the kill, he realized his army had been greatly diminished in size. Fearing a defeat, he reluctantly agreed to the truce.

"Both sides agreed that there would be no more war between them. Gwynn would rule everything that came from peace and love and Dougall would rule everything that came from fear and hate. It was a treaty that Dougall begrudgingly agreed to, secretly vowing to find a way to defeat his other half.

"So, both sides continued to nurture the beings they had created. They scattered them throughout the Universe to live their lives, giving each one of them a soul so they would know where they belonged if ever they were called back to their ruler. Gwynn granted his souls special powers so they could learn how to live in harmony with the Universe. They learned how to harvest the powers of the worlds around them and they lived happily, enjoying their freedom. Eventually, Gwynn wanted all his souls to come back to him and live with him in tranquility and peace.

"Dougall didn't share in this philosophy, he wanted to rule alone. His souls meant nothing to him; he only needed them to win his battle against Gwynn. He was afraid to give them too many powers, he didn't want them to overthrow him, and so he filled them with a false sense of knowledge. He made them reliant on wealth and power and made them believe this was their only way to salvation. Souls were expendable to him and it was because of this that his numbers started to dwindle. He needed to recruit more.

"Every soul that is made, whether by Gwynn or by Dougall, is created in the image of Edric. Each one has a part of Gwynn and a part of Dougall in them. To help the soul decide which part shall dominate, each side created beings to help them on their journey. Gwynn created Soul-healers and Dougall created Soul-stealers. You already know about the Soul-healers and, as you can guess, the Soul-stealers are their counterparts. They are sent by Dougall to collect souls for his army. These souls are then used as his foot soldiers, the first to die in battle. Soul-stealers are pure evil and know many ways to lure a soul away from good. They use their weaknesses against them, promising them eternal happiness if only they would follow them. Their ways are cruel and unforgiving and we must always be on the lookout for them," she finished with an exuberance Whisper could feel from across the table, and then she looked down at her empty coffee cup and her mood totally switched. "I'm going to get another, do you want one?"

"No, thank you," answered Whisper, trying to comprehend everything she had just been told. When Alannis got back she sat in a chair closer to Whisper.

"It's a lot to grasp in one day, isn't it?" she asked.

"Just a bit," Whisper answered.

"I'm sorry it has to be this way. In a perfect world you would have been able to come through this the right way, not so fast and stressful. But, there really is no time."

"Everyone keeps saying that but I don't understand why. What's the hurry?" Whisper asked.

"I'm going to tell you because I think you could probably handle the truth now," She took a drink of her coffee before she continued. "Whisper, Dougall thinks his army is almost complete. He has been collecting souls for a very long time now and he has kept them safe, away from anyone who might influence them to go the other way. He is preparing to wage war and this time he intends to win, there will be no survivors. All he needs now is one soul." Whisper looked at her in disbelief and waited for her to tell her more.

"After that first war, Gwynn created a group of warriors that would guard his kingdom. He didn't trust Dougall and wanted to keep himself safe. These warriors were specially trained and could fight beyond anyone else's capabilities. When Dougall found out about them he was furious and did everything he could to try and destroy them but nothing worked. Finally, he called a meeting with Gwynn and accused him of a breach of the treaty. He threatened death to every soul, even his own, unless Gwynn got rid of these warriors. Gwynn had to do something but he could not bring himself to destroy them, so he hid them throughout the Universe. Dougall was happy with this because he knew that, without the protection of Gwynn, the warriors would become vulnerable. He started to search the Universe for them, wanting to recruit them and have them fight in his army but, when he found them, he discovered they would rather sacrifice themselves than fight for him. This frustrated him but he never gave up. He kept finding them and one after the other they refused to work with him until, finally, one day he convinced one of them to come to his side. Having won this small victory, he continued on his quest to acquire more of them.

"The soul whom you are about to try and save is one of these warriors, the last to be precise. Dougall knows where he is now and will try anything to get him on his side. He already found him once before and was defeated but he has vowed not to let that happen again. We must hurry and keep this soul on our side or our battle with Dougall will be lost and evil will rule this Universe forever. Time is running out and everything depends on this one soul."

"And you want me to do this?" Whisper couldn't believe they had given such an important task to her. What were they thinking? She couldn't possibly save this soul. She just found out who she was!

"We have no choice, it is you that this soul has called and nothing can change that now," she said. Whisper sat there for a moment, stunned.

"You mean all I have to do is save this soul to save the Universe," she said sarcastically. "Anything else? Maybe change the size of the sun or shuffle the planets around while I'm at it?

127

This is crazy; absurd!"

"I know it sounds overwhelming," Alannis reached over and tried to calm Whisper down.

"How will I ever be ready?" Whisper asked; panic taking hold of her body.

"We'll teach you," she said. "You just have to concentrate and let the power of your being take hold of you." Whisper sat back in her chair and tried to convince herself that what Alannis said could happen.

'I could save this soul, couldn't I?' she thought, but in the back of her mind doubt peeked out at her and she felt a wave of fear cross over her heart.

Chapter 10

When Cael left Rob he was so upset. He couldn't believe that Mr. Yamanaka had never told him that he was Jiro's brother. He had never even told him his name. How could he do that? He drove around aimlessly for awhile and finally ended up on the highway out of the city. He knew where he was heading, a place where he had been going almost his whole life, a little spot out in the foothills. He knew it was the only place where his mind could relax and he could really think about the things that had happened in the last couple of days. He parked his Jeep in the little gravel parking lot and got out and walked down the long path to his favourite spot. It was in the woods, at the foot of a small mountain, with the river running just a few feet away. The snow had still not entirely melted out there which was good because it meant it was unlikely he would see any people around. In the summer this place was starting to attract a lot of people like tourists, hikers and picnickers but in the winter and spring it was still pretty quiet. There wasn't very many people that came out there now except, maybe, the occasional off-roader and Cael hadn't seen any or heard any.

He always loved it out there. His parents first brought him there when he was very young. They camped and fished and hiked. They always had a lot of fun and spent quite a bit of time there before his father's job got too busy for him to take time off. Still, though, when he turned sixteen and got his license, he was out there again either with friends or without. He brought his first girlfriend out there and enjoyed his first kiss right under the tree he was sitting under now. Sometimes he would camp or fish and he could take his Jeep far back in the bush if he wanted, which he often did just to get away from people. Right now, though, all he wanted to do was sit and think, away from the city with no people around, just him and nature. He sat there for hours, watching the water flow by, until the sun started to disappear and the woods started to fade into darkness. He finally decided sitting outside as the night grew colder was not a good idea. The temperature could cool down quickly out there. He had not solved anything when he got back into his Jeep. How could he? Nothing had changed since he got there. But being there and breathing in the fresh mountain air started to settle his mind.

He picked up a burger on his way home and ate it in his apartment, watching some mindless reality show on TV. He left his computer turned off and decided he would check his emails tomorrow. Right then, all he wanted to do was sit on the couch and not think about anything. He called his mother to tell her about his meeting with Rob and that Jiro was Mr. Yamanaka's brother. She didn't sound very surprised and he figured she was busy. He asked her if she needed any help with the service and she said no, in fact, she had a time and place already. He would phone Rob with the information in the morning. He told her Mr. Yamanaka's first name just in case she needed it. She thanked him and said goodbye. He hung up the phone and went and got a pop out of the fridge. He must have stayed up very late because when he finally went to bed the only thing on TV was a bunch of infomercials. He went to his room, stripped down, turned his radio on and got into bed where he lay awake for a while before going to sleep.

While he slept, he dreamed. He was being chased in a dark forest. There was a cool mist in the air and yet he could feel perspiration on his face. There was a deep silence and every twig or dry leaf he stepped on crackled with a thunderous explosion in his ears. His breath came heavy and mixed with the beating of his heart as he made his way through the maze of trees. He had no idea who was trying to catch him; he just felt the urgency of his escape. Panic was starting to take a grip on his sanity. As he ran, figures kept appearing from behind the gigantic trees, some he knew and some he had never seen before. Jiro was there, pointing towards a path that led up a steep hill. His legs were burning with exhaustion and he balked at the thought of climbing this steep incline, but Jiro kept pointing emphatically. He started to climb and just when he thought he could go no further, Taro suddenly appeared at the top and waved him up. This gave him a surge of energy and he made it in just a few short strides but when he got there, Taro was gone. He stood there, frantically searching for his friend. Then the woods filled with a diabolical laughter which made him stop short. He started to feel himself fill with a rage that he had never felt before. Someone, or something, called his name from behind and he turned to face whatever it was. What he saw made him take a step back. His parents stood there, lifeless, looking as if all their essence had been drained from them. Their faces were pale and blank and their eyes stared straight ahead, looking right through him. He called them but they didn't move, didn't even blink. It was like they were unaware of anything going on around them. He started to go to them and then stopped when he saw a dark figure appear behind them. The laughter returned and he instantly knew that it came from this thing. Was it a man? He couldn't tell because its face was hidden behind a black hood. His blood froze and he quickly looked around for a way to escape. Then he saw the figure lift its hands and he saw, for the first time, that it held an axe within its grasp. It was then that he knew he could do nothing to save his parents; it was too late. He stood, paralyzed with fear, and watched as the axe came down in slow motion. As it came in contact with the top of his father's head, he woke up with jolt.

He sat straight up and immediately checked the clock, 6:00 a.m. There was no way he could sleep now. He rubbed his eyes and ran his hand through his hair. All this stress was starting to give him nightmares now, he thought as he swung his legs over the side of his bed. He grabbed his robe and headed for the bathroom. He may as well have a shower and start his day early again. While he stood in the hot water, he tried to make sense of his dream. Taro had once told him that your dreams could reveal a lot about your life. Some dreams could tell you about an ailment you didn't know you had, some could reveal a piece of your past you had forgotten about, some could show you a glimpse of your future and some, the most common ones, could help you deal with whatever was plaguing your life at the time. The trick was trying to figure out which dream you were having by deciphering all the symbolism that occurred in it. That's where he always ran into difficulties. There were so many different meanings for each symbol that he often got lost in the translation.

He tried to pick out the different symbols of this dream but there seemed to be so many. The forest could have significant meaning but so too could the mist and darkness. The fact that someone was chasing him could just be left over fear from the shooting. Seeing Jiro and Taro there and then having them suddenly disappear could mean that they were once there for him to rely on for advice but now they were gone from his life. His parents and the dark figure were the three things he could not explain. Maybe, subconsciously, he was worried that his parents could be in danger. After all, he had already lost one person very close to him. He contemplated all of these things as he got out of the shower and got dressed.

He wasn't hungry yet, having eaten the hamburger way too late the night before. He went to the fridge and poured himself a glass of juice. There was not much food in there and he made a mental note to go shopping later. He walked over to his living room window and looked out at the city. It was very much alive already this morning. As the city grew the morning traffic got busier and busier. If you didn't get an early start chances were you'd be caught in some kind of traffic jam. He was glad he didn't have to join that rat race. Staying at home was just fine with him. He walked back to the kitchen and put his glass in the sink. Now that he had no judo he wondered how he was going to fill his days. He used to go for a quick workout in the morning and then again later in the day for a more intensive one. But now he wondered if he would even bother to find another dojo. He didn't think he could go back to his old Rocky Mountain club. Being taught by Rob did not really appeal to him. Maybe he'd just take some time off for a while, find something else to occupy himself. He thought about this as he looked around his apartment. Then his eyes came to rest on his computer and he let out a sigh and walked over to it.

"Better check those emails," he said out loud, "there's probably a lot."

He was right; there were over eighty messages. He rolled his eyes and pulled his chair closer to the computer, knowing he would be stuck there for some time going through all this junk. And that's just what most of it was, too, junk. He started going down the sender's names, opening the ones he knew and deleting the ones that could go straight to the recycling bin. He got about three quarters of the way through when one of the names jumped out at him: Jiro Yamanaka.

'It couldn't be could it?' he thought, as he stared at the name again. Then he looked at when it was sent; this morning at six o'clock, right when he had woken up from his nightmare. He opened it up and began to read.

When the ocean cries we do not know
For the tears it sheds it does not show
When the sun laughs we do not see
For its brilliance still escapes me
But when one so close turns away
We feel the sadness of the day
And when one we love falls in shade
We cannot see our fate is laid
And when the shadow calls our name
Our life will never be the same
So turn your face toward the sun
And let your fate become undone

'That was it, just this poem?' Cael read it over and over. What could it possibly mean? Why would Jiro send this to him? What was he trying to tell him and where exactly was he? Cael saved the email in a new folder and shut off his computer. The email was too much; there was no way he could continue to work. He had to figure out why Jiro would send such a peculiar poem with no explanation.

Now that he knew Jiro and Taro were brothers, many things began to cross his mind. Perhaps whoever killed Taro was now after Jiro. Didn't Taro say, right before he got shot, that he had something important to tell him? He said that he had been sent to teach him something from ancient times and that Cael, himself, was someone special. But, if that was the case, why would they kill Taro? Why wouldn't they just try to kill him? None of this made sense, or did it? Maybe that's why Jiro went away so suddenly. Maybe he knew about the ancient teaching and why Cael was so special and figured, with Taro gone, they'd come after him now. The same question still lingered in his mind, though, why not kill him? Because they *knew* he didn't know anything. It was as simple as that. They knew that as long as he was in the dark, he would be no threat to them. That would mean they were watching him, waiting for him to realize his own fate. *Fate,* that word was in the poem.

Cael turned the computer back on and retrieved the email from the saved folder. He read it again with a whole new perspective. Could this be a warning? Was Jiro trying to tell him who to look out for, who could be a danger to him? Cael thought about this as he reread the poem:

> *When the ocean cries we do not know*
> *For the tears it sheds it does not show*
> *When the sun laughs we do not see*
> *For its brilliance still escapes me*

Does this mean he had been blind to what was happening around him and that he needed to wake up and look for some sort of sign, something that would help him solve his friend's murder?

> *But when one so close turns away*
> *We feel the sadness of the day*

Could this be referring to Taro's death?

> *And when one we love falls in shade*
> *We cannot see our fate is laid*
> *And when the shadow calls our name*
> *Our life will never be the same*
> *So turn your face toward the sun*
> *And let your fate become undone*

This, he was sure, was his warning. Someone close to him, someone he loved and trusted had turned on him and was now watching him and waiting to…what? Kill him? But who? He was not close with very many people. He pretty much stuck to himself most of the time. There was Taro, Rob; whom he hadn't even seen in years, a couple of guys he went 4x4ing with and his parents, not a lot…

The dream!! It all came back to him now. In his dream, Jiro and Taro had been urging him up the hill and at the top of that hill his parents stood there. They were emotionless, standing there as if the only thing that remained of them were the empty shells of their bodies. In fact, it was from the shadows behind them that his name had been called, just like in the poem. Then that dark, ominous figure brought down his axe, forever destroying the two people he loved so much.

Cael thought about his mom and dad. They were just here

two days ago. They had seemed so concerned about him, had even agreed to help him with the memorial service, although very reluctantly. Surely, there was nothing wrong with them. There couldn't be. Then he remembered all their questions. They wanted to know everything; what he knew, who he had seen, what had been said and they even wanted to know how much the police knew. And then, when he mentioned talking to Jiro, his mother seemed irritated with the idea then quickly agreed with him after looking at his dad. And last night, when he told her that Jiro and Taro were brothers, she didn't sound surprised at all, like she already knew. Then he remembered something that sent chills up his spine. When he was in that room at the hospital, right after Mr. Yamanaka had been shot, he tried to phone his mother and there was no answer, not even the voice mail was on. He remembered how odd this was for a woman who had always been so addicted to her phone and hated missing any calls. He tried his father's cell phone that day, as well, and it was also shut off. Yet, his father had said they tried to get a hold of him *after* they heard his messages. What messages? He hadn't left any. Where did they say they were? The country markets.

That was easy enough to check. He Googled all the country markets around the city and in no time at all he had a whole list of websites to visit. He started clicking on each one and felt his heart sink. One after the other they each said the same thing: 'Sorry, Closed; Will Open Again June 1'. They lied! Suddenly two of the lines of the poem made complete sense to him.

And when the shadows call our name
Our life will never be the same

Chapter 11

Whisper woke up early the next morning because she wanted to get off to a good start. Today was the day she was supposed to start her special training. Alannis was going to show her how to communicate with her Flatliner, that's what she started to refer to him as since she didn't know his name yet. Alannis touched on the subject yesterday at dinner. She and Aria took Whisper upstairs, as promised, after her lesson was finished. They ate in the same room Aria had brought her to two days before. Was it only two days? It seemed like a lifetime ago to Whisper, she had learned so much in such a short amount of time. The meal was delicious *again* and, just like the first time, Whisper overate.

While they ate, Alannis told Whisper that the training she would be doing with her would involve mind reading, dream walking and thought transference. Alannis warned her to get a good night's sleep because this type of work would be very draining. To their surprise Whisper didn't put up any protests about it. Now that she understood the magnitude of her task, she was more than willing to put in all the hours it took to get herself ready.

After their meal, they sat and talked about many things.

Whisper learned a lot about Atlantis and made a promise to herself to go there after all this soul healing business was over. Alannis explained how they had been working with crystals for thousands of years now and that they could do far more than just light up a room. The crystals had become their only source of power and did everything from running their machines to powering their household appliances. They could even generate heat in their homes and, just recently, they had been put into all their vehicles, including their elaborate flying vessels. The Atlanteans *could* mind-port but only in the world of Chrystalline. In Atlantis, they still had to rely on some sort of vehicle to get around.   These crystals fascinated Whisper and she learned that, once put into use, they would last forever, never diminishing nor eroding away. She also learned that Atlantis was not the only world that had these crystals. She told us that every dimension had them but they just didn't know how to harvest their power. It was one of the first things that had brought her to Chrystalline; she wanted to teach the people there how to use these remarkable rocks.

They must have sat there for a few hours, talking and getting to know each other without the pressures of saving the Universe. Whisper really liked the two women. She was starting to feel a sisterhood with them. Aria shared some funny stories of her own too. She told them about one that occurred at the school recently. Tanner and Jackson, two boys in Whisper's Choral class, were brought to her office one day. It seemed they thought they could sneak into the girl's locker room to have a peek, typical male behaviour in any dimension but, what they didn't realize, was that the girls in the locker room that day were a group of seniors who had just finished a class in mind control and were anxious to try out what they learned. Those poor boys didn't know what hit them. They waltzed into Aria's office wearing colourful dresses and loads of makeup. They had big, goofy grins on their faces and were singing love songs at the top of their lungs to any female that came within ten feet of them, even the school secretary. It was all Aria could do to keep from laughing. They got suspended for three days but not before they walked through the school in their dresses at lunchtime, when everyone was out in the hallways. Whisper remembered the incident and how her and her friends had laughed at them.

After the conversation died down and the women were feeling tired from the meal and all the laughter, they decided they should all go back to their rooms for the evening. Aria went to Whisper's for awhile. They watched a couple of movies, made popcorn and giggled. Whisper could tell she was trying hard to pick up their friendship where it had left off. Whisper didn't mind; she liked having someone around to talk to. Aria stayed into the evening and then left, yawning and stretching, obviously ready to go to bed.

Whisper was tired too but there was something she wanted to do first. Take a bath! Ever since she laid eyes on the enormous tub in the bathroom, she wanted to try it out. She went into the bathroom and found a bottle of bath bubbles under the sink. She turned on the taps and filled the bath with warm water and lots of bubbles. A beautiful fragrance filled the room and she started to feel relaxed even before she slipped into the water. She must have stayed in the tub for a good forty five minutes before the water started to cool down and she decided to get out. She felt good, calm and rested. When she climbed into bed, she barely got under the sheets before sleep overcame her.

#

She was fully dressed and walking behind Marcus, ready for her training to begin. She decided not to tell Aria she was awake, wanting her friend to take advantage of a couple of extra hours of sleep. There was nothing she could do while Whisper was with Alannis anyway. Marcus led her to the lounge and told her to make herself comfortable while he let Alannis know she was there. Whisper walked over to the back table and made herself a cup of tea. She took a sip and looked around the room. The same two women from the other day were there again, reading books from the shelves. There was no one else there, it was still very early. She started to walk to the table that had become their usual meeting place. She just about reached her destination…

WHAM!!

'I know this sound,' she thought as she started to feel her surroundings slowly fade away.

WHAM!! WHAM!! WHAM!!

#

Cael threw another book across the room. He was furious; he had never felt this angry before. How could they? What kind of evil game were they playing? His parents, his own flesh and blood!! Was it true that they could have had something to do with Mr. Yamanaka's death? But why? How? He stood there, hands on his hips and trembling with rage. When he finally made the connection with the help of his dream and Jiro's cryptic poem, he sat in the chair unable to even breathe. Then, as his mind started to comprehend what it all meant, his rage started to take hold of him and he cracked.

#

Whisper couldn't believe it. It had happened again. She was standing in what looked like someone's living room. There was a huge window looking out at a busy city and beyond that some mountains. There was a very old looking brown sofa in the middle of the room. She looked over to where the book that had just whizzed by her head came from and let out a little gasp. It was the man, *her* Flatliner, standing there in front of her. He wore nothing but a pair of old looking pants leaving half his body bare. She marvelled at the smoothness of his chest and the outline of his muscles. He obviously worked out. She felt a tiny quiver in her stomach and slowly tried to breathe again. Her eyes followed the line of his body up to his face and again she found it hard to breathe.

"You're so beautiful," she said as she stared into his eyes.

144

"What? Who's there?" Cael was starting to get a familiar feeling and he knew he was no longer alone.

"Can you hear me?" Whisper decided to come right out and try to talk to him. Cael looked across the room, trying to see the source of his feelings.

"I know you're here. Show yourself!!" He took on a defensive stance, waiting for an attack.

"I'm not here to hurt you. I'm here to help." She took a couple of steps towards him. He seemed to relax a little. "My name is Whisper."

"Where are you?" He reached out like a blind man looking for an object that might block his path. He was desperately trying to make contact with the being he was sure was there.

"I'm right here," she said. She was right in front of him now. She could smell the fresh scent of soap on his skin. It was intoxicating. She searched his face for some sign that he could feel her there. She reached out with a trembling hand and touched his arm. He froze and she could tell that he, too, could feel the electricity that surged through their bodies as they made contact. He started to calm down.

"I can feel you," he said. Whisper flushed and jumped back. "No, don't let go, you make me feel better. Please, I trust you." She reached for his arm again. She felt the surge of electricity again and this time she smiled shyly. The fury Cael felt at his parents slowly subsided and a peace started to come over him. He didn't know what had a hold of him but he liked it and didn't want it to let go.

Whisper stood there with his arm in her grasp for what seemed like an eternity. She could feel his emotions becoming calmer. She closed her eyes, lost in his presence. Was she supposed to feel this way about her Flatliner? She was completely taken by his quiet, inner strength. She had to fight the desire to stay with him. She opened her eyes and could see that, he too, was standing there with his eyes closed, perhaps trying to feel her presence as well. She tried not to stare at him but it was hard. She started to look around the room and was drawn to a small box, similar to a TV, on the desk behind him. Its screen was full of words and it lit up the small area around it. She knew what they called those things, computers, and it was their way of sharing information. Whisper shook her head, she couldn't figure these people out. They had never even tried mind communication; instead they relied on machines to do everything for them, even think. She tried to focus on the computer's screen. It was a list of some sort. The word 'Market' appeared in every single item along with the name of a place. A list of shops, she presumed. Then she noticed the upturned chair and crumpled up paper. She looked at the screen and then back at her Flatliner, why had this list of Markets made him so angry? She didn't get it.

"Whisper!! Whisper!!" A distant voice was calling her name. "You have to come back now!!"

'Come back now? But why?' She didn't want to let him go. She felt at home here, comfortable, like she belonged. The voice called for her again, and she felt a slight tug on her free arm. With great reluctance she finally let go and bid her Flatliner a silent goodbye and slowly drifted back to her world.

#

She came back to her body and opened her eyes to see a huge mess on the floor. She must have dropped her tea when she got pulled to the Earth dimension and now her cup lay broken in a puddle of tea.

"Oh, man, what a klutz I am," she said as she lifted her head to search for something to clean up the mess. Four sets of eyes met her gaze as she straightened up; four sets of very astonished looking eyes. She jumped back and gasped, her hand flying up to cover her open mouth. Alannis, Aria, Marcus and Miles were lined up in front of her, waiting for her to say something.

"Whisper, what happened?" Alannis looked very upset. "We were worried. Where did you go just now?"

"I-I-I was pulled by my…er…a Flatliner. He pulled me to his world, I-I didn't want to go." She was afraid they'd be mad at her.

"But that can't be!!" exclaimed Aria. "She's not supposed to be able to do that. Not here, not now."

"I think we should go sit down, shall we," Miles said, looking around, trying not to attract attention.

"But I should really clean this mess up," Whisper said, not wanting to leave it for someone else to do.

"Don't worry, I'll get it." Marcus pointed his finger at the mess and suddenly everything disappeared, no more cup, no more spill, nothing. Whisper had never seen anything like it before. She stared at the now empty spot in disbelief.

"That's amazing. How'd you do that?" she asked.

"It's not important right now," Marcus said, totally unimpressed by what he had just done.

"But, I've never seen anyone do that before. I mean I've heard there are some people who have mastered the art of…"

"Whisper! We must talk about what just happened with you," Alannis sounded upset. "You can get Marcus to teach you about Elemental Displacement later."

"Sorry," Whisper said quietly. She could tell this was a serious matter. They all took a seat around a table.

"You have to tell us exactly what happened just now," Alannis said. "We were on our way here when we heard Aria scream. When we got here you were standing there like you were in some kind of a trance. We tried to call to you but you didn't seem to be able to hear us, not until I grabbed your arm." It was like when Whisper's father had found her the other day, she never heard him either until he grabbed her.

"Well, I was walking to the table with my tea when suddenly I heard a loud bang," she explained. "Then boom, I was pulled into this room, like a living room, it had a huge window with a view of beautiful mountains. I think I was in the Earth dimension." The others were starting to lose their patience with her; they didn't want to know about the scenery. She quickly continued. "Then I saw this guy standing there. He looked really upset and he was throwing books across the room, one almost went straight through me."

"Did you do anything to bring yourself there?" This was Miles, trying to analyze the situation. "Maybe wish you could meet the soul you're meant to save?"

"No!" Whisper was kind of mad they'd think she'd do something like that. "It was just like before when I saw this same guy at the hospital." They all looked at her, stunned, like they didn't know what she was talking about. "You do know about that don't you?"

"No," Aria said, sounding surprised, "at least I didn't, did any of you?" They all shook their heads. Whisper couldn't believe this, they had no clue she had already been pulled to her Flatliner? But they had to know; why else would they bring her here?

"But I thought you knew. I thought that's why I'm here. You know, I've been pulled to save a soul so now I have to learn how." She searched their eyes for some kind of understanding.

"Whisper, we brought you here because one of our sources discovered a spy at the school and we feared for your safety. We had no idea you had already been pulled," Alannis looked very grave. "When did this happen?"

149

"The other day, when I got grounded from cheating on that test." Aria and Alannis shared a worried look. "I had to walk home and on my way I heard a loud bang and suddenly I was in a hospital somewhere. I could feel someone in the building was very angry and I found him in a small room. He looked upset, like he had lost someone close to him. It's weird; I think he knew I was there too, just like today."

"What do you mean, he knew you were there?" It was Marcus this time looking quite interested in what Whisper had to say.

"I mean, I jumped when he pounded his fist onto this counter, and I let out a little yelp. He turned around and asked who was in the room like he heard me," she said. "Then today when I talked out loud, he did the same thing. I think this guy is very sensitive to what's around him. Anyway, today he looked upset about something that had come up on his computer; at least I think that's why he was upset."

"What makes you think that?" asked Alannis.

"Because he had crumpled the papers on his desk and knocked over his chair as if he wanted to get away from what it said." It made sense to Whisper that it was the computer that had upset him. "Honestly, I don't know why a list of markets around town would upset anybody though." Alannis let out a small gasp and looked at Miles and Marcus.

"He knows," she said.

"Knows what?" Whisper asked. "And who is this spy at

150

my school?" Alannis seemed more willing to answer the second question.

"Your teacher, Miss Foster, the one who gave you that test. She set it up so you would have to cheat one way or the other." Whisper was shocked. Miss Foster? No way!

"How did she do that?" she asked.

"By playing with the clocks, she made it appear to only you that you were running out of time and so would have to cheat. It's a good thing Aria was at the school or we never would have known," said Alannis. "Miss Foster knows your father's reputation for being strict and that, if you were caught, he would probably ground you and then they could keep a better eye on you."

"But why would they want to do that, I wasn't going anywhere?" she asked.

"Because they must have found out about the Mirai somehow," Alannis concluded.

"Mirai? I have no idea what you're talking about," Whisper said. Alannis looked at her and decided she better tell her what was going on.

"We are not alone in our quest to win this war. There are a group of beings from far away who have come to help us. They have stayed in their own constellation away from everything that could influence them and have become as close to perfect as a species can be. Like all of us, they were created in the image of Edric and have learned to eliminate any traces of Dougall. For a long time they refused to get involved in any kind of fighting but now they feel they have no choice. They still won't get into any physical battle, having only a tolerance for peace and understanding, but they can help us with knowledge and their knowledge is extraordinary," Alannis finished and Miles continued.

"Yes, these beings have the ability to see the future and they came here a few weeks ago with a very important prediction. They knew about you and your calling to save this soul. They also knew that you could be pulled to him any time, although they could not say exactly when. We just assumed it hadn't come yet."

"But who are these creatures and where are they now?" Whisper asked.

"Like we said they are called the Mirai and they come from the Trylinnian Constellation. There are two of them here staying in the same dorms as you," said Marcus.

"Really? Can I meet them?" She looked at them anxiously.

"You've already seen them," said Marcus with a smile on his face.

"I have? When?" Whisper didn't remember seeing anybody unusual.

"Over there, reading. They seem to have a fascination for books." Whisper stared over at the two women she had overlooked so easily every time she came in there. They were

152

busy looking for another book to read. Just then the door opened and a person came in that Whisper had never seen before. He scanned the room quickly, spotted their group, and headed straight for their table. Whisper looked at the others anxiously but they seemed relieved to see him.

"I came as soon as you called Master Miles," he said as he bowed to the people at the table. He carried himself with a quiet elegance and looked like he came from the Earth's Japan land.

"Jiro, so good of you to respond so quickly," Miles stood up and clapped Jiro on the back in welcome. "I'm afraid we're going to have to start Whisper's training a little earlier than expected. Something has come up that has made it imperative that she know everything to defend herself and fast.

Chapter 12

Jiro, Whisper was told, was a master in the art of defence, not only in this world but in many others as well. He was a Cross-over and had been around for many centuries and had lived in many different worlds. He had even spent some time in Atlantis where he met Alannis. They became close friends while he was there. He taught her some defence training while she, in return, taught him about the crystals. He became fascinated with them and soon conquered the art of controlling their power. When he left he started a small quest to find other crystals in other worlds to see what powers they could hold. He discovered that, along with their electrical power, they could also be used for healing which no one in Atlantis knew about. He rushed back there to share his findings and soon the Atlanteans were practicing this new found technique on their population. It proved to be an unparalleled find, bringing relief to many ailing people. From that day forward Jiro was regarded with great respect in Atlantis and called on many times to join in their holidays and celebrations.

Whisper was allowed to go back to her room and change into something she could work out in, which was a relief because she didn't think the tight jeans and small red pumps she had put on when she got dressed would be much good in a gym. She chose a black pair of sweat pants and a big grey t-shirt from her closet and put her hair up in a ponytail off her face, a small miracle in itself. She looked on the shelves of shoes and grabbed a simple black pair of sneakers and headed for the door. Marcus was waiting for her in the hallway when she came out and he brought her back upstairs to the lounge without uttering a single word. It was okay, she was starting to get used to his need for silence. When they got back, Jiro jumped up from the table to greet them.

"Good. You are ready, I see," he said. "Time to go. Did you eat well this morning?"

"Yeah, I had an apple, a bowl of yogurt and a glass of milk," she said, proudly. Usually she wouldn't be caught dead eating such healthy food but she figured if that's what they stocked her fridge with then that's what she should eat. Jiro turned to Alannis, who was still sitting at the table. Aria and Miles were nowhere to be seen.

"I will see you later and we will finish this discussion," he smiled and bowed.

"I look forward to it," Alannis smiled and nodded. Did Whisper detect a trace of red run across the Atlantean's cheeks? She laughed to herself.

Jiro gestured for Whisper to follow him, which she did. She was getting used to following people around blindly here. They left and went to the door right across the hall. That was quick, not too far to walk. Jiro took a key out of his pocket that

155

looked more like a stick to Whisper. He pushed it in the hole above the doorknob and a loud click filled the hallway. He pulled the door open and they stepped inside.

Never before in all of Whisper's life had she seen anything like this room. The wonders of this strange little fortress were limitless. When they entered she could have sworn they were outside. They were standing in a lush, green forest with huge trees that looked to be covered with a rich green moss on their trunks and full, leafy branches that extended into eternity. The ground was covered with a thick carpet of grass that Whisper felt the urge to run her bare toes through. She could hear birds singing and tilted her head to catch their words. There was a fragrance of sweet pine mixed with the aroma of roses and when she looked around she could see that the roses were growing everywhere and in every color. This must be where they got the roses in her room from. She could feel warm sunshine on her face but when she looked up she could see no sky.

"Pretty impressive don't you think?" Jiro had noticed the look of awe on her face.

"Uh-huh," she said, stupidly, unable to piece together any words.

"I'm glad you like it. I must confess I had a small hand in helping to build this room," he said.

"Room? But it's not a room. It can't be. We have to be outside somewhere." She stood there, looking around, amazed at the beauty of it.

156

"No, I can assure you, we are still inside and we are still twelve feet underground."

"But how can we be? Those trees must be thirty feet tall!" She craned her neck to try to see the top of them.

"They appear to be don't they? It's all a trick Whisper, an illusion to fool your eyes, but if you really think about it, *could* there be trees that tall in here? No, it would be impossible." Whisper looked at him and tried to understand what he meant. "You're eyes can be your biggest enemy sometimes. They can take all the logic from your brain and convince you something is one thing when it is really something else." He closed his eyes and the forest faded away and in its place appeared a dingy old gym with washed out walls and old, torn up mats. Whisper sighed in disappointment.

"Not so appealing, is it?" he asked. She shook her head, wishing the forest would come back. This room was very depressing. Jiro laughed at her expression, then closed his eyes again and within a few seconds the forest returned. "The mind may know the truth but the eyes are very hard to please. I prefer the room this way as well."

After this, they began their training. Jiro did not take it easy on her just because she was new at this. No, as a matter of fact, she found herself flat out on her back with the wind knocked out of her throughout most of the class. They worked so hard she could just imagine her aching muscles in the morning. Now, she knew why they put that huge tub in her room, she would need it to soak away all the pains from the class.

First, they started with some stretching which showed Whisper's flexibility left much to be desired. Next, they went on to punches and kicks with Jiro yelling instructions and counting with every different move he showed her. After what seemed like hours of repeating every move over and over again, Jiro decided it was time to spar. Whisper kind of liked this part. She liked having a living target to try to kick or punch but Jiro was good and very fast. They started on the grass and she could feel, with every passing moment that her body was starting to grasp the moves more quickly. It was like her muscles were starting to remember how to do this. Just when she thought she was getting better, her concentration broke and Jiro kicked out her legs and she ended up on her back again.

"Come on! Concentrate!" he yelled at her. She hopped up, feeling stupid, and returned to the defensive stance he taught her earlier. She started to think harder about what she was doing and eventually she got better, a lot better. She came at him and he dodged to the right, just what she wanted him to do. She had anticipated this and grabbed his arm and came in. Their bodies met as she swept her foot behind the back of his leg and pushed. He was already off balance when she pushed and he fell easily to the ground. Immediately, without thinking, she jumped on him and wrapped her legs around his waist and her arms around his neck and squeezed. She was so blinded by her need to eliminate her enemy that she didn't realize at first that he was trying to tap out. She let go and he slowly stood up, coughing and holding his throat.

"I'm sorry," she said, reaching to help him. "I-I didn't notice you tapping, I was too focused on choking you out."

"Very well done, young Whisper!" he laughed and coughed as he straightened up and looked at her. "You are remembering everything that was taught to you before. Tell me, do you remember this?" He jumped straight up. Whisper was taken by surprise and spun around, trying to see where he had come back down.

"W-where'd you go?" she yelled out.

"Ah, this time you must *count* on your eyes to find me. Look up." She looked up and saw the slender teacher standing on a sturdy looking branch of a tree about fifteen feet off the ground.

"How'd you get up there?" she asked.

"I flew," he replied with a smile on his face. It was another trick, like the room. No one could really fly, could they?

"Show me," she stated.

"Okay, come up here and I will." Whisper looked up at him, and then looked at the tree. There didn't' seem to be any way to climb up. The lowest branch was the one he was on so she walked around the trunk and felt the bark to see if there was some way she could get a foothold on it. She felt a tap on her shoulder and jumped, her heart skipping a few beats. He stood behind her with that stupid grin on his face.

159

"What the…?" She looked back up at the branch which now stood empty.

"You were taking too long," he said.

"But I don't know how to fly," she said as she looked at him in disbelief.

"There are many things you know how to do but you have convinced yourself that you can't." He pointed at his chest and continued. "In here you remember everything but you have let your eyes and your mind forget it. You must close your eyes and let what is in here show your mind how to do what you believe to be impossible." He took her hands in his and they closed their eyes.

"Let your mind relax and allow your heart to lead the way." She started to relax and tried to listen to what was inside her heart. Nothing. She tried harder, even started to tremble with the effort. Her grip on his hands tightened.

"You are trying too hard. Empty your thoughts and just be." She loosened her hands and tried not to think. Was it working? Was her mind empty? It didn't feel empty. She could hear a bird in the distance. What was it trying to sing? She strained so she could hear it better.

"Whisper! Empty your thoughts!" He sensed her mind had not let go and was getting annoyed with her. It was hard to totally empty your mind; she'd never done it before. She always had a dozen things running through her brain.

She tried again, this time adamant about getting it right.

160

She let her whole body relax and put all her trust in her heart, letting her mind rely on it to guide her through. She stood like this for a few minutes, feeling a quiet calm wash over her. She could feel her mind starting to let go. She felt light and full of air. She could no longer feel the ground beneath her feet and when she felt the need to open her eyes she was not surprised to see that she was several feet above the ground, resting on the same branch that Jiro had occupied minutes before. What she didn't expect, however, was that he was no longer in front of her holding her hands. She hadn't even felt him let go. The sudden realization that she was alone up there made her stumble and quickly race to the solid structure of the tree trunk to hold onto tightly. She heard laughter rise up from below.

"Whisper, you made it up there, why reach for the tree for help now?" he yelled.

"Because, you're not here to keep me from falling," she yelled back.

"But, you didn't need me to get up there; you certainly don't need me to *stay* up there. Have more confidence in what you can do. You have learned in minutes what it takes great warriors years to accomplish. Now, come back down here, we have more work to do." Get down? But how? It was way too high to jump. Then she realized that if she was able to get *up* than she should be able to get *down*. She closed her eyes and relaxed her mind. It was easier this time and before she knew it, she was standing in front of Jiro with a renewed sense of pride in herself and a willingness to learn more.

By the time Jiro thought they had enough, Whisper was tired but also excited with her progress. She could barely move but that didn't stop her from wanting to learn more. When she realized that she had the power to levitate herself high in the air, she couldn't be stopped. She started to feel there was nothing she couldn't do. He taught her to somersault in midair and come down with a kick to the throat. She twisted and did countless spins, shooting out her hands in hard punches, striking anything that came near her. She could go twenty feet up and twenty feet sideways and not lose control of any of her defences. He tried everything to throw her off balance and nothing was working anymore. She was fast on her feet, agile in her movements and intelligent in her strategy. She was starting to feel invincible. Finally, he held up his hand in protest. He was out of breath and bent over, leaning on his knee.

"Enough, young Whisper," he panted, "we should save some things for tomorrow."

"But I get it. I understand what I'm doing. We can't quit now. Please, just a few more minutes?" She looked at him pleadingly.

"No, we will continue tomorrow." That was it, he spoke with strong conviction. Her jubilation died down and she gave in to the fact that their workout was over for the day. Without the excitement of working out she realized just how exhausted she was and grimaced as she tried to stretch out her back. He saw this and said so.

"Ah, young Whisper, I see that I was right in stopping for the day. You look like you need nourishment and rest."

"Yeah, I guess I could go for a long nap right about now," she wiped her brow and discovered how sweaty she had become, "and a shower."

"No sleep for you. You may shower and eat but then Miss Alannis will be waiting for you when you are done."

"Alannis? Why?" Whisper didn't think she could cope with any more lessons today.

"You must make up for the class you should have had with her this morning. It is just as important as your defence lesson, maybe even more. She has so many things to show you. You are very lucky to have such a fine teacher." She could tell by the way he spoke of her that he had great admiration for the woman. Whisper followed him to the door and thanked him for the workout. He bowed to her then they departed. Whisper went off in search of Marcus to let her down to her room and Jiro returned to the lounge, probably hoping to meet up with Alannis again.

#

Whisper got to her room and had a somewhat speedy shower. It was hard to be too quick. Once the hot water hit her aching muscles she didn't want to move, but then she started to feel guilty that Alannis was somewhere, waiting for her and she began to hurry a little more. She dried off and got dressed into

163

some comfortable clothes; a loose fitting pair of jeans and a big blue hoodie. She was just finishing the impossible task of combing through her wet hair when there was a knock at the door.

"Aria?" she said when she answered the door and saw her friend standing there.

"Hi, Whisper," she said. "I heard your workout with Jiro went quite well."

"Yeah, it was fun. It took me a while to get the hang of it but once I did I loved it!"

"That's good!" She sounded happy for Whisper. "I'm glad some things are getting easier for you."

"Do you want to come in?"

"Oh, no, in fact, I was wondering if you'd like to come over to my place for something to eat. I knew you wouldn't have time to rest *and* make a good meal before seeing Alannis so I took the liberty of making something for you." That sounded good to Whisper. She was starved, but the thought of going into the kitchen and making food just did not appeal to her right now.

"Thank you," she said sincerely to Aria. "Let me grab my shoes." She put on her sneakers and followed Aria to her room.

The meal was delicious. Aria didn't skip on anything. She had made sandwiches and cut up vegetables with dip. There was hot cheese melted over crispy taco chips with salsa and guacamole on the side. She had water and juice to drink and, for dessert, she had cut up all kinds of fruit and placed them delicately on little plates. It was delicious and Whisper ate every bite. She must have been hungrier than she realized. Aria laughed at the way she gobbled everything up.

"Slow down, you still have a bit more time. If you eat too fast you're going to make yourself sick," she said as she cleared away some of the empty dishes.

"I'm sorry, it's just all so good," Whisper apologized while she chewed on a big chunk of honeydew melon. "Thank you so much. That workout with Jiro must have made me famished." She took a drink of water to wash everything down.

"No problem, I'm glad you liked it."

"Aria, do all of us know how to fight like Jiro?" Whisper asked.

"Oh, yes, being a Soul-healer can be very dangerous," she said. "There are evil forces everywhere trying to undo the work that we do and they don't fool around. Once they realize what we're doing they'll try anything to get rid of us. You know, take out the competition to make it easier for them."

"Does it ever work?"

"For the most part, no, but there have been some Soul-healers that have been badly damaged. So much so that sometimes they must rest for centuries before they're allowed to return to any kind of life," she finished.

"But have any, you know, gone bad?" This question had been bugging Whisper for a while now. She couldn't imagine that a Soul-healer could be swayed but if it was possible she'd like to know how they could be tempted.

"Yeah, there've been a few." All of a sudden she didn't look well, her cheery exterior had gone away and Whisper could see that she didn't wish to continue. She started clearing away more dishes. "I think it's time to go meet Alannis. I'll call Marcus to meet you at the top of the stairs."

"Okay," Whisper said, seeing that she had somehow upset Aria. "Thanks again for all this food, maybe I can do it for you sometime."

"Sure," she said, still looking a bit upset.

#

Alannis was waiting at their usual table, holding her ever present cup of coffee. She seemed to really have a liking for this beverage. When she saw Whisper she smiled, put her cup down and got up to meet her.

"Are we staying in here again?" asked Whisper.

"No, not this time, we need a more peaceful room than this." She pushed her long white sleeves up her arms a bit and reached to open the door. She turned to say something.

"I know, I know, just follow you," Whisper said before Alannis had the chance. She laughed and led the way.

This time they headed down the hall toward the stairway that led to the dorms and stopped just short of it. To the left was a door that appeared to be made of out of metal. It was a greyish silvery color and had a bit of a shine to it. She reached up the sleeve of her right arm and pulled out a long silver key. She placed it in the lock and a familiar 'click' could be heard throughout the hallway.

"After you," she said as she held the door open for Whisper. There was a well lit spiral stairway that wound around and around for a long way, going even deeper than the floor the dorms were on. Whisper followed it and started to feel dizzy from the constant circular motion she had to take. The stairs were very narrow with only enough width for one person at a time to occupy each step but Whisper could feel Alannis right behind her.

"How far do these stairs go?" she asked, thinking that, perhaps, there was no end to them.

"Not much further, we're almost there."

"Okay." They kept going for another few minutes and then, finally, they came to another shiny door. Whisper looked back up at the long staircase, dreading the fact that when they were done they would have to climb back up them. She turned and looked at the door again, wondering if she'd need a key.

"Just turn the handle and the door will open." Whisper did, it opened and she stepped inside. They were in a room that looked like space. They were surrounded by black and what looked like stars that were scattered everywhere, twinkling and shining as if they were alive. In the distance Whisper could see a planet that looked very much like theirs and further on, her eyes picked out a brightness that could only be the sun. She saw a meteor shoot past. She was amazed by the room, wondering if it was some kind of movie theatre that generated images on every surface; the walls, the floor, the ceiling. The silence in the room was overwhelming; it was so quiet that Whisper could hear her heart beat.

"This is called the Celestial Room," Alannis said. Whisper had almost forgotten that she was still there. "Watch this." She closed the door and all of a sudden Whisper felt her body lose all its heaviness. Her feet lifted from the ground and she started to float up in the air.

"What's going on?" She sounded a bit panicked and Alannis laughed at the girl's uncertainty.

"We've lost our gravity," she answered as she turned somersaults in front of Whisper. Her dress and hair seemed to float around her, giving her a sort of glow. Whisper was mesmerized by it. "We now feel exactly as we would if we truly were out in space. This is my favourite room to be in. Try a flip; it's so easy to do in here." Whisper tried, getting caught up in Alannis' enthusiasm. It *was* easy! It was different than being able to jump high with Jiro. There were no restrictions, no worry of falling. There was no thinking, just being. Whisper liked the room too, she felt at peace there. They continued their acrobatics for a few more minutes and then Alannis' voice took on a serious tone.

"Okay, now that you've grown accustomed to the room, it is time to begin our lesson," she said, coming to a stop in front of the girl. "I want you to relax and listen to my words." Whisper let her body hang loose and tried to get herself into a horizontal position. She closed her eyes and focused on Alannis' voice.

"Let us begin with what you know," she began. "You already know how to read some minds. You do it all the time when you peek into other worlds, we all do. We find it amusing to try and guess what a person is thinking then reading their thoughts to see if we were right. But, you also know that this ability has its limits. If a mind is advanced and senses your intrusion they can turn themselves off to you, block your advances. This is why you can't read my mind, or Aria's or almost everyone else here in Chrystalline; we are far too advanced here for that." Whisper knew this; otherwise she might be inclined to cheat on her tests at school. Being able to read the smart kid's mind would be a real plus. "I'm going to teach you how to break down our barriers and get into our thoughts. But I must warn you, we only do this when it is absolutely necessary. We don't invade the private thoughts of a person just because we're curious. No, we only use this ability when we really have to." She floated over to Whisper and placed her hands on either side of her temples.

"I want you to concentrate on your inner eye. We all have one and it sits right here." She placed her hand on a spot just between Whisper's eyes and up a little on her forehead. "As I told you before, we were all created in the image of Edric and Edric had three eyes; two to see the Universe from the outside and one to see it from within. When Gwynn and Dougall made

169

us they assumed we would never need this third eye so they covered it up, buried it deep within our minds. Little did they know that eventually, some beings would learn how to peel away this cover and discover its true purpose and begin to use it. It took thousands of years of practice to accomplish this feat and these beings would only pass on their knowledge to those they felt were worthy. All Soul-healers use it and some Cross-overs and even some Flatliners have the ability to see through this eye.

"Once we uncover your inner eye you will be able to read minds and transfer your thoughts which will be helpful when you're trying to communicate with the soul that has called for your help. Without these abilities he would never know who you are or what your purpose is. Because he can never see you, communication through the mind is vital. With mind reading you can read his thoughts and with mind transference he can see yours."

"What do you mean, he can never see me?" The thought of not being able to appear before her Flatliner was kind of off-setting for Whisper. She was looking forward to meeting him, he intrigued her.

"Well, not in the physical sense, but there are other ways they can see you and get to know you."

"C-can *you* read my mind?" Whisper wondered if Alannis knew about her fascination with her Flatliner. If she could read her mind, she would know everything Whisper was thinking.

"If I wanted to I could but I have no need to do so. It would be a horrible invasion of your privacy and a misuse of trust. I only use my abilities when I'm healing a soul or when I'm fighting an enemy."

"An enemy? You can read their minds?" Whisper asked, wondering what it was like to actually fight someone. "Can they read mine as well?"

"Yes, they can, unless you learn to block them out which I'll teach you to do later on," she explained. "Anyway, like I was saying, you must be able to hear the thoughts of the one you're helping so you can understand what emotions are driving them. When you know this, you can help guide them to a better road. It is a fine line to walk between guiding and instructing. We must not tell them what to do. We can only show them the path, whether they take it or not is up to them."

"But if this is all I can do then why all the pressure to get it right?" Whisper asked, letting herself come to a more vertical position so she could look Alannis in the eye.

"Because some souls are not even able to *see* the path. This is your job, to make them see that there are other ways laid out for them. Some souls are so angry, they turn their back on everything. They're stubborn and don't want any help. They believe they can do it on their own and will get angry if you try to assist them in any way. Some souls are so distraught, they give up and don't care what happens to them and then there are the confused ones. These are the souls that are on the precipice of

171

knowing something but not sure what it is. They don't know which direction they should go but they're eager for answers. The one thing that all these souls have in common, no matter what their emotion, is that they're very vulnerable and can become easy prey for the Soul-stealers."

"If we open our third eye," Alannis continued, "it makes our job easier and quicker. Now, to do this we are going to go through a series of meditative exercises."

"How many of these exercises will we have to do?" asked Whisper.

"I don't know. Usually it doesn't take too long after you've been awakened but, with you, it could be different. On the one hand you're awakening came early yet, on the other hand, you obviously have used some of these abilities already."

"What do you mean?"

"When you went to the Earth dimension, this soul of yours felt your presence, even knew when you were talking. I think you used your abilities and didn't even know it."

'Or he used his,' Whisper thought.

"I think this proves that it's not going to take very long to uncover your inner eye."

"I hope you're right." Whisper was very doubtful.

"Even if I'm wrong, we have to open it one way or another, but I don't think I am." She floated over to the wall and touched a button that Whisper hadn't noticed before. The room filled with soft music that put her mind at ease. Alannis floated back and asked. "Are you ready to begin?"

"I guess." Then Whisper remembered something that she wanted to ask. "By the way, what is dream walking?"

"Dream walking is exactly what it sounds like," Alannis explained as she tilted Whisper back down into a horizontal position. "You can communicate with others through dreams. It's like being in a virtual world, you can introduce yourself, you can touch, smell and even taste just like you would out here but it all takes place in a dream. It's pretty neat; I'll show you how to do it later."

She floated off to Whisper's left and told her to close her eyes and concentrate but Whisper just couldn't. All she could think about was what Alannis just told her. Was it possible that Whisper could actually meet her Flatliner inside his dreams? Would he then be able to see her, talk to her and maybe even touch her? She felt a rush of warmth run through her body again. She was so busy thinking about all the possibilities that it took here at least three meditative exercises before she could really concentrate on what Alannis was telling her.

Chapter 13

Cael picked up the chair that laid on the floor. He was so angry when he realized his parents had lied to him that he started to tear apart his apartment. Then something weird happened, something he couldn't explain. He felt the presence again, the same one that was with him in the room at the hospital the other day. He sensed it and then he physically felt it. It was like it had touched him, had held his arm to calm him down. He looked down at his arm and rubbed it gently. It worked, too. In fact, it not only calmed him down, it sent a shock up his arm that left him a bit unbalanced. Then, just like that, it disappeared.

At first he thought that it was a ghost then he changed his mind. He knew what it was like to be the presence of a ghost; he had seen one before when he was small. This was something different, something much more than an apparition. It seemed to know him and wanted to comfort him. He felt good in its presence, safe and peaceful. He thought of this as he picked up the things he threw across the room and tidied up.

He had so many things to think about today, he didn't know where to begin. He figured he'd call a few of the markets, make sure they were really closed. He hadn't pieced together what he would say to his parents yet. He thought he should keep quiet until after the memorial service the next day. There was no need to spoil that. How ironic it would be if his parents *did* have something to do with Mr. Yamanaka's death, which Cael wasn't sure if they did, and then planned his service. It would certainly keep any suspicion away from them.

He really only had one question he wanted to ask them if his suspicions were right. Why? That's the one thing that kept confusing him, why? If Taro really did get shot because he was trying to tell Cael something important then why would his own parents do it? Were they working for someone else; someone who was a part of something much bigger? Why would they be a part of something like that? There were so many questions and he didn't know who to go to for answers. Who could he trust? He sighed because he knew there was no one.

He promised to let Rob know about the service and figured he could go visit the dojo again to tell him. He could also take him up on his offer to have lunch with him. It would get him out of the apartment for a while and take his mind off of things. They could catch up on old times. He went to the phone and gave his friend a call. Rob was happy to hear from him and they made plans to meet at the dojo at around twelve thirty. He hung up and went and got dressed. When he returned he went back to the computer and started calling the markets listed on the computer.

#

Half an hour later, it was just as he thought, not one of the country markets was open full time yet. Some were open just on the weekends and only in the afternoon. They would all open

175

with their longer hours, from eight in the morning to eight in the evening on June first. What he would do with this information, he still didn't know. Could he wait until after the service to say something? He was beginning to doubt that. Perhaps he should phone his mother right now and demand some answers. He reached for the phone and started to dial, and then stopped. What would he say? Was he really ready to believe that his parents were that evil? He put the phone back down. He should check his email. Jiro had sent him one message maybe he had sent him another. He scanned the incoming mail for the familiar name and there it was; Jiro Yamanaka. It was recent too, just within the last ten minutes. He clicked it open and read:

Quiet is the gentle breeze
That blows across the land with ease
But noisy is the howling wind
That meets with anger from within
When one is filled with bitter pain
Silence shall remain his name
To keep your head within the storm
Will bring you aid to keep you warm

Cael reread the poem again and knew exactly what it meant; Jiro wanted him to stay silent. He must not say anything to his parents. He must keep quiet until someone came to him and offered to help. He was pretty sure it would be Jiro coming to help him. Why else would he be sending Cael these messages? If that was the case, then Cael hoped he would come soon. He needed better answers than the cryptic poems he had to decipher.

He went to shut down his computer but before he did, he changed the password. He couldn't take the risk of anyone hacking into it and finding these emails.

He planned to do some grocery shopping after his lunch with Rob, but until then he had no plans. He decided to take it easy, unplug his phone, lock his door, and even take a nap. Tomorrow he would see his mom and dad and he had to be prepared for that moment. He would have to pretend that he didn't know anything and that would be hard to do. He wished that the presence he felt earlier could be with him tomorrow. He knew it would help him to keep calm. He lie back on his couch and thought about it as he slowly drifted off to sleep.

When he woke up, he was a little more rested, but it wasn't long before anxiety reared its ugly head again. He had overslept and realized he was going to be late for his lunch. He gave Rob a quick call, apologized and said he would be there in twenty minutes. Rob didn't sound too upset, he was running a bit late himself and would appreciate the extra time to get some things finished.

#

Their lunch went well. They spent it reminiscing about old times together. Cael actually enjoyed the way Rob seemed to *only* remember the fights that *he* won. They talked about what all the kids that bullied them were doing now. Rob said he heard that one of them was now living on the streets, heavily addicted to crystal meth. Sometimes there really was karma in the

Universe he said. Cael told him that one of the mean kids he knew was now in his third year of law school and doing quite well. Sometimes people grew up and the Universe forgave. Rob didn't think so. There would be justice for him in the future. They talked for a couple of hours and when he left, Cael was starting to feel like himself again.

He went shopping after that, filling his cart with an even balance of healthy food and junk food. He picked up a six pack of beer and headed home. He checked his email as soon as he got in and was a little disappointed when he found nothing new. He was just starting to put away his groceries when the phone rang. He looked at the caller ID and saw that it was his mother's cell. Should he answer? He didn't really want to, but he supposed she would get suspicious if he didn't or, worse, come over to check on him.

"Hello?"

"Cael? Where've you been, I've been trying to call you all day?" She sounded anxious.

"I went out with an old friend for lunch, and then I went grocery shopping. My fridge was getting empty." He was actually amused at the sound of panic in her voice.

"A friend? What friend?" He could just imagine her heartbeat getting faster.

"Rob," he said.

"Oh." He could hear her calm down, sounding very relieved. He guessed Rob was okay to see. He thought he'd test her a bit.

"Yeah, it was nice to get together again," he smiled as he contemplated the effect of his next sentence. "By the way, he heard from Sensei Jiro again." Silence; nothing on the other end. "Mom? You still there?"

"Yes," she sounded angry. "What did *he* have to say?"

"Nothing, Rob told him when the memorial service was and asked if he'd be coming." This was a lie but he knew his mother didn't know that nor would she ever find out. Her and Rob had always disliked one another.

"And?" she asked, trying to sound calm.

"And...I don't think he'll make it. Too bad, though, I would have liked to talk to him."

"Me too."

'Oh I just bet you would,' he thought.

"Anyway, that's not why you called is it?" It was hard to keep the anger out of his voice. She ignored it.

"I wanted to ask what kind of music you wanted played tomorrow." This was a lie, he knew it. She had never wanted his opinion on anything before, let alone music. She was checking up on him, seeing how much he knew.

"Music? I don't know, whatever you choose will be fine," he said trying to keep his voice calm as he broke the pencil he had picked up when he answered the phone.

"Oh, okay, I just thought that because Mr. Yamanaka was Japanese, you might want Japanese music or something," she

179

said and Cael started to feel the fury in his body.

"I don't think it matters, Mom, Mr. Yamanaka is dead and won't care what music is played."

"Cael, are you okay?" she asked.

"Yeah, I'm just tired that's all."

"Do you want to come over for supper? Your father would love to see you."

"No, that's okay. I'm still pretty full from lunch. I'm just going to stay in tonight."

"Okay," she sounded relieved that he had said no, "I'll see you tomorrow then?"

"Okay, sure, bye." He didn't wait for her to say goodbye, he was too angry. He had to learn to control his emotions or tomorrow would be a disaster.

#

Cael's mother had rented the tiny chapel that was attached to a funeral home that served the farming communities just outside the city. It was a good thirty minute drive for Cael from his apartment and he almost got lost on the way. The service was to begin at nine thirty in the morning which just seemed ridiculous to him. How his mother ever expected anyone to get out of bed, get dressed and make it way out here by nine thirty was unbelievable. Then he remembered that his mother didn't really care who showed up. She had no feelings for Mr. Yamanaka or for those who cared for him. This whole memorial service was just a way to keep any suspicion from her.

Still, he must admit, she did do a good job of decorating the little chapel. There were bouquets of spring flowers at the beginning of every pew and, at the altar, there were vases full of daisies, tulips and lilies. It was very tastefully done. She booked an organist to play soft music as everyone arrived and then again when the guests filed out. She asked the funeral director to preside over the service and he did a very respectable job. He allowed for people to come up to the front and talk about Mr. Yamanaka if they wanted to and Cael took this opportunity to pay tribute to his friend. He could hardly contain his sorrow while he spoke and then his eyes came to rest on his parents who were sitting in the front pew. Anger started to seethe within him and it pushed his sorrow away and he quickly finished and returned to his seat, clenching and unclenching his fists. After him, Rob got up and said a few words on behalf of the Judo community. All in all, it was a very simple service and Cael knew that his friend would have liked it.

There were not very many people there, further confirmation that Mr. Yamanaka liked to keep to himself, and so it didn't take long for the chapel to empty out. Cael spotted Rob and noticed that he brought a woman with him, a very beautiful woman, and he walked over to introduce himself.

"Cael, it was a nice service. You're mother did a good job," Rob said as he shook his hand.

"Thank you, I'm glad you could make it," he replied, as he turned his head to the woman. She was tall, slender and very shapely. She wore a simple black dress that showed off her ivory skin and her dark red hair. Cael noticed how heavy her makeup was and thought it inappropriate for a funeral.

"Robbie, aren't you going to introduce your handsome, young friend to me?" Cael didn't like her. As soon as she spoke, it was as if he could see the poison dripping from her mouth. All of a sudden he felt cold inside and wished he hadn't come over but his mother was lurking in the background and facing her wasn't a pleasant idea either.

"I'm sorry. Cael this is Stephanie. Stephanie this is Cael." She reached out to shake Cael's hand but he quickly put them both in his pocket and shivered as if he were cold. She took her hand back and laughed as if she didn't notice his rejection.

"Cael, how nice to meet you, Robbie has told me so much about you," she said.

"Really?" He looked over her head at Rob who was shaking his head in denial at her remark. "I hear you're the new secretary at the dojo. Do you like it?"

"It's a job. I meet very interesting people there all the time," she said with a glance at Rob. Immediately his cheeks flushed and Cael looked away.

"I hear Jiro has kept in touch with you since he left," Cael stated.

"Is that what Robbie told you?" she laughed. "Well, I hate to disappoint you but I've not heard from the quiet Sensei since he took leave. I do wish he would let me know what's going on; it would be so nice to let the students know when he'll be back. I mean Robbie is doing a good job but Jiro is so much more experienced. Have you heard from him?"

"No, I'm afraid I haven't talked to Jiro for a few years now," Cael answered.

"I told Cael he could come back to the club if he wanted, no charge," Rob told Stephanie.

"Did you? And what did you say?" She looked at Cael with her intense brown eyes.

"I said I'd think about it." He could tell that she didn't believe him. He had no intention of ever going back.

"What are you three discussing?" His mother had walked up to the group without Cael noticing. Hearing her voice sent a rush of anger through him.

"Nothing much," said Cael. "Mother, have you ever met Stephanie? She's Jiro's secretary at the club." He noticed a flicker of recognition between the two as they shook hands and introduced themselves to each other.

"Well, Robbie, we should get going, the gym won't run itself." Stephanie seemed to want to make a quick exit.

"I guess you're right, as always," Rob said. "Don't be a stranger and come by every once in a while okay?"

"Okay," Cael said as he walked them to their car and watched them get in.

"She seemed very nice, don't you think?" asked his mother. He put his hands in his pockets again and clenched his jaw shut. He couldn't look her in the face right then so he stared after Rob's car as it pulled away.

"I guess," he said. He didn't want to have a long conversation with her so he tried to figure out what to say that would get him out of there quickly.

"You did a nice job with the service, thank you," he tilted his head and peered at her out of the corner of his eye. "Too bad it had to be way out here and so early."

"Yeah, well, it was the only place I could find on such short notice." She was glaring at him now, sensing his coldness toward her. "Do you want to come over for a while; it would mean so much to your dad." He turned to see his father talking with the funeral director.

"No, I don't think that would be a good idea," he said casually.

"Are you sure?"

"Yeah, I think I might take a drive, maybe check out those country markets you like so much." He turned and looked her directly in the eye. She stared back at him and he couldn't tell if she had understood his comment.

"That sounds interesting," she said as if she were only half listening. "If there's anything else we can do…"

"No, I'll be fine. Say goodbye to Dad for me okay?"

"I'll do that," she said coldly and turned away.

He almost ran to his Jeep, he couldn't get away fast enough. As he pulled out of the parking lot he caught a glimpse

184

of his dad walking over to his mom with his arms held out as if asking what happened. His mother turned and stared at Cael in his departing Jeep and he felt a cold chill run down his body. That was not his mother, not the mother he knew, the one that had raised him. This woman was cold and calculating and he wondered where his real mother had gone.

Chapter 14

"Is this report accurate?" asked Dougall as he scanned through the thick folder the woman put on his desk. He was sitting in his office which was huge, featuring a large desk, a built in bar and a big movie screen that was set into the only solid wall in the room. The rest of the room was made up of windows all showing the same view, the blackness of space. He liked feeling like he was in the middle of nowhere; it threw people off just a little. He wanted this ship to be placed just far enough out of the reach of any curious eyes.

When he started building his army, he took the name 'Almighty', mainly for the peons of the Earth dimension. Once they heard his omnipresent name they practically begged to be in his army. They were a foolish people, so easy to manipulate. He just had to tell them there was a cause to fight for and they were there, no questions asked, ready to give their lives if they had to. Every one of them wanting to be martyrs. They were a joke and he would feel nothing when they were sacrificed.

"Yes, sir, we have our best men on it." The woman was a whiny little thing, always sucking up, thought Dougall. Always saying 'Yes sir,' 'No sir', it was annoying. He would be much happier when he could get rid of her.

"I'm sure you do, but I must have some sort of verification. I can't just wipe out two of my best people and then find out I made a mistake." He spent a lot of time placing these two into the roles of Gladys and Hal Fraser.

"Yes, sir," Dougall winced at the words, "I'll find you what you need as soon as possible."

"Sooner than that, I hope," he said, staring right into the woman's eyes.

'She's kind of beautiful,' he thought, 'but I don't have time for play right now, perhaps later.' He smiled at the thought.

"Yes, sir," she said then turned and left.

Dougall let out a heavy sigh as he watched her go. Too bad she was so annoying. He thought he was lucky to have found her. She seemed to have come to him out of nowhere. He had heard that somehow she had gotten to the Earth dimension from the Abyss dimension. Apparently, a little known, centuries old portal leading directly to the Earth dimension brought her there. The Abyssians have a reputation for causing great corruption wherever they go and are often assassinated when discovered. So the woman had shown great courage in coming this far. Dougall admired that but she was still annoying.

#

Jezebel had roamed the Earth dimension for a few hundred years, disguising herself as different people and enjoying her many conquests. She had lovers everywhere, too many to keep count, not that it mattered, one was just like the

187

next and none could ever satisfy her. When she grew tired of them she would kill them and dispose of them, feeling nothing in the process.

Eventually her travels led her to one of Dougall's many foot soldiers who immediately fell desperately in love with her. As usual, she used him for her own desires until she got bored and got ready to dispose of him. Sensing his time with her was ending, he revealed his role in Dougall's army. She became fascinated with this Dougall and begged to be introduced to him. Finally, fearing it was the only way to keep her, the man arranged a meeting between the two.

When she met Dougall, she was immediately in awe of his power and he was excited by her beauty. They came together and became inseparable. The first thing they did was get rid of the man that had introduced them. It was an elaborate sacrifice that they arranged to be watched by others as an example. They had such fun with it. The woman was at the mercy of Dougall and found herself doing whatever she could to please him, a role she had never played before. Dougall, however, was becoming tired of her and soon even her beauty could not hold his attention.

Seeing that her appeal was waning, she became desperate to stay with him, knowing what would happen if she fell out of favour. She looked for anything that would please him, asking whoever she met what it was that Dougall wanted most. This is when she heard the story of the 'last warrior'. This was it!

Finally, she had found the one thing that would keep her in the good graces of her lover. All she would have to do was find this 'last warrior' and bring him to Dougall. A task not easily accomplished. From what she knew of these warriors they had a special bond to Gwynn, Dougall's arch enemy. This made it almost impossible to convince them to switch to the other side. It had been done once before, though, and she was positive she would find a way to do it again. So, she studied day and night, learning everything about the warriors of Gwynn and when she was ready she returned to the Earth dimension to look for him. She knew the places a warrior would gravitate to and that's where she began her impossible search.

She knew a warrior would be drawn to places where they could hone their skill at fighting, after all, they were supposedly the best fighters ever created. But when they were scattered and hidden they were given new bodies and new minds and they would have to relearn everything that was ever taught to them. To do this Gwynn had secretly sent special teachers to guide them in their training and the woman was sure that this would make it easier to find him. Now, she was looking for two very distinct persons instead of just one and they should be joined in an unbreakable bond. Just when she thought her task would be impossible to achieve and she would suffer the fate of being tossed aside by Dougall, she stumbled into the Mountain Judo club.

As soon as she walked into the gym, she knew she had

found it. She could sense it in her bones. This was the way to the warrior. When the head sensei introduced himself as a man *named* Jiro Yamanaka, she was positive she had found the special teacher. She persuaded him to hire her as a secretary where she could quietly observe the students of his class. When she was introduced to a young student named Rob, she thought she had found the warrior. She turned her charm towards him to lure the truth out of him and discovered she had been wrong. The man had turned out to be like any other man, full of greed and lust. The 'last warrior' would be a man full of high standards and morals, of this she was sure. She knew, however, that she should not leave because she was convinced this would be the place that would lead her to him.

Her instincts paid off one day when she answered the phone and heard the voice of the true teacher. He had said that he wanted to talk to his brother, Jiro, and immediately she understood why she had felt the connection between the sensei and the warrior. His name was Taro Yamanaka and she used all her resources to track him down and follow him. She was sitting outside his gym when she spotted a black Jeep pull up outside. When the door opened and a young man jumped out, she let out a gasp. It was him! She was positive this time. All this time and she had finally found him and what a find he was! She didn't expect him to look so appealing. If it hadn't been for her desperate love for Dougall, she would have tried very hard to conquer this man.

She brought all this information back to Dougall immediately and together they devised a plan to win this warrior's trust. She was relieved, Dougall seemed to be pleased with her and she wanted to do more. They decided to reach this man through his emotions. They would need to get close to him and manipulate his life. It was hard; he had no close friends, no girlfriends and no siblings. It seemed all he ever did was work, which he did at home, and train. Taro Yamanaka was out of the question, he was sent by Gwynn and there was no way he would ever work for Dougall. So they went to the only other important people in his life, his parents.

Jezebel knew just what to do for that as well; Kern and Maura. They were the king and queen of the Abyss and were the reason she left in the first place. Maura had been fiercely jealous of Jezebel's beauty, worried that her husband would be tempted by her. She locked her in the dungeon of the palace and had the guards whip her daily, sure that she could destroy her beauty. It didn't work, though, Kern was still drawn to Jezebel and visited her in her prison almost as many times as she was whipped. When Maura found out she flew into a rage and banished Jezebel from the Abyss forever. Jezebel hated them both. They were evil and thought that they ruled over everything and could do as they pleased. They needed to be reminded of how inconsequential they really were. She suggested them to Dougall and he agreed that they would fit nicely into their plan. He had them sent up from the Abyss and explained the plan to them and they were

191

only too happy to agree, they never really had a choice. Dougall had tested Kern out on a few jobs and he had proven himself worthy in his master's eyes. When the time was right Gladys and Hal Fraser's souls were ripped from their bodies and thrown away. Dougall had no use for them; Gwynn could come and pick them up for all he cared. Their bodies were left for Kern and Maura to enter and begin their assault on the warrior's emotions.

Immediately, Jezebel had regretted suggesting these two idiots to Dougall. When they got to the Earth dimension they had no idea how to behave in that world. They made so many stupid mistakes, but the worst was their total lack of respect for the intelligence of the people involved. They never even checked up on Taro Yamanaka so, when he started to suspect that Jezebel was a servant of Dougall, it was almost too late to stop him from talking to the warrior. She met with them and commanded that they take care of the problem before Dougall found out. And they did too, in a way that was so typical of their antics. They killed the warrior's teacher. It only made the problem worse. By breaking the sacred bond that Gwynn had placed on the warrior and his teacher, they uncovered the only emotion that could call his Soul-healer.

Dougall knew this Soul-healer and was not particularly thrilled to have to face her again. She caused so much destruction to his army the last time she faced him that he would rather leave the warrior than fight her again. Jezebel's powerful lover was furious when he learned of the turn of events and almost

192

destroyed Kern when he came to visit him. Then Dougall had an idea and a plan started to form, a plan Jezebel didn't like at all. Dougall decided he wanted to keep Kern under close watch as long as he could deliver the girl along with the warrior. The *t*hought rejuvenated him, he remembered how beautiful she was, even more so than Jezebel, and the idea of having her for his own exhilarated him. And her power would complement the warrior's perfectly.

Jezebel was in turmoil and didn't know what to do. She couldn't let this girl take her place, not now when she had worked so hard to please him. She started to feel anger towards Dougall and tried to see a way to change things. When Jiro took off because of a warning from Taro, she had an idea. It seemed so easy. She must let the warrior know everything that was happening, suggest to him that there were evil forces working against him and he must not trust anyone. If he could figure out that his parents were the enemy and not confide in them or trust them, there would be no chance that Kern and Maura could convince him to turn to Dougall, therefore, keeping the girl away too. It was brilliant and all she would have to do was send a few poems to the warrior with messages she knew he could decipher and then present Dougall with the evidence of Kern and Maura's ineptness once more. It had worked. She walked back into the office with a copy of the emails sent to the warrior and a willing witness to the cold exchange between mother and son at the memorial service.

Dougall looked at the blonde boy and wondered what this woman was up to.

"Sir, I brought you your proof." She laid the copies on his desk. "This boy can tell you about the meeting at the service." Rob stepped forward, still not totally understanding where he was and who this man was before him.

"Well, speak up boy!" Dougall didn't really have time for this woman's little play toys.

"I-it's true, I've n-never seen Cael express such hatred towards his m-mother. It was like he wanted to kill her." Rob stepped back hoping his part was done and he could leave. Dougall read the files and shook his head. Jezebel was right, something had to be done.

"I don't believe he'll *have* to kill them. Are you finished playing with your toy." Dougall asked her with a look in his eyes she had not seen in a while.

"Yes." She gulped and had one of the foot soldiers escort Rob back to the Earth dimension. Dougall reached for her and she came to him quickly and buried her head in his chest. This was what she wanted more than anything else.

"Well, my dear, shall we watch a couple of souls beg for mercy?" he laughed as he started to walk her to the door.

"Oh, yes, my love, let's do just that and then…" She let the question hang in the air.

"And then, we'll see," he laughed again as he lead the woman away with a firm grip around her waist.

Chapter 15

The police were starting to rope off the highway. This was going to be a messy one, probably have the road closed well into the night. Red hated these kinds of accidents, they always had the same old story; driver falls asleep at the wheel, wanders over the centre line and right into the path of the biggest bloody semi on the road. The driver of the truck never has a scratch on him and the people in the other vehicle have to be scraped off the engine and put into bags. He'd better call his wife and tell her he'd be late for dinner.

#

Cael went to his favourite spot again after the service. His mother had given him such an evil look and he felt so disturbed that he needed to go somewhere where he could relax and clear his mind. She seemed so angry and he wasn't sure going home was exactly the best idea. How long would it be before she would be knocking on his door? The thought frightened him just a bit, knowing now that something was definitely wrong with her. He thought it better if he disappeared for a while, go somewhere no one would think to look for him.

It seemed a little colder today than it was the other day he thought as he stood, trying to skip flat rocks across the river. He decided he should do something to keep warm, maybe take a hike. He went to the Jeep and grabbed a thicker coat and a bottle of water he had thrown in there that morning before he left, just in case of an emergency. You never knew what could happen when you drove out on some of these country roads.

He figured he would start up the trail that would take him down past the small waterfall and then, eventually, up through the abandoned beaver dams. Whenever he went to the dams it felt like he was stepping back in time, a place frozen in the exact same way it had been long ago. Beavers had been building dams along this river for hundreds of years; it was one of the reasons that humans first came to the area. It used to house dozens of the creatures until they started getting trapped and killed for their pelts. The place where he was going still had about a dozen of the amazing structures still standing. Long ago abandoned, they now stood hauntingly alone surrounded only by the thick forest and the small ponds they had created. Now ducks, squirrels, chipmunks and the occasional lost bear were the only animals that wandered through there.

He hiked for almost two hours before the trail by the river ended and started winding up the side of a hill. This part of the trek continued on for another twenty minutes before it flattened out and he saw the first of the dams. It was hard to believe that the river once ran through here, he thought as he came up to a huge stump. He had no idea where the rest of the tree had gone. He scanned the ponds wondering if it had been used for one of the dams. He brushed the light covering of snow off the stump and sat down. He took a drink of water and closed his eyes then took in a deep breath.

He remembered the first time he found this spot. He was twelve and his mom and dad had pitched a tent not far from where the Jeep was parked now. In those days everyone would camp wherever they wanted to. Not like it was now. Now they had campgrounds with campsites that had to be booked weeks in advance. He remembered his mom and dad were getting everything unpacked and set up and he was bored. They told him to go explore which he was only too happy to do. He wandered around everywhere, losing all track of time and eventually found these dams. He was just as taken with them then as he was now. He spent hours running around, exploring every inch of them. Finally, he noticed the shadows getting longer and the sun slipping away and decided to head back to camp. He said farewell to his private playground and hurried back.

His parents were frantic. They were searching for him all over and were about to go to the Ranger's Station to report him missing and get help. They were sure he was lost or hurt. How could he be? He never got lost nor had he ever been afraid while he was in the woods. It was like he belonged there amongst the wildlife and the trees. His mother was so upset, fearing he would never come back to her. He could still feel the wetness of her tears as she held him tight.

The memory slowly faded and Cael felt dampness on his

face and knew he was crying. What happened? Everything seemed to be unwinding. What seemed like such a simple life was now gone. His teacher was gone, his parents were acting strange and may be responsible for Taro's death. The only person he could talk to was just an email message on a computer somewhere. Where could he turn? He put his head in his hands and tried to think about what he could do. He prayed for guidance, for some sign that it would all work out. That somehow he would get through this.

'You must have faith, Cael, help will come.'

He jerked his head up as soon as he heard the voice. There she stood, floating just over the pond in front of him, her robe billowing out around her. He could see her long sleeves as she held her hands out to him in a gesture of kindness. Her long hair shone in the sunlight. He knew, immediately, that it was the same lady that came to him before. He stood up and started toward her then looked down and realized he couldn't walk through the water, it was like a bog and he would sink.

"What can I do?" he pleaded.

'Have patience,' she answered in a beautiful sing-song voice.

"But I feel so lost," he cried out.

'That will pass. One will come,' she said.

"I know, Jiro. He's been writing to me. But when?" The woman stopped and he could detect a bit of hesitation in her movement.

'Do not listen to Jiro, it is a trick. He is not the one you should be looking for.'

"What? But who is?" Now what? The one person he thought he could trust and now this ghost was telling him not to.

'One will come,' she said as she started to fade away.

"No, come back, I have more to ask you. Please, come back!" But it was too late, the lady was gone.

#

It only took him a little over an hour to get back to his Jeep and when he did, he had mixed feelings. He was happy that someone was finally coming to help him but he was confused about who it might be. He was positive it was Jiro but the ghost had told him not to listen to the Sensei. He knew this ghost, she had been watching out for him for a long time. He would go home and look at those emails one more time.

He was thinking of this as he drove down the highway. It was the same road that would take him past the funeral home he was at in the morning. He was leaning his arm on the window and listening to a CD, when he noticed the long line of traffic ahead.

'What now!?' he asked himself as he pulled to a stop behind a red pickup. All he wanted to do was go home and now he was stuck in a traffic jam in the middle of the country.

He sat in his car for almost an hour before anything moved and it was another half hour before he came to the blockade of police cars and fire trucks. They had closed down almost all lanes of traffic only leaving one open and alternating it between east and west bound cars. He came to a halt again as the traffic heading west was guided through. Cael rolled down his window and spoke to the police officer standing just off to the side, making sure the cars were doing what they were supposed to.

"Big accident?" Cael asked.

"Yeah, car and semi. Not too pretty," the officer replied.

"Oh, man," Cael said, shaking his head, knowing that there were probably fatalities. "How many people?"

"I'm not sure, there's not much left of the car," he said as he waved through the last few cars. "Semi's okay though, hardly a scratch on it. It's just got an expensive Range Rover as a hood ornament now." Cael looked at the officer curiously.

'Did he say Range Rover?' he asked himself. 'It couldn't be. It had been a long time since the service this morning. They would have headed home hours ago.'

"Hey!" the officer called again. "It's your turn, you can go!"

"Sorry," he said as he put the Jeep in gear and slowly moved forward. As he passed the fire truck blocking off the lanes of the highway, the carnage of the accident came into view. He could see the front of the black semi and, at first; it didn't look like anything was wrong with it. Then, as he got closer, he could start to make out the crushed outline of a vehicle. It was almost impossible to tell what color it was let alone what make and model. There was a yellow blanket draped over what was once the front seat and there was glass everywhere. He saw a heavy set man dressed in blue jeans, a red jacket and a baseball cap off to the side, talking to a couple of police officers. Cael assumed it was the truck driver by the look of shock still etched on his face. There was debris littering the road and ditch, mostly from the car which was all twisted. He couldn't tell one part from the other. He kept moving slowly forward, craning his neck and focusing his eyes, trying to see something that identified the car. He started to make out the words Range Rover written across the back then the silver color started to come into view. His stomach tightened and he forced himself to search out the license plate.

When his father had bought his Range Rover it was not only because he could finally afford an expensive car after all his years of hard work at the bank but it was also because his parents genuinely loved the vehicle. He remembered how crazy he thought they were when they actually went to Registries and purchased a personalized license plate: THE BEST it read.

He slammed his foot on his brake pedal and stared at those same two words now written on the license plate of the smashed up car. The car behind him just missed sliding into his Jeep and the man laid on his horn and threw up his arms, yelling and swearing. Cael didn't hear him; he just kept staring at the license plate. One of the officers off to the side looked up to see why there was a sudden outburst of honking and screaming. He looked at the black Jeep and then at the line of cars piling up behind it. He headed over with a look of anger on his face.

'God damned rubber-necker,' the officer thought to himself. 'What, is he mad we have the bodies covered up?' He knocked on the window to get Cael's attention. Cael just sat there, the officer knocked louder.

"Sir? I'm going to have to ask you to keep it moving. There's a long line behind you." Cael turned his head and looked at the officer.

'Holy mother, he's as white as ghost!' thought the officer.

"Sir, are you okay?" He gestured for Cael to roll down his window, which he did slowly. "Sir?"

"I-I think I know this vehicle."

"Is that right?" The officer could tell by the look on Cael's face that he was telling the truth. "How can you tell?"

"The license plate," Cael pointed, "it belongs to my parents." The officer turned and noticed that the license plate was untouched and in plain view for everyone to see. He looked back at Cael and recognized the look of shock on his face. It was the same look he saw on so many faces when he had to inform them that a loved one had been killed.

'Jesus Christ!' he thought. 'What a way to find out your parents were dead.'

"Sir, you'd better pull over." He directed Cael to the shoulder of the highway, not too far from where the trucker stood and told him to hang on. He walked back to his cruiser and spoke into the radio.

"Could we have some psychiatric help to the accident out here on Highway 14 west?" He proceeded to fill in his dispatch on the situation. Then he popped open the glove box and grabbed his roll of antacid tablets. This was going to be one of those days he thought as he walked back to the black Jeep.

Chapter 16

Alannis got up early. Yesterday had been a good session with Whisper and she couldn't wait to get started again today. She was just making her way to the lounge when Marcus rushed up behind her.

"We have to talk!" he said, looking a little anxious.

"Sure, let's go to the lounge, I could use a cup of cof…"

"No, we have to talk in the Chamber. Come on, everyone else is waiting." He took her arm and hurried her toward the door that led to the giant freezer. Kisho was gone and, instead, there was another guard there; one Alannis barely knew.

'This must be important,' she thought as they went through one freezer and into the next. This time they had to move some boxes and go through a hidden trapdoor in the floor. Once through, they pulled the door shut and Marcus concentrated on moving the boxes back in place with his mind. With that accomplished they headed down the seemingly endless ladder until they reached the bottom. Here was a room a bit smaller than the freezer above and just about as cold. They were surrounded by steel walls and Marcus took out a different key ring than his usual one. This one held three metal shapes; a triangle, a square and a circle. He chose the circle and laid it flat against one of the metal walls. All of a sudden a blue light lit up the circle and the steel wall disappeared only to come back once they had passed through.

They were now in a long, rectangular room with eight doors. Each door opened up into a brick wall but only one of these walls could be opened. Marcus and Alannis approached the third door on the left where he now chose the triangle. He opened the door and laid the shape flat against the brick wall. It started to glow a fiery red and, like the steel wall before it, disappeared. They walked through and turned to watch the brick wall come back in place.

This time the choice of doors was cut in half and they were spread evenly around a circular room. Their shoes echoed off the black and white tiled floor as they walked to the door directly across from them. The square was the only shape left and Marcus held it in his hand as he opened the door. Facing them was a wall of water that seemed to have no beginning and no end and not one drop dripped into the round room. Had they not had the key and tried to reach into the water with their bare hands it would have rushed out and flooded the room in seconds. He placed the square flat against the water and it glowed green and this time a tunnel was created through the water, allowing them to pass, untouched, and then filling back in with a splash as they walked through.

When they got to the end they were standing on a beautiful beach with warm white sand beneath their feet. If they were to turn around, all they would see was the calm blue ocean and the clear sky above. There was no trace of the door or the circular room. In front of them stood the most amazing city ever built here or on any other planet. Marcus looked at Alannis and smiled.

"Welcome home," he said.

"It's so good to see my Atlantis again," she said as she took in a deep breath. "They're already in the Chamber you said?"

"Yes, and they have sent Aria to watch over Whisper while we are here. We must hurry!" He started walking at a fast pace towards the city and Alannis followed.

Atlantis was one of those worlds that seemed to have gotten everything right. It was no wonder that so many other worlds tried to imitate them. There were always visitors from many different places coming to admire their beauty and learn their secrets. The Atlanteans never seemed to mind either; in fact, they were happy to share their knowledge and even traveled to far off places to teach other worlds how to use their different inventions. That's how many mysterious objects had ended up in different places. Some worlds used these inventions and some set them off to the side only to be forgotten over the passing years.

Atlantis had a superior society as well. There was no crime nor had there been for many millennia now. They understood how to treat each other and how to govern in fairness and in peace. They eliminated the need for money, trading goods and services fairly and without malice. They were an enlightened people who understood their souls and opened their minds. Everyone worked together and all were equal. It was a world described by many who visited as the perfect place; paradise.

The Atlanteans did have a fixation, however, and you could see it wherever you went. Atlantis had a love for the architecture from the Earth dimension. There was an incredible library at the center of the city designed in the style of the ancient Greeks. The roads were designed after the German autobahn with a transport system made to duplicate the Tokyo subways. The many sporting events could be viewed in the massive Roman-like Coliseum just a few blocks from the library and there were skyscrapers in the downtown that looked an awful lot like New York City. But the real variety of cultural architecture could be found in the houses the Atlanteans lived in. They ranged from Victorian mansions to Mexican haciendas, from Swiss alpine cottages to Native American tepees and from Hollywood bungalows to African grass huts. It was the most amazing sight to see and everyone that came here was awed by how it all seemed to flow together effortlessly.

When travelling through the city, the superior technology that Atlantis was known for became apparent. Being unable to mind-port here, the Atlanteans had spent a lot of time on perfecting their vehicles. The sky was dotted with flying vessels and the road held many models of flow cars, a vehicle made of a material that held no gravitational pull and powered by a crystal that kept it just above the ground and propelled it forward, backwards or sideways. There were elaborate fountains that danced to music being piped out through the streets. There were stores lit up by bright lights of every colour and everything was powered by crystals similar to the ones back at the fortress.

The room that they were headed for was in the library at the center of the city. This building was not only a place that held every book ever written in Atlantis but it also held 'the Chamber' on its top floor. This was a room where the governors of Atlantis sat and discussed matters of their world and made decisions that would better all. It was a very private and trusted place with no threat of intruders. It had become the place where the matter of the last warrior could be talked about and where their plans to bring him back to Gwynn's army could be discussed.

Alannis led the way once they entered the library and Marcus followed her willingly. There were always two guards posted outside the Chamber and she nodded a hello to them as she opened the door to go inside. There was a huge wooden table that filled up the room and it was surrounded by chairs, enough to sit thirteen, the usual number of governors. Alannis looked around at the people she had come to trust with her life; Miles, Jiro, Astra and Gelraen the Mirai from the Trylinnian Constellation, and finally Kisho who was seated beside the two gnomes that had been sitting at the table in the lounge the first day Whisper had walked in. They were here to represent the

Lorynth dimension and the vested interest they held in seeing that the last warrior move to the side of Gwynn.

Alannis slowly scanned the faces of the men and women at the table, trying to read their expressions. She stopped when she spied a figure at the back of the room with his back turned. Her eyes looked at him curiously and then her face changed to an expression of recognition and disbelief. She did not expect this and she smiled and ran toward the man who now held his arms open to welcome his wife in a loving embrace.

"Taro!" She barely got his name out as she found his lips and kissed him passionately. He kissed her back and then broke away and looked down into her eyes. "But how? I was told you weren't ready, that you wouldn't be for years. Oh, darling, how can this be?"

"It's amazing what Gwynn can do when he really wants to." Alannis didn't know whether to laugh or cry and decided she would hold him tightly and not let go.

"I was so scared this time," she said. "I thought that, maybe, they had finally gotten it right." He pulled her face up towards his so he could look straight into her eyes.

"They were amateurs. They used regular bullets and didn't even come close to my head," he reassured her. "You know that the only way to kill me would be to close my third eye permanently. For some reason Dougall kept this little secret to himself, they only aimed for my heart."

"I'm so glad Dougall can be such an idiot sometimes,"

Alannis said and kissed her husband one more time.

"Ahem! If you two are finished with your-um-*hellos*, we have business to attend to." Alannis blushed at Jiro's words and slowly looked over at him only to see a big smirk across his face. The rest of the room was looking away, trying not to laugh.

"You knew!" She narrowed her eyes and pointed at him accusingly. "You knew Taro was coming back and didn't say anything to me. How could you just let me suffer like that, thinking it would be years before I saw him again?" She was mad at Jiro but her overwhelming joy of having Taro back was greatly overshadowing it.

"Hold on! It was Taro who told me not to tell you. I wanted to but I have to do what my brother tells me to, he is stronger than me you know." Alannis looked from one to the other with her hands on her hips and her lips pursed. Then she threw up her arms in defeat and let out a huge sigh.

"Oh, what can I do? You two are as thick as thieves," she laughed. "I'm just glad to have you back, my love."

"Good, now come and sit," Jiro said and Taro and Alannis took their seats beside each other. Miles took control of the meeting from there.

"First of all, before we go any further, Alannis how was your session with Whisper in the Celestial Room yesterday?" he asked.

"Unbelievable!" said Alannis. "As we all thought, she had already regained partial use of most of her powers without

210

even realizing it. She can now do mind reading and thought transference perfectly and she has made great strides in her telekinetic power. Aria told me she learned to control the crystals in her room within minutes, something that takes even an Atlantean longer to master." Everyone at the table seemed impressed at how strong Whisper had become.

"That's good and, Jiro, what about her defensive skills?" Miles directed his attention towards the slender martial arts trainer.

"I'd have to say her knowledge of fighting has never gone away. After only half a lesson she was beating me at every turn. She conquered levitation and control of her body in minutes. She didn't want to stop after four hours of constant fighting, it was amazing and it was I that had to call for a break." There was no shame in admitting how tired she had made him.

"Excellent. All this information is good but is it enough? Do you feel she is ready to meet Cael?" Miles looked at both of them with an expression of anxiousness.

"What? Now? I don't know. Should she be?" Alannis asked. Jiro was just as baffled and wondered what this man was getting at.

"She is good, yes, but there are many things she still must learn," said Jiro. "For instance, the art of controlling the elements has not even been brought up to her."

"Yes, and we never even touched on dream walking yet," added Alannis.

"There may not be time." All eyes turned to Taro as he spoke these words. Miles sat back down and let him take over the meeting. "There has been drastic events taking place in the last two days in the Earth dimension and Cael may need our interference sooner than we thought. Gwynn has been keeping a close eye on his brother and has discovered something very disturbing."

"What's that?" asked Alannis.

"Dougall has taken a very unpredictable creature under his wing and doesn't even realize it. He has let his beastly passion for beautiful women get in the way of his thinking by uniting with Jezebel, the harlot from the Abyss dimension. It was she that first discovered the warrior and reported it to Dougall. She has been living there under the disguise of Stephanie, the secretary Jiro hired for his club. She knew she was close to finding Cael when she met my brother but it wasn't until we talked to each other on the phone that she realized it was really me she was looking for. What she didn't count on, though, was that I recognized her, as well. I warned my brother to leave the Earth dimension immediately. I was sure I could contain her but she proved to be trickier than I thought.

"She brought up her long time rivals from the Abyss dimension to take over the bodies of Cael's parents. The goal was to try and manipulate him into coming to Dougall. Gwynn was beside himself when he saw how carelessly the souls of these two people were tossed aside. Dougall believed Jezebel was doing everything she could to please him and had no reason to question her actions. Everything was going according to the woman's plans until Whisper entered the picture.

"When Cael believed me to be dead and our broken bond was heard by Whisper she came rushing into his life like a tidal wave, whether she wanted to or not. No one had anticipated this except the Mirai." He nodded towards the two women to acknowledge their participation in all of this. "Now she is pulled to him whenever he is overwhelmed by anger, a fact that Jezebel is unaware of. If she had known she might have put a stop to her plans.

"When Dougall found out about Whisper he let his passion take over again. He remembers her from their last battle and his urge to have her as his own has resurfaced. So now, he wants both Cael and Whisper and is determined to get them. But he has unwisely forgotten about Jezebel. She's obsessed with Dougall and will do anything to keep him for herself. She has found a way to tell Cael who his parents really are, leaving Dougall no choice but to eliminate them. He has no idea Jezebel planned it this way. She's a clever and determined woman. She still intends to deliver Cael to Dougall but she will never allow him to get his hands on Whisper, even if it means killing them. But it is far worse than that." He stopped and looked at Astra and Gelraen, urging them to share their vision.

"We believe that Dougall is close to discovering Jezebel's betrayal and will be outraged when he does," Astra

213

said in a melodic voice.

"His only option," continued Gelraen, "will be to come to the Earth dimension, himself, and take Cael away with him. That way he will be able persuade the warrior to join him." They all knew what this would entail.

The people at the table stared at the two women as they spoke these last few words. They were the prophets of the Universe and what they said always came true. If Dougall did that, he would be breaking all laws that governed the treaty signed so long ago. Everyone knew, though, that he was desperate and breaking the treaty didn't matter as long as he could get Cael to work with him. The situation was dire and they knew they had to move fast.

"What can we do?" asked Alannis.

"We must send Whisper to Cael to warn him of the danger and then we must go to the Earth dimension, ourselves, and retrieve him before Dougall finds out about Jezebel." Jiro explained. It was the only solution that made sense.

"But that will mean that we're breaking the treaty ourselves won't it?" asked Marcus.

"Not if we send Whisper," Taro said quietly.

"But she will be vulnerable, they could kill her there!" Alannis looked at her husband to see if there was some other way.

"I know, but there is nothing else we can do," he said.

"When does she have to go?" Jiro asked.

"Tomorrow." He raised his hand to stop the protests. "We will send her on a dream walk tonight after we have filled her in on everything that's going on. There is no hiding information from her now, she must know all and be prepared for anything." With that the meeting ended and Alannis' joy of having her husband back was temporarily put aside while they prepared themselves for what must be done.

Chapter 17

Whisper sat there stunned as she looked around at the faces staring back at her. What they were telling her was hard to comprehend. They were in the lounge and had pulled two tables together to accommodate all of them. Aria was with Whisper all day. It was nice to take a break from the lessons for awhile. When the telecommunicator buzzed about an hour ago, it was Aria who answered it. She was told to bring Whisper upstairs and Marcus would escort them both to the lounge. The whole trip was made in an uncomfortable silence. Now, here they sat, all of them explaining things to Whisper with a note of urgency in their voices and a look of concern on their faces. She stared from one person to the other as they each took turns talking.

She learned her Flatliner's name was Cael. When she heard it for the first time Whisper felt a deeper connection to him. They told her that he was in terrible danger because Dougall was going to come down to the Earth dimension and capture him and torture him until he agreed to fight on his side. They said that only Whisper could stop it. She wondered if it was all real or if she was imagining the whole thing. She felt a pull on her emotions when they explained all the things Cael had been through over the past week. She remembered how beautiful he was and how he had made her feel when his eyes seemed to look at her. The shock that ran up through their bodies when they touched was so real and she smiled as she recalled the memories. That was how she knew she'd go to help him. There was no choice, they were connected somehow and she had to put any fears she had aside and go.

Since arriving in the lounge, one man had been doing most of the talking. It was a man Whisper had never met before and, finally, she asked who he was. Alannis looked embarrassed that she hadn't introduced him earlier.

"This is Taro, Jiro's brother and," she paused to hold his hand, "my husband."

"You're what?" Whisper thought that Jiro had a thing for her and that she had felt the same. They seemed to enjoy each other's company and were always having deep conversations with each other that Whisper just assumed she was with Jiro.

"My husband. He was hurt recently and Jiro has been keeping me informed of his condition. As you can tell, he has made a complete recovery." She looked so happy and suddenly all her meetings with Jiro made sense. Whisper reached out to shake his hand.

"It is so nice to meet you, Whisper." He took hold of the girl's hand and her face froze as she gripped his hand, unable to let go. She was propelled into a flood of memories that chronicled almost every day that he had spent with Cael. She saw Cael through his eyes when he was young and fragile. She saw his determination and strength as he learned the art of defence. She saw him as he confided in his teacher his fears and sorrows about not being able to fit in and she saw him in anguish as he cried over the bloody body of the man he had grown to love. All these images flashed through Whisper's mind in a matter of seconds and when it was over she let go. She was tired from the impact of the memories but was happy to know so much more about Cael.

"You were a fine teacher," she said to him. Everyone looked at her in surprise. They hadn't told Whisper that Taro was Cael's teacher. "He misses you and will be happy to know you are all right." Taro was impressed by her ability to read his thoughts. Alannis, however, wasn't. She knew Whisper's telepathic abilities were strong and had come a long way.

"We can't tell Cael about Taro right now, it would be too much for his mind to handle," Alannis said.

"I know, I was just anticipating the future, you know, for when I bring him back here." This was Whisper's way of telling them that she would go to the Earth dimension and do what they told her to. Aria was the first to realize this and came to her friend and hugged her tightly. She looked at Whisper with tears in her eyes.

"Are you sure?" she asked.

"Yes," said Whisper, "and don't cry, I'll be fine." The others were breathing a sigh of relief.

"But you don't understand, in the Earth dimension you're

not invincible. You can be killed and this Jezebel woman will want to do just that." She sounded upset and worried. Alannis came over and put her arm around Aria and gently guided her away from Whisper.

"Whisper will not be alone, I will be with her and so will Miles and Marcus," she explained, trying to calm her down.

"But why not Jiro and Taro? They're the best fighters, shouldn't they go too?" Aria pleaded.

"They can't go," Whisper said, seeing what Aria was too upset to realize. "They would be recognized too easily and then we would definitely be in trouble."

"I guess." She was starting to understand that there was no other way. "Can I go?" Whisper looked at her friend and felt her heart ache for her total commitment to their friendship.

"Aria, I'll be fine," Whisper tried to reassure her. "You *must* stay here. If you come, you're life will be in jeopardy as well and I wouldn't be able to think with fear of losing you. You're my best friend and I'll need you here when I get back," she laughed. "Besides, I'm not too bad of a fighter, myself, right Jiro?"

"Uh-yes, you are very good, young Whisper." The room filled with laughter. Aria seemed a little more at ease after hearing this.

"Okay, it's getting late and if I'm going to warn Cael that we're coming I need a lesson on how to do this dream walking thing. Alannis?" Whisper got up from the table and headed for the door, pretty sure that Alannis was following *her* this time. She didn't want to stay here any longer; she just wanted to get started before she lost her nerve.

#

Cael finished signing all the necessary paperwork with a sigh of relief that the day was almost over. The police officer that told him to pull over had insisted he talk to someone that could help him deal with his sudden grief. He finally agreed but refused to ride in the ambulance they sent, choosing to follow it to the hospital in his Jeep instead. Thankfully, they pulled away from the scene before they started to extract the bodies of his parents from the wreckage.

He still didn't know how he felt about the accident. He was upset, of course, and shocked. He probably should be feeling more but he couldn't. He felt like he lost his parents when he found out that they were lying to him. Right now he felt so alone. At least when his parents were there, no matter what he thought of them, they were still a link to his past. They were a part of him. He just wanted go home, have something to eat and relax.

There would be no one to call about the deaths. Both sets of grandparents had died when he was young and he couldn't recall any aunts or uncles. His parents, like himself, had no siblings. As he thought about it, he supposed he would be the last of the Fraser's now. He would phone the bank in the morning and inform them that his dad would never be coming to work again. Then he would have to search for all their legal documents he was sure his father had put away somewhere. There must be a will; he didn't know, they never said anything to him. Maybe somebody at the bank would know. In any case, he would go to their house tomorrow and try to find any papers that might help him settle their affairs. Then he would have to arrange funerals. He'd probably contact the same guy who did Taro's service that morning. There was so much to do and he couldn't think straight. He needed to go home.

He stopped for another burger on his way, thinking that it was becoming a bad habit but he just didn't want to take the time to cook. He let himself in and turned on his lights. Everything was how he had left it that morning, yet so much of his life had changed. He put his burger and fries down on the coffee table and went to change; he would have a shower in the morning. He grabbed a bottle of water out of the fridge and flopped down on the couch and reached for the remote. The evening news was on when he turned on the TV and there, staring him in the face, was the horrific image of the wreck which took his parents' lives. He should have known it would be on. He remembered seeing the news van arriving as he was pulling out to follow the ambulance. He started flipping through the channels and settled on a station showing ultimate fighting. There was a time when he had contemplated training for this kind of fighting. It had been a brief lapse of vanity when he was sixteen and wanted to be adored by everyone, especially the girls. He eventually came to his senses and gave up his dream of getting punched and kicked in the face every night. He knew that, no matter how good of shape he was in, his body wouldn't be able to handle that kind of constant punishment. That's when he decided to concentrate more on his computers.

He ate his hamburger and sat back and watched the fights. It turned out to be a marathon of fights, showing the best of the best from the last ten years. He was happy for this, now he could keep it on one channel and not worry about running across any more news stories about the accident. He watched about half a dozen fights then made himself more comfortable on the couch by grabbing a pillow and blanket and turning off all the lights. He watched about three more fights before he finally fell asleep.

#

Whisper lie in her bed in her apartment and was finding it a little difficult going to sleep knowing that Alannis and Aria were in the next room waiting anxiously. Did they think she would just fall asleep instantly, walk right into Cael's head, tell him everything that was going on, say bye, see ya later, then come back, wake up and tell them everything was A-okay? She didn't think it worked that way. In fact, she was *sure* it didn't work that way. Learning how to dream walk had been easy enough, the fundamentals seemed pretty basic, but applying it might be a little different. She needed time to adjust her sleep, relax her inner eye and turn it toward Cael's. They needed to connect on a subconscious level.

Two things had to happen before any of this could work.

222

First, Whisper needed to travel within the realm of dreamscape and second, Cael needed to be receptive to her intrusion into his thoughts. She tried to concentrate harder, force herself to fall asleep. She tossed and turned under the mass of pillows piled on top of her. The light in the room got darker and darker. Time was quickly passing and she couldn't fall asleep! She got up and strode into the living room. Alannis and Aria were sitting quietly on the couch, watching a movie. Watching a movie!? No wonder she couldn't sleep, the electricity from the TV must have thrown her senses off. Then she remembered it was powered by the crystal, but it still must have been emitting something that interfered with her ability to fall asleep. They both turned their heads toward her as she came further into the room.

"Look, guys, I know you mean well but, seriously, I can FEEL you out here," she explained. "I've tried and tried but I just can't do it. I can't fall asleep!" They looked at her blankly and then back at each another.

"Okay, you're right; we'll go to Aria's if it will help." Aria started to protest but Alannis touched her on the knee. Whisper searched Aria's face.

"Okay, sure," she said, and then smiled. "That way we can get something to eat, I'm starved. We didn't want to make any noise out here." They got up and turned off the TV. Whisper was relieved that they agreed to leave so easily. She walked them to the door and before they could ask she offered.

"I will come right over as soon as I wake up."

"Promise?" Aria looked her straight in the eyes to be sure she wasn't lying.

"Promise," Whisper vowed and gave them each a hug. When they left, she locked the door, making sure no one would sneak in after she fell asleep.

With the two women gone, sleep came easy and quick. Whisper was tired. It had been a long week with so many things happening. Even the meeting tonight was exhausting. She met so many people she didn't even know existed a week ago. The events of the week raced through her mind as her eyelids fell heavily shut and her mind started to drift away.

#

Whisper was in a forest again but it didn't feel like the dark one from her nightmare a few short days ago. She was by herself and she could feel the hot sun on her face and smell the sweet aroma of the wild flowers. She was wearing a light blue dress that came down just below her knees. It was cinched in at the waist and the soft, airy material felt cool against her body. There were no sleeves, only thin straps that hung effortlessly from her shoulders. She was barefoot making her feel young and free. Her hair came down in waves of soft curls down her back and she could feel it bounce in the wind as she walked down the forest path without a care in the world.

But where was Cael? Wasn't he supposed to be here with her? She stopped and looked around. She could hear a river nearby and walked through the trees determined to find it. She

224

didn't have far to go, it was just past a few tall pines and a row of wild strawberry bushes. She felt a pull to follow the water upstream and stopped occasionally to toss a pebble in or pick a flower. There didn't seem to be any hurry at all. Eventually, she decided to leave the river and started to climb a hill. There was a bird fluttering about and she tried to catch it. She would get it just within her grasp and it would hover right in front of her eyes before flying away. She laughed at this game and didn't realize how far she'd come until she stopped to look around and noticed strange things around her.

She was standing in a small clearing with not many trees. There were little bodies of water, like ponds, scattered around and ducks were happily swimming around on them. She saw strange structures sitting out in the middle of the water and she wondered what they were. They looked like little mounds of sticks and twigs. Each one about the same size with logs built up on either side. They were causing the water to flow like little waterfalls. The sticks seemed to be stripped bare of any leaves or bark and she thought to herself, 'What strange little houses.' She looked around to see if she could spot the creatures that lived in these houses, and that was when she saw him.

He was sitting on a tree stump with his back to her and instantly she knew it was Cael. She stood there, staring at him for a few minutes, studying his posture and feeling reluctant to go any nearer. She was nervous and knew it wasn't the mission that was making her feel that way. She remembered how his eyes had seemed to pierce through her, how his body had taken her breath away and how his voice had sent shivers through her. She was nervous knowing this would be the first time he would be able to see her. Suddenly she felt shy and awkward. She looked down at her ugly feet and wished she had shoes on.

The bird returned and flew just above her head, making her jump in surprise. She waved her arms to swoosh it away and, when she finally got it to fly off, she fixed her hair and straightened her dress.

'What a mess that blasted bird has made of my hair!' she said to herself as she finished fixing everything and returned her focus on Cael. He was standing now, his arms at his side. He wore a loose pair of jeans and a white t-shirt, his hair looking a little dishevelled. Whisper's heart skipped a beat as she realized he was looking at her and, by the looks of it, her appearance had startled him because it seemed to wipe all the colour away from his face.

'Oh, great,' she thought, 'I must look horrible; maybe that bird crapped on me or something.' She started twisting and turning to see if she could see anything.

'Who is she?' thought Cael, as he stood there staring at the young woman in front of him. He had been sitting and watching a family of ducks when he had heard a twig snap. He turned and spotted movement out of the corner of his eye. Immediately he stood up when he realized it was a person. It was a girl and she was jumping around waving her arms at something he couldn't see and looking quite comical as she did it. He was becoming amused at her antics and then she stopped when she realized he had gotten up. He had to catch his breath when her eyes came to rest on his.

She was beautiful, unlike any other woman he had ever seen. She wore a blue dress that showed just a hint of her slender figure. Her hair was brown and shining alluringly in the sun. It looked soft and he felt an urge to reach out and touch it and run his fingers through it. Her face was young, with delicate white skin. She had soft features with warm and tender lips and she looked at him with eyes that were the clearest blue he had ever seen. She looked down at the ground then slowly peeked up through her eyelashes and gave him an awkward half smile. His heart began to beat loudly, threatening to leap out of his chest and he could feel himself starting to break out into a cold sweat.

#

Whisper stood there for a few minutes, feeling awkward and wondering how she would ever manage to get any words out. Then she remembered why she was there; there were a lot of people depending on her to get this right. She had to pull herself together. Sure, he was cute, but she couldn't let that distract her. She had to talk to him.

'Heart, could you please calm down?' she pleaded with herself. She took in a few deep breaths, trying to focus as she closed her eyes, stretched out her arms and flattened her hands the way Alannis had shown her when they started their meditation exercises.

'What the hell is she doing?' thought Cael as he watched her going through some strange stretches. He had decided to talk to this woman but now he wasn't so sure. He approached her slowly.

When Whisper opened her eyes again he was walking towards her, waving a hand and smiling. She felt butterflies take off in her stomach and her cheeks flushed.

"Concentrate!!" she scolded herself.

"Excuse me?" he asked, looking at her strangely. She hadn't realized she had spoken out loud.

"Uh-um I said hi!" she tried to sound calm. "Nice to m-meet you, my name is Whisper." She held out her hand for him to shake. He looked at her with an odd expression, and then slowly came closer so he could take her hand.

"Hello, Whisper, my name is…ow!" They touched and it was the same as before, like an electric shock ran through their bodies. They both let go and shook out their hands and tried to recover from the tingling sensation it left behind. "Holy…what was that?!" Cael exclaimed.

"I don't know." She tried to shrug it off. "What was your name?"

"Oh, yeah, I'm Cael, pleased to meet you." They stood there staring at each other, not knowing what to say. Then they both tried to talk at once, and then laughed nervously.

"You go first," he said, putting his hands in his back

pockets.

"I'm curious; do you know what those little mounds of sticks are? They look like houses of some sort but I'm not sure what kind of creature could build such a structure." He looked at her like she was insane.

"You're kidding, right?" he asked, smiling.

'What did I say?' she thought it was a reasonable question.

"You don't know what a beaver dam is?" He was laughing now and Whisper started to get a little angry.

"Of course I know what it is, I was just seeing if you did." She stuck her chin out defiantly, but knew her face was turning red.

"I'm sorry; I didn't mean to upset you," he said, regretfully. "You're not from around here are you?"

"No, not really," she said.

"Where are you from?" he asked, offering her a seat on the old tree stump, which she politely declined.

"I was sent here to help you." She watched for his reaction.

"You?" He looked mortified. This couldn't be the help he had been so desperately waiting for. "All this stuff that's been happening in my life, and they sent you?!!"

"What's that supposed to mean?" The anger in Whisper's voice echoed the anger she felt inside.

"It's just that…well…" he was stumbling over his words,

not knowing what to say, "I get the feeling that whatever it is that's going on, it can't be good. It has to be dangerous........They sent you?!?" He looked frustrated and shook his head in disbelief.

"And what is wrong with me?" She couldn't believe he was questioning her ability to help him. Of all the male chauvinistic...were all males in every world like this?

"N-nothing's wrong with you, I mean, you're incredibly beautiful and all, but honestly, look at you! You're so small and delicate looking. How can you possibly help me?"

'He thinks I'm beautiful!' she thought, temporarily forgetting the fact that he had just insulted her. 'No, he said incredibly...Hey! Wait a minute!! Who does he think he is, saying I'm too small?'

"I'm not that delicate! I could whip your butt!" He laughed at her threat. She was furious now. "Don't believe me? Come on, I'll show you."

"You're serious!" He looked at her with amusement, thinking that she was just kidding. "I have to warn you, I've trained in Judo for years."

"What's Judo?" Whisper asked.

"Seriously? You've never heard of beaver dams and now Judo? Where are you from?" He looked at her like she was an alien or something.

"A place where neither of those things exist, obviously!" she said nastily. "Now, come on, are we going to fight or not?"

"Okay, but it's a shame that pretty dress is going to get ruined." He smiled at her smugly.

"I wouldn't be so sure of yourself," she said as she waved him on. Still smiling, he lazily went to grab her wrist and sweep her feet out from under her. In a flash, Whisper jumped over his head and kicked out the back of his knees. Cael fell to the ground, grabbing his legs in pain. She crossed her arms and smiled.

"Hey!" He stood up and faced her, looking a little more serious. He started at her, quicker this time. She waited for him to grab her wrist. When he did, she immediately countered and flipped him onto his back. Then, still holding his arm, she got on the ground and dug one of her heels into his armpit and the other into the crook of his neck and wrenched his arm in an attempt to break it in half. Within seconds he was tapping frantically on the ground with his free hand and pleading with her to let go, which she did. They stood up and Whisper brushed the dirt off of her dress.

"Not so small and delicate now am I?" she said, feeling a bit superior over him.

"Okay, okay, you've made your point," he said, rubbing his arm. "Where'd you learn all that?"

"I had a very good teacher," she said.

"Look, if I call a truce, will you tell me where you come from and how you can help me figure out what the hell is going on around here?" He looked at her with his big blue eyes and her anger at him was forgotten. She knew that she could talk to him now, the ice had been broken and she didn't feel so nervous anymore.

"Okay," she said. He put out his hand and she looked at it hesitantly. Would the shock still be there? She took a chance and grabbed his hand in a friendly shake. The shock was there, but it had dulled and now the feeling was something they could both tolerate, even start to enjoy.

Chapter 18

When Whisper finally finished talking to Cael, he knew everything. He knew that they were inside his dream and he knew who Whisper was and how she had gotten there. She told him that his parents were really good people and that they were taken over by two evil beings that worked for a man named Dougall, whom she explained, was trying to take over the Universe. She told him that Stephanie was really a woman named Jezebel and that she also worked with Dougall and would stop at nothing to see Whisper dead and him captured. She explained who Gwynn was and that he had created a group of warriors with supreme fighting capabilities a long time ago. Cael was one of these warriors and Dougall wanted him on his side. Dougall knew where he was now, thanks to Jezebel and was coming to get him. It was his own choice whether he wanted to go with Dougall or Gwynn. It was an easy choice, he said; he wanted no part of Dougall or his evil ways. If that was the case, she told him there was plan to help him escape to a better and safer place. He was relieved that all of his questions were answered and he looked forward to meeting everyone when he was awake. Then he questioned whether or not he would even remember any of this in the morning and Whisper assured him that he would.

She explained what a portal was and told him he would have to travel through one to get to Chrystalline. They would have to do the same to come here, she explained, because she would be traveling with people that couldn't get here any other way. She asked if he could meet them there. He agreed and asked where it was. She told him that it was not far from where they were now. He just needed to follow the river to the base of a mountain where he would find a formation made up of three large boulders and a golden tree. He knew the place, he said, he had gone there once after he first got his license.

When he was sixteen, Cael had snuck a couple of beers out of the fridge at home and drove up there, figuring he was old enough to do whatever he pleased. There were too many people hiking around the falls that day and he felt too scared to drink anywhere near them so he walked and walked until he found some privacy amongst these huge rocks. He remembered that there was an evergreen in the center, except it wasn't green at all. It looked like it had some sort of disease or something because the needles had turned a light brownish color, but when the sun hit it, it turned gold. He stared at it in awe and then felt guilty about the beer. He sat there for awhile and tossed the beer out on his way back to his car.

That sounded like the place, all right. Whisper was glad he knew how to get there. Their conversation was coming to an end. She could feel her body starting to wake up. She looked over her shoulder to make sure her path back was still there. Cael sensed that she was getting ready to go and a look of disappointment came over his face.

"Do you have to go?" he asked.

"Yes, I can only stay in your dream for a short time. You must not get stuck here, this world isn't real," she answered.

"But it feels real," he said, looking around at all the beauty surrounding them, "more real than anything in my waking world."

"It's not, though, and to stay here could prove too dangerous for you, it could even cost you your life," she was very serious now. "Cael, you must be strong and remember that we're here for you."

"It feels good to know that I'm not alone." He looked down and kicked the ground. "I'm sorry I was so mean to you earlier."

"It's okay," she said, with a smile. "I guess I am small…"

"…and beautiful." He took a deep breath and looked into her eyes. Whisper's smile faded and she flushed with a heat that came from within and quickly looked away.

"I-I have to go," she could barely get the words out as she started to tremble inside. He reached for her arm and pulled her close. She weakly struggled to get away. "I can't…I…"

"It's just a dream, right? Who's it going to hurt? No one will know." He lifted her face so she was looking in his eyes and then he kissed her. She should have been angry, outraged, by his assumption that he could just kiss her like that but she wasn't. Instead, she melted in his arms as he held her. She felt the passion in his kiss and, for a brief moment, she returned it but she had to stop. This couldn't be! Whisper was his Soul-healer! These feelings could not exist between the two of them! She pushed away from him.

"You shouldn't have done that," she said to him, shaking her head.

"Don't worry; I'll behave in real life," he smiled. She looked at him, sadly, then turned and ran back the way she had come, tears flowing down her face.

#

Whisper woke up with her head buried beneath a pillow. She was sobbing with tears of anger and frustration. 'How could I have let that happen? I really blew it now.' she chastised herself. She couldn't believe she had let Cael take so much control over her. She didn't know what to do, who she should tell or even if she should tell. The thought of seeing the disappointment on the faces of her friends made her feel sick. Maybe she wouldn't have to say anything. Maybe he wouldn't remember kissing her. She could act like she didn't know about it, like that part of the dream happened *after* she left, that it was part of *his* dream only. It would be hard to pretend though because, like it or not, she enjoyed the kiss. In fact, if she had her choice, she would stay in his arms forever even if it meant staying in his dream.

She slowly crawled out of bed and headed for the bathroom. She looked in the mirror and cringed at her reflection. She didn't look so good. Her hair was all messy and in knots, her face was pale and streaked with tears and her eyes were red and puffy. She had to pull herself together, not look so desperate. She had to go to Aria's and tell them everything had gone smoothly. Cael believed her and would be there, waiting for them when they went through the portal. She had a few minutes so she got in the shower and tried to clear her head.

#

Cael could still feel the moistness of her lips as he stretched out his arms and legs. His face held a big stupid grin and his eyes were still closed. He could sense the light from the sun on the back of his eyelids but he was reluctant to open them. He wanted to savour the memory of Whisper as long as he could. He couldn't wait to see her again. He figured he could still go to his parents' house and look for any important papers; he still had time to do that. He could phone the bank, as well, in fact, he could probably do that pretty soon. With that, he decided he'd better get up and have a shower. He finished stretching and opened his eyes only to have his heart stop, terror gripping his insides.

"Good morning, sleepy head. Pleasant dreams I presume?" It was Stephanie, or Jezebel, as Whisper had called her. How she had gotten in, he didn't know. He tried to sit up and push himself to the far side of the couch by kicking his feet

237

in the now twisted blanket wrapped around him.

"What the hell are you doing in here?" His body was starting to recover from the initial shock of seeing this woman's face.

"That's no way to greet a beautiful woman when she wakes you up," Jezebel said as she reached out and stroked Cael's leg. He quickly pulled it away from her toxic touch.

"You'd better explain yourself lady, before I call the cops." Cael reached behind him for the phone he knew always sat on the end table beside the couch. The blow came quick and hard and he winced at the pain in the back of his hand as he quickly pulled it back to him.

"What the…who else is here?" Cael turned his head around and caught a glimpse of blonde hair. "Rob? What's going on?"

"You should learn to be a little nicer, my friend," Rob said as he walked around to the front of the couch. Jezebel smiled up at him and then uncoiled her body slowly from the couch and wrapped her arms around his waist.

"Such a well trained pet, don't you think?" Rob seemed amused by her words, as she ran her hands up his back and through his hair, then she leaned over and nibbled at the corner of his ear. All the time, her eyes never left Cael's and she smiled seductively at him. Now that she was standing in the light of the window, Cael could see that any trace of the quiet secretary was gone. She wore a black, leather skirt that came up about mid-thigh and a short waisted red jacket that covered a black lacy tank top. Her auburn hair was curled back off her face which was thickly covered with make-up. She looked every bit the part of a harlot and Cael could hardly contain his hatred for her.

"What do you want?" Cael spoke quietly through gritted teeth, his eyes showing all his anger. There was nothing he could do, he was cornered. Rob smiled as he realized his long time opponent was about to give in. Jez had been right; there really wasn't much to Cael Fraser.

"Oh, darling, don't look so angry. I only want you to come with me for a ride, show me some sights. I'm new here, don't you know?" she said, teasingly.

"Why don't you get your *pet* to show you?" She laughed at his attempt to belittle Rob.

"I much prefer your company right now," she said. "Now, go on to your room and get dressed, we don't have any time to waste."

Cael looked from one to the other and realized he had no choice. He would have to bide his time and wait for an opportunity to get away. He had no idea what she wanted but figured he would find out soon enough. He went to his room to get dressed.

"Oh, you earth men are so obliging," she said, as she watched him walk away with a glint of wanting in her eye. Rob noticed this and cleared his throat in an obvious attempt to attract her attention. She slowly turned her head towards him and dropped her smile.

"Stop with the jealousy routine. Haven't I shown you how much you mean to me?" He smiled at her and she had to keep from tearing his throat out. Despite her sudden distaste for this fool, she had to keep him around. He had become useful in her recent quest. She needed his protection against Cael. If not for him, she might not have been able to learn so much about this warrior.

When they had found Cael sleeping this morning, Jezebel's intention was to take him to Dougall before that cheap little Soul-healer could come and ruin everything. She figured if it could be done quickly, maybe her lover would forget his desire to have the girl as well. She was about to wake him when he spoke the girl's name. This threw her off her plan and she proceeded to search his mind for any information. She wasn't very good at mind reading; the Abyss was not a world full of eager teachers. Besides, her companions usually had their thoughts written all over their faces. She was pretty sure she was reading Cael's correctly, though. She saw him and that girl in an embrace and her blood began to boil. This proved that they had met already and a new plan formed in her head. This could be her chance to wipe the girl out for good; all she needed was for Cael to take her to his little girlfriend. It shouldn't be too hard; she had seen a forest in his mind and knew that this must be where the girl was hiding.

Cael came back in the room fully dressed and fully

prepared. Whisper had warned him that this woman would be able to read his mind, so he tried very hard to keep all thoughts of her and their plans out of his head. Instead, he concentrated on the tasks he had originally planned for the day.

"Ah, very nice," Jezebel said as she looked Cael up and down. He had on a pair of black jeans and a long sleeved grey shirt. He glared at her as she smiled back at him.

"Where are we going?" he asked.

"What, no argument?" She threw Cael his coat and they headed for the door with Rob bringing up the rear. "We're going for a ride in the country. We'll take your Jeep. Rob's Mustang is nice but totally useless in the woods." Cael looked back at Rob and wondered why he took this woman's insults.

"Woods?" Cael asked. "Why would we be going into the woods?"

"Because, I saw a lovely image this morning and I can't get it out of my head. I wanted to see the live version of it." She was laughing gently to herself.

"What are you talking about?" asked Cael, trying to fish out information from her. They were in the hallway now, walking single file towards the stairwell.

"Come on; don't play dumb, you know what I'm talking about." Cael came to a stop and turned to face her. His heart was pounding and his fury was rising.

"Look, lady, I don't know who you are or what you want but I'm not taking you anywhere." He started to walk past her when Rob reached for his arm to pull him down. He had anticipated the move and tossed Rob's hand away and shoved his friend up against the wall.

"You're still way too predictable my friend," Cael glared into Rob's face.

"Boys, boys, boys!" yelled Jezebel. "Why don't you let poor Robbie go and quit resisting? You're going to help me whether you want to or not." She held up a weapon Cael had never seen before. It sort of looked like a gun but not any gun he had ever seen. It had a long narrow barrel and it sat in Jezebel's hand perfectly like it was moulded to fit there. Cael stared at it and wondered what it was and what it could do when, all of a sudden, she pointed it at the floor two feet from him and fired. A blue light flashed from the end of the barrel and within seconds there was a two foot wide hole in the floor. There was no noise or anything, the floor just vanished.

"Jesus! What'd you do that for?" Cael was angry now. "I do live here you know." He stared at the hole, angry now.

"Just wanted you to know that I do have ways of making you listen to me," she said, and then she looked at Rob. "I thought you told me that you could beat this guy. What happened?"

"Yeah, well, it's been awhile. He's had special training," Rob looked ashamed as he said this. "Next time."

"Yeah, right." Jezebel looked at Cael. "Shall we?" After seeing what that gun could do Cael knew he had to obey.

After they got into the Jeep, Cael and Jezebel in the front, Rob in the back, he started the engine and looked at the woman sitting next to him.

"Where to?" he asked.

"I want you to take me to the place where I saw you and that girl in your head this morning." For the first time Cael started to feel a bit of panic. What did she see? His entire dream? Did she know the plans that were made?

"And like I told *you* before, I don't know what you're talking about." How long could he put her off? Not long, she took out the gun and pointed it at his head.

"Cael, darling, I'm going to keep this brief," she said. "My name is Jezebel and I work for a man named Dougall. He wants you badly and I intend to deliver you to him. But first, I must take care of this girl. She poses a threat to Dougall and I must do everything I can to protect him. I know you know where she is. I saw your dream, you kissed her then you called out her name. She is somewhere in the woods and you know where, so take me to her now!"

"It was a dream; I've never seen that woman before. She was just some made up woman in my dream. *I* don't even know who she is." Cael hoped he sounded convincing enough. He was pretty sure the only thing that Jezebel saw of the dream was the kiss. If he could convince her that it meant nothing, just some fantasy, then, maybe, he could keep Whisper safe.

"You know I might have believed you," she said, "if you

243

hadn't called out her name. You see, I know her name. Dougall has mentioned it enough times, Whisper I believe? I also know that the kiss you shared with her was much too real to just be a dream. You were remembering it, not dreaming it. Now, take me to her, before I start to lose my patience!"

Cael put the Jeep in reverse and pulled out of the parking lot. He had to think fast. Her tone of voice when she mentioned Whisper and Dougall told him she was jealous, dangerously jealous. Whisper didn't pose a threat to Dougall at all; he wanted her and this woman was not about to let that happen. He looked in the rear-view mirror at Rob in the backseat and wondered if he knew that she didn't really care about him. He kind of felt sorry for him, his ego had finally cost him. She was just using him, and probably wouldn't hesitate to get rid of him if she had to. Jezebel shifted in her seat and smiled, knowingly.

The rest of the drive was made in silence as Cael decided he knew just the place he could take this woman, a place where she would get totally lost. Now, he had to figure out a way to get that gun off of her.

Chapter 19

Whisper finished repeating everything that was said in her dream walk with Cael, minus the kiss, of course. Aria and Alannis were thrilled that Cael accepted everything so easily and thought that, maybe, his warrior inside was starting to awaken. Taro told Alannis that Cael was a strong soul and with a little encouragement from the right people he would again become the warrior he once was. It would be tough, though; Gwynn had hidden his warriors well, even from themselves. That was one of the reasons most of them ended up as Flatliners, it was harder for them to remember who they were if they were buried inside a soul that was so spiritually undeveloped.

"So, we proceed then," said Alannis. "We should go tell Marcus and Miles to get ready. I only have a few things to do before I go. You told him three o'clock right?"

"Yeah." Whisper wanted to tell Alannis something, something she'd been thinking about ever since she explained to Aria why she couldn't come. "Alannis, I've been thinking and, well, I want you to stay here too."

"What are you talking about?" Alannis looked at her as if she was joking.

"I mean it. Cael knows we're coming, in fact, he'll be right there waiting at the portal," Whisper explained. "We won't even have to go anywhere to get him. We'll just come out, grab him and head back. The whole thing will only take a couple of minutes. We won't really need you."

"But what if...?"

"There won't be any what ifs. I think you should stay here."

"Wait a minute." She sounded a little ticked off. "If you think this is going to be easy and you won't need me..."

"Yeah, I do think it's going to be easy," Whisper stated simply. "Besides, you're a Soul-healer like me and Aria and I don't want you to get hurt just like I don't want Aria to get hurt. I've really come to like you two over the past couple of days. You've kind of grown on me."

"She's got a point," Aria added, happy that she might not be the only one missing out on all the fun. Alannis turned and glared at her. "Well, she does."

"I don't need your opinion. You're just mad that you don't get to go." Aria looked away, obviously hurt by her remarks. "I *have* to go."

"Why? I'm sure Miles and Marcus can handle themselves and I know I can. I don't think we really need you." Whisper didn't want to sound too conceited but it was the only way to convince Alannis to stay. "Anyway, I think Taro might want to spend just a little bit more time with you. I mean how long did he see you, like, twenty minutes yesterday? I think he might want more time than that." She could tell that this hit a nerve with

246

Alannis and she seemed to hesitate just a bit.

"Well, maybe…" She was wavering. Whisper could feel a sense of satisfaction come over her and a big grin appeared on her face. "Don't get too excited. We have to clear it with everyone else first."

"Fine," I said, knowing that it wouldn't be a problem.

#

The others were quite happy to hear that Cael would be meeting them at the portal. They also agreed that Alannis would not be needed and could stay behind. With the ease in which Cael agreed to the plan, Marcus and Miles would be enough to accompany Whisper through to the Earth dimension. The twins were thrilled to have the extra responsibility and Taro was ecstatic to have his wife by his side for awhile. If the truth were to be told, he was probably a little nervous about sending her to the Earth dimension anyway.

By two forty-five they were ready. They went down to the basement, to the portal room that Marcus and Alannis used to get to Atlantis. The room held portals to all dimensions. This time Marcus used the keys in a different order and on different doors. Whisper found it fascinating that he knew exactly which door opened where and which key would open it. She also wondered if he was the only one who knew all the various patterns leading to all the different portals. From the way Miles followed behind his brother it was apparent that he didn't possess the same knowledge but he didn't seem to be upset by it, maybe he had a talent of his own.

It took almost a full fifteen minutes to arrive at the circular room and when they did Marcus chose the door directly to the left. There was no water when he opened it this time. Instead, it was a mushy, yellowish color that looked like the inside of a beehive. He placed the key against it and the path was opened.

"This is it," he said, "the last door." Whisper followed him inside, knowing that in a few short moments she would be face to face with Cael. No dream this time, no thought presence, just the two of them in a real world. She shivered in anticipation.

They walked through the portal and arrived in a small area that was enclosed by three huge boulders. When Whisper looked back she saw no doorway, only a beautiful tree that was shining a golden color in the afternoon sun. She looked up to see how tall it was and discovered that the color carried right up to the very tip of the tree. It was an incredible sight to see. She was amazed to think that they had just walked out of this colourful tree.

"Where is he?" Miles asked.

"What do you mean? Is he not here?" Whisper asked, looking around for Cael.

"I don't see him," Miles said.

"Maybe he got tired of waiting. Are we on time?" she asked. There had to be a reason he wasn't there.

"Yes, three o'clock exactly," stated Marcus.

248

"Maybe he went down to the river," she offered. "It's just over there."

"You wait here," said Marcus. Miles and Whisper stood there, silent, while they waited for him to come back.

"Nothing, he's not there. I looked up and down along the river, too," he said when he came back a few minutes later.

"M-maybe he got held up somewhere. We should just sit and wait a few minutes." She didn't want to give in to the panic she was starting to feel. Miles must have felt the same way.

"That's a good idea. We'll wait thirty minutes. If he doesn't show up, we'll start searching." Marcus agreed and the three of them picked a spot to sit and wait.

'Where could he be?' Whisper asked herself. She tried to concentrate and get in tune with his mind thinking, maybe, if she could communicate with him she could find out where he was.

#

Cael was starting to get angry at the predicament he had gotten himself into. So far he had managed to convince Jezebel that Whisper was hiding at a spot that was nowhere near the place of the portal. They drove a good twenty miles past the falls and then took a dirt road halfway up a mountain on the opposite side of the highway. He knew that if he took her here he could get her out walking on a long, twisting trail that would take a few hours to complete. There should be plenty of opportunities to disarm her on this trek.

By now, he realized that she was not very good at reading

249

his thoughts. He tried to test her abilities with outrageous thoughts of him and Whisper, thoughts he knew she wouldn't be able to resist invading and commenting on. She seemed to not be aware of them. Besides, he could tell when she was trying to read his mind because she had to concentrate real hard and her eyes would narrow and her eyebrows would crinkle together with the effort of it. Knowing this he could put ideas in his head to confuse her. It worked quite well and she was starting to trust his thoughts more and more.

"Cael, really, how much further do we have to go? If you haven't noticed, I don't exactly have on hiking boots." Yes, he had noticed how she was struggling in her high heels; it was all part of his plan actually.

"I told you, when I saw her, she was at the top of this mountain. Whether or not she's still there is another thing all together." The mountain they were climbing was a popular one amongst hikers. It wasn't very tall, only about eight thousand feet and more than half of that was covered by the dirt road. There were no steep rock faces to climb, making it a hike even a small child could make. Still, it would be a chore for Rob and Jezebel to reach the summit. They had no water and neither one of them had ever hiked before. With the cool weather lately, the mountain was pretty empty right now which was what Cael wanted. He couldn't stand it if any innocent people got hurt.

The main reason he chose this particular hike was because, once you got to the top, you were in the open and exposed to the elements. There were no trees, therefor, no shelter from the wind. On a day like today the wind could be blowing around eighty miles per hour and it would be cold. This would be his chance to disarm Jezebel and make his escape. Her feet would be so chewed up by the climb that she would never be able to follow him. His one problem would be Rob, but judging by his struggle with the hike so far, that might prove to be easier than he thought. He only hoped he could accomplish all of this and still get to the portal before Whisper got there.

It took a couple of hours but, once they got to the top, the wind was howling just as he thought it would. Jezebel had long ago ripped the heels off of her shoes and now she stood in the wind with her hair blown into masses of stringy knots, her clothes were dirty and stained with sweat and, now that the wind was blowing in her face, her eyes were watering and her make-up streaked down her face.

'Now, she looks like the witch she truly is,' thought Cael with a smile. Rob was standing beside her, hunched over and leaning on his knees, trying to gulp in air in an attempt to regulate his breathing.

"Where…is…she?" She looked like she was out of patience. Cael stood up straight, with his hands in his back pockets; he hadn't even broken a sweat. He searched the area nonchalantly.

"I don't see her." He smiled back at Jezebel. "Perhaps she went exploring." That did it, except it wasn't Jezebel who lost it;

251

it was Rob.

"You son-of-a…" He straightened up and came at Cael. "Is this your idea of a joke?" It was easy for Cael to defend his attack; he was too tired to launch any kind of real assault. Cael just waited until he was almost on him, stepped to the side and stuck out his foot. Rob went down hard, falling face first to the ground and then rolling over a pile of rocks. He heard him grunt in pain but never looked down at him; instead, he kept his eyes on the woman.

"Really, Robbie, you're proving to be more of a detriment then a help." Jezebel looked totally disgusted in him. "Would you please pick yourself up and come and stand over here by me." Rob slowly got up and returned to her side, his shoulders slumped over, looking defeated. Cael looked at him sympathetically. What a horrible road he had chosen for himself.

"Robbie does have a point, though," she said. "Just what were you thinking, dragging us way up here? Is this your way of amusing yourself?"

"Honestly, this is where I left her." He tried to sound convincing.

"Then where is she?" She started to grip the gun in her hand a little tighter and Cael concentrated on keeping his calm.

"Perhaps I should call for her," he said. Jezebel's head popped up, she hadn't thought of that maybe that would bring the girl out.

"Okay, try it." Cael moved towards her a little more and

put his hands up to his mouth.

"Whisper!!" he shouted. No answer, not like he expected one. He tried again. "Whisper!!" Jezebel and Rob looked around, fully expecting to see the girl emerge from the woods.

"Maybe we should go further along the summit," said Cael, wanting to get them completely in the open so the wind could hit them full on. Rob started out but Jezebel stayed where she was.

"You two go, I'll watch from here." Was she on to him? He looked at her and tried to figure out what she was thinking, maybe it was her sore feet. He looked down and noticed she had slipped her shoes off. Her nylons had torn and she had scratches on her legs and her feet looked all blistered and bleeding. He returned his look to her face and she smiled embarrassingly at her appearance and tried to straighten her hair.

'Vanity,' thought Cael with a smile, 'it may just save my life.'

He and Rob started out to the middle of the ridge at the top of the small mountain. The wind really picked up out there and it was hard to stand up straight. It was also hard to hear what anyone was saying. There was no way either of them would be able to hear Jezebel way out there. Cael had almost gotten to the spot where he would try to make his escape. He stopped and Rob looked at him curiously. He was standing there, hunched over against the wind and holding his coat tightly closed. Cael put his hands up to his mouth again.

"Whisper!! It's okay you can come out." As he yelled he turned in a circle so he could see what Jezebel was doing. She was standing there, shivering, the gun hanging loosely from her hand. She was searching the trees, looking for Whisper, hardly paying attention to the two of them. Cael knew his time had come and that he would have to act fast, he had no idea how far that gun could reach. He slowly positioned himself so that Rob was standing between him and Jezebel, all the time he kept yelling for Whisper. When he got just above a small cliff he made his move.

Without any hesitation he jumped backwards, knowing that there was a small ledge about four feet down. From there, he quickly got down on his stomach and shimmied himself over the ledge until he found the foothold of a branch that belonged to a two hundred year old Douglas fir that had embedded itself into the side of the mountain.

He had climbed this tree many times when he was a kid. He had started sliding down the tree when he heard a loud tremble come from above. He looked up and caught a glimpse of Rob trying desperately to claw his way over the cliff. Above him, Jezebel stood, looking for something to shoot at. Cael kept climbing and finally came to the bottom of the tree. He jumped down into the bushes and ran. He made it and there was no way those two could follow him, not through here. This was his territory and they had no idea where they were or where any of these paths led. He looked at his watch, one fifty-five, he would be late. Hopefully, they would wait for him. It could take him at least an hour and a half to get to the portal.

Chapter 20

Dougall learned of Jezebel's little escapade through a spy he had placed strategically in the woods. The spy saw Cael arrive on the mountain path with Jezebel and some blonde kid and proceeded to follow them. When he saw her attempt to force Cael to bring out the girl known as Whisper, his curiosity was piqued. He came close to the clearing, wondering how this would all work out. He could sense the warrior was lying but it was obvious the wench didn't realize it.

When Cael made his escape and started running, the spy immediately went to Dougall. Dougall was furious! What was that stupid woman thinking? Why was she taking matters into her own hands? The idea was to convince Cael that coming to his side was the right thing to do, use a little mental persuasion to lure him here, not kidnap him. Now, he would want nothing to do with him. He would fight Dougall's attempts with all his powers. And why was she looking for Whisper? Was she planning to bring them both here together? Did she really want to please him that much? Foolishness, that's what it was.

Because Dougall was oblivious to Jezebel's deep love for him, he had no idea her ultimate goal was to kill Whisper to keep her away from him. If he had, he would have planned her demise immediately. Instead, he made plans to go to the Earth dimension to try and fix what she had done. He would find Cael and bring him back here, there was no choice now. Then he would try everything within his powers to control his mind and persuade him to join forces with him. Then he would use him to lure Whisper here. He sent the spy back to learn more.

By the time the spy returned, Dougall was ready to go. He must talk to Jezebel and send her away for awhile. She could take her little plaything with her if she wanted but she must not be allowed to mess up anything else. If she fought too much he would get rid of her. It would be a small sacrifice but he could easily replace her. In fact, Whisper could take her place, which was the plan he was contemplating anyway. The only trouble was that they had the beautiful little Soul-healer locked up in that blasted fortress; no one could get to her in there. But he knew that if he tortured the soul of the warrior long enough the girl would be forced to come to his aid.

"Sir, there has been a drastic change of events." The spy was out of breath and excited by the news.

"What is it?" Dougall was annoyed that his thought process was interrupted.

"The girl, Whisper, she has come to the Earth dimension!" Dougall stopped what he was doing and stared at the spy.

"What?"

"Whisper, she arrived through the portal in the woods not

long ago. She came with a couple of Cross-overs. It seems she has made actual contact with the warrior and they planned to meet there, which is probably why she didn't come with very much protection," the spy said.

"So, that means she is at the portal right now?"

"No, she left when Cael didn't show up. She is making her way to the city now."

"And Cael?" asked Dougall.

"He is on his way to the portal. Jezebel delayed their meeting just long enough for Whisper to take leave," explained the spy.

"Well, well, well, the harlot proves useful after all." Dougall laughed out loud. "We cannot allow the warrior and the healer to meet and, under no circumstances, can they use that portal. Go there and destroy it. I will go talk to my lovely Jezebel."

"Right away, master." The spy ran out to obey his orders. Dougall put on his Earthly clothes, a pair of blue jeans, a white dress shirt and a black leather jacket. He was getting a little excited; he had waited a long time to start the battle again. He put on a pair of dark sun glasses and started his descent to the Earth dimension.

Chapter 21

Cael started to get close to the portal at around four o'clock. It took him just a little longer than he thought. With the snow still lying on the ground, traveling through the woods on foot was difficult. He didn't stop once since making his escape for fear that somehow his two captors had found a way to track him. Now, as he ran along the river, he began to feel fatigued. He stopped briefly to get a drink of water then continued on his way. His only thought was that soon he would see Whisper and he would be able to hold her, for real this time. This pushed him forward and he started to pick up his pace.

When he finally got to the portal, nothing could have prepared him for what happened there. The small hideaway was gone, it was completely destroyed. The boulders were smashed into small pieces and the beautiful, golden tree was chopped down and burned beyond recognition. He saw golden needles lying all around the ground like tears that were shed by the giant tree in its final moments of life. Who did this? He began to feel a surge of rage within and he walked over to one of the broken boulders and picked up a piece of it. He squeezed it in his hand, anger taking total control of him. The rock crumbled and he looked at the dust that remained, astonished at his own strength.

Slowly he let the particles fall to the ground.

#

WHAM!!

Whisper was running with Miles and Marcus by her side for about half an hour now. When Cael didn't show up, they decided to go look for him at his apartment, figuring something had gone wrong to prevent him from meeting them there. They almost made it to the edge of the forest when the familiar sensation of being pulled stopped Whisper dead in her tracks. Within seconds she was gone.

She was back at the spot where the portal was supposed to be except that it wasn't there anymore. Something horrible happened to it. She stood there, in shock, watching the tree burn. She looked around at the rest of the destruction and saw Cael sitting by one of the crushed boulders. She headed towards him.

"Cael?" He looked up, recognizing the feel of her presence.

"Whisper, is that you?" He stood up and looked around, trying to figure out where she was.

"Cael, I'm over here." Whisper reached out and touched his arm. He jumped at first then smiled at the familiar shock.

"Whisper, what happened? Where are you?" She concentrated hard and tried to send her thoughts to him clearly.

"You were late, where were you?" He looked her way and smiled.

"It's so good to hear your voice."

'Well, that's good, my lessons with Alannis had worked,' she thought as she realized he had no trouble hearing her.

"Tell me, why were you late? Did something happen?" she asked. His smiled faded.

"The woman, Jezebel, she was there in my apartment when I woke up. She wanted me to take her to you."

"To me? But why would she think *you* could take her to me?" A small smile appeared on his face.

"She saw my dream." Whisper's heart sank and she let go of his arm. "No! Don't let go! She only saw the end part; she has no idea of our plans or of the portal. She only knows that we met somewhere in the forest and that we kissed."

Whisper started to walk away. It was her fault; she should never have let him kiss her. Now everything was ruined. She came there feeling superior, like she could do anything. 'I don't need help,' she had told Alannis. Now, look at this mess. Miles and Marcus were stuck there, Cael was exposed and right out in the open for Dougall to come and get and there was nothing she could do. All because of a stupid kiss.

'Oh why did I give in to his embrace?' she asked herself. 'Why do I feel so damned attracted to him?'

"Whisper?" He was standing there, reaching out his arm, trying to find her. She had to forget her attraction to him and remember her job to keep his soul safe. She grabbed his arm again. He smiled at the touch.

"Cael, think hard, are you sure she didn't know about the

261

portal?" she asked urgently, ignoring his smile.

"Yes," he said. "I took her somewhere else, to lead her away from here. She's probably wandering around lost by now."

"Then who destroyed this portal?" Whisper asked, fearing the worst. "Did you see anyone else?"

"No, we were on top of a mountain in the middle of nowhere. There was no one else there, trust me, I would have known if there was." She looked around at the trees that surrounded them. There had to be someone else. Someone knew they were there and was blocking their way back to Chrystalline. She had to think of a way out of this. They all needed to gather together and find a new portal. This was Marcus' talent; Whisper just hoped he was ready for the challenge.

"Cael, you must go to the place in our dream. The place with the little stick houses." She was taking control of the situation, her attraction for him set aside.

"You mean the beaver dams?" He laughed at her definition of them.

"Yes, and you can't take this lightly, we're in serious trouble."

"Sorry, okay, I'll meet you there. Do you know the way?" he asked, looking a little guilty and feeling embarrassed for laughing.

"Yes, I can find it but we're quite far away right now. It will take us a good twenty minutes to get there. Just go there and hide. Stay out of sight and if you hear anything, run! I will find you later," she said, trying to stress the urgency of the situation.

"But how will you find me?" he asked.

"I think I know the emotion that pulls me to you, anger. If you get angry, really angry, I will come to you," she said. "Now, go! I must get back to my friends."

"Okay and be careful," he said.

"I will and Cael?" Whisper needed to be sure he understood this next part. "You have to forget that we kissed. It was wrong, we can't be together. I am your Soul-healer and there's no place for those kinds of emotions between us." She tried to make her words sound final, not leaving any room for questions.

"But, I…" he started.

"No, I mean it, the kiss never happened and I *will* deny it." She let go of his arm and let herself drift back to Miles and Marcus.

#

Cael stood there for a few minutes after her presence left and thought about what she said. Was she right? Was the kiss they shared a mistake? She seemed to think so, but he wasn't so sure. How could something that felt so right be wrong? No, that would be a nasty joke to be played on him. If he wasn't meant to feel anything for Whisper, than he would know it. He started to head off to the beaver dams, thinking he would play along with her little game of denial for awhile, but eventually, there would have to be some way of convincing her that the kiss was right and that there was nothing wrong with that.

He made his way back down to the river, and then stopped for another drink. He wished he had something to eat, he was starved. He hadn't eaten all day. He stood up and stretched and wondered just who destroyed the portal and if they were watching him right now? He twisted his back to make it look like he was getting some kinks out, but he was really scanning the trees, looking for anything unusual. He knew how to tell when there was a predator in the woods, not that he was ever bothered by bears or cougars, but they were out there. When something came through the forest, the birds would stop singing and the squirrels would start chattering, warning each other. It was a whole elaborate system that the animals used. He learned to read their little warnings a long time ago; it was probably what kept him safe from any dangerous encounters all these years. Right now, there didn't seem to be anything around. The sounds of the forest were carrying on like normal. He stopped stretching and headed for the beaver dams.

#

Miles and Marcus stopped when Whisper went to see Cael. They realized what was happening and knew she would come back to her body shortly and inform them of what was going on. While they waited, they found a place to sit and rest. They didn't have too long to wait.

"We have to change course," she said when she got back, afraid of how they were going to react when she told them about

264

the portal.

"Is he there, at the portal?" asked Marcus.

"No, I've sent him somewhere else to meet us," she said as she started to head back in the direction they just came from. "Come on, we'll talk as we walk."

"Whisper, why are we not going back to the portal?" Miles knew something was wrong. She had to tell them what happened but she didn't want it to slow them down.

"Because it's gone," she said bluntly, not knowing any other way to say it.

"Gone, but where did it go?" asked Marcus, obviously not comprehending what Whisper was saying.

"It's just gone, that's all." The twins stopped walking and looked at her angrily.

"Whisper, you must tell us what's going on. We are here together as a team and it would be useless to all of us if information is withheld. We must know what you know," Miles said.

"Okay, okay." She stopped and looked at her two comrades. "I'm sorry; I just didn't know how to tell you. Somebody destroyed it."

"Destroyed it, how?" asked Marcus, slipping his hand in his pocket to grasp his keys.

"Destroyed it, you know, they smashed the boulders, chopped down the tree and set it on fire. There's nothing left of it." She tried to sound as if it didn't matter, that it wasn't going to ruin their plans but she knew it did.

"But who did it? Did Dougall come here already?" For the first time since she met them, Whisper saw a small crack in the twins' stiff exterior. They looked genuinely afraid. She made the decision to stop and talk it over with them, try to make some plans. Miles was right; they were all in this together.

"Okay, let's talk about this," she said. "I don't know if Dougall is here, but someone destroyed that portal and all I can do is tell you what I do know, which isn't much. I just know who did *not* do it."

"And who did *not* do it?" asked Marcus.

"Jezebel. She kidnapped Cael this morning. He led her far away from here, making sure there was no way she could find us, and then he escaped. When he got to the golden tree it was already destroyed. He got angry when he saw what happened and that's how I got pulled to him." She looked at the two men, trying to read their reactions.

"She kidnapped him? She wasn't wasting any time was she?" Miles said. "But why would she make him take her out here? What was she looking for?"

"Me," answered Whisper, "she caught the end of our conversation in my dream walk and saw us talking in the forest. She thinks that I've been here since yesterday and she was forcing Cael to show her where."

"But that means she must be acting on her own and wants you dead before Dougall finds out anything," said Miles.

266

"And it also means that she will be desperate now that Cael has escaped. She must find him before Dougall finds out about her little caper this morning," Marcus added. The two of them were thinking out loud between themselves.

"Did you say Cael went immediately to the portal when he escaped?" asked Miles.

"Yeah, that's what he said."

"And Jezebel would not be able to beat him there?" he asked.

"I don't think she even knows there is a portal," Whisper said. She could see that Miles was formulating an idea in his head. Marcus could see it as well.

"What are you thinking, Miles?" he asked.

"I'm thinking we need to get to Cael fast!!" he said as he started to walk quickly.

"Wait! Tell us what's wrong." He stopped and turned to them.

"Don't you see? Cael left Jezebel to head for the portal where we sat for half an hour waiting for him. There's no possible way Jezebel could have beaten him there and us not seen her, but someone did. Someone came after we left and before Cael showed up. Could it be Dougall? But that would mean that he knows everything that's happened today. Would he spend his time smashing apart a portal or punishing Jezebel? I think he would prefer the latter; menial tasks are not his forte. No, it wasn't Dougall, he had help."

"Then who was it?" asked Whisper.

"I think it was a spy," he said and Marcus gasped.

"You don't mean…?"

"Who else could destroy something like that so quickly?" Whisper had no idea what they were talking about but she wanted to find out.

"We have to go now!!" Marcus grabbed her arm and started running, Miles on her other side.

"Tell me who could have destroyed the portal? Who is this spy?" They were going pretty fast.

"Someone you don't ever want to meet. Now, tell me how far until we get to Cael?"

"It's by the portal, about twenty minutes away." She could see them exchange looks of grave concern and then they started to run even faster. Whisper wished, for the first time, that they could mind-port here.

#

"You stupid, idiotic, sorry excuse for a man! How can anyone be that careless. I told you how important it was to keep Cael with us." Jezebel yelled at Rob all the way down the mountain. She was furious that Cael escaped but she knew that it was as much her fault as it was Rob's. She should have known he'd been tricking her, but she trusted him. Everything in his mind told her he wasn't lying. Oh, how could she be so stupid!? Now, all she had to show for this day, which started out so promising, were clothes ready for the trash and feet she could barely walk on. Rob piggy backed her down most of the mountain.

"I'm sorry, Jez, I told you it was windy out there, I could barely stand straight. When he went over the edge, I didn't even hear him jump. He's fast and he knows this area. I told you, he grew up out here." He apologized just as much as she yelled at him. He didn't want her to be angry with him, not now when his feelings were so strong for her. He fell hopelessly in love with Jezebel the first time he saw her. She was beautiful and she treated him like he was special, the only man that could make her happy. It was great at first but lately, since all this stuff with Cael came about, she was mean and nasty to him. He should have dumped her but he just couldn't bring himself to do it.

They carried on down the same path they came up hours before. It was starting to get dark and the last thing either of them wanted was to be out in these woods at night. Hopefully, Cael abandoned any idea of retrieving his Jeep and they could drive home. If they had to walk, there was no way they would make it tonight, it was too far. It was getting cold and they would have to find some way to keep warm. They were hungry as well and they didn't bring any food or water with them. All this made Jezebel angry again and she started yelling at Rob once more.

"I can't believe I trusted you to watch him! You're such an imbecile! You make me…" They emerged into the tiny parking lot at the end of the long dirt road. The Jeep was still sitting there but there was another vehicle parked there as well.

Jezebel stopped talking when she spotted the large, black Hummer. Its windows were tinted black but she didn't need to see the person sitting inside to know who it was.

"Put me down!" she whispered to Rob. He did and then straightened out his back. He looked at the Hummer and wondered who else could be out here hiking so late in the evening. He started to walk towards the Jeep when Jezebel reached out and grabbed his arm to stop him. "Wait!"

The door to the Hummer opened and a figure got out. It was a man Rob had seen once before, yesterday actually, when Jez took him to that strange place. She wanted him to tell this man that he saw Cael argue with his mother. Rob didn't like the man, he was spooked by him then and he didn't feel any better now.

"Well, well, look what we have here." Dougall glided halfway over to them, his hands in the front pockets of his jeans. He wore sunglasses so they couldn't see his eyes. Jezebel stood, frozen, beside Rob. "Kind of a strange day for a hike don't you think?"

"D-Dougall, What are you doing here?" She was starting to tremble with fear.

"That's funny. You come down the side of a mountain in a skirt and, um, let's see, high heels, I guess, and no vehicle in sight," he looked around the lot as he spoke; resting his eyes on Cael's Jeep, "unless you've stolen this one, and you question *my* appearance here?"

"No, we didn't steal that, it's..." Jezebel elbowed Rob in the ribs before he could say anymore.

"Yes?" Dougall smiled in anticipation of an explanation.

"What Rob is trying to say is…" she tried to pull herself together, straightening her skirt as she walked towards him with no sign of the pain in her feet, "that we came up here with Cael in his Jeep; he drove. He wanted to show us this beautiful trail. Only problem is, he's much better at hiking than we are. He had a huge lead on us coming down. Is he here yet?" She stopped and looked around, pretending to search for him. Dougall threw his head back and roared with laughter. He could hardly contain himself. The woman really was quite amusing. How could she possibly think her lies would go unnoticed?

"And the gun?" He pointed to the weapon she still held in her hand.

"Bears?" She looked at him innocently. It only took seconds for him to cross the rest of the parking lot and stand, towering before her, his sunglasses in his hand so she could see the full fury in his eyes.

"DON'T PLAY GAMES WITH ME WENCH!" Her legs felt weak and she tried to turn her eyes away. "LOOK AT ME!"

"Y-yes s-sir." Her voice was barely audible as she turned her eyes towards the man she loved. All she saw there was hatred and she started to die inside. He raised his hand as if to strike her and she shrank away in fear. Rob started to take a step forward than thought better of it.

271

"Don't ever call me sir again. I can't stand it."

"Okay, I won't." She felt some sort of reprieve that he didn't hit her.

"Why are you here? And don't lie, I can tell." He crossed his arms in front of his chest and waited for her explanation.

"Okay, I'll tell you." She swallowed hard and tried to keep her voice steady. "I went to Cael's apartment this morning. I wanted to bring him to you; I know how anxious you are to have him. When I got there he was sleeping and he called out the girl's name. I looked into his head and saw them together in the woods, so I thought that if I could get him to take me to her I could bring both of them to you together, just like you wanted."

"You did this without my say so?" he asked.

"I wanted to surprise you." She looked at him like a little girl, too innocent to get mad at. Dougall knew better.

"You had no right to interfere with my plans." He took her face in his hand and squeezed it tight, staring deep into her eyes. "Did you think I couldn't handle things on my own?" She tried to shake her head but his grip was too tight. Her eyes were wide with fear now. Rob stood quietly out of the way, not wanting to draw any attention to himself.

"You've almost ruined everything." He let go of her face and she rubbed it, trying to smooth away the pain he caused. "I'm going to tell you what's going to happen now and you're going to agree or, I swear, I will make your death very long and very painful." She nodded her head quickly trying to hold back tears; something she never shed before in her life.

"You will go back to the Abyss dimension and stay in your dungeon until I come for you. You can take this *thing* with you if you want." He pointed at Rob. "I don't want to hear from you or see you and if you even try to come out before I am ready for you, I will know and, trust me, I will not be so kind next time." Jezebel let out a sob as she felt her world come crumbling down.

"Do you understand me?"

"Y-yes, I do." Dougall snapped his fingers and the back door to the Hummer opened and out came a man Jezebel knew well. He was a monster who took pleasure in torturing people for Dougall. He was tall and heavy, weighing about three hundred pounds with a large, bald head and long hairy arms. His face was burned severely at one time, leaving it full of grotesque scars. One eye had lost its eyelid and sat there, half exposed. His lips were burned off and his teeth remained in a permanent grin. He was hideous and Jezebel usually did everything she could to avoid him. She took a step back when she saw him.

"Come now, don't tell me you're afraid of Bayha, he likes you so." Dougall smiled and put his sunglasses back on. "You may bring the Hummer to the place I told you about when you have finished," he said to the huge man.

"Yes, master." Bayha grinned even harder with anticipation. Jezebel looked at Dougall, panic written all over her face.

"W-where are you going?" she yelled.

"I think I'll take a walk. These woods seem so inviting!" He laughed as he left the three of them standing there.

Chapter 22

Whisper was right. It took them exactly twenty minutes to arrive at the little stick houses. When they got there, however, Cael was nowhere to be seen. They looked around the strange place, searching for him, with a sense of panic creeping in.

"Where is he?" Whisper was getting more and more anxious.

"Did you tell him to wait?" asked Marcus.

"Yes, I told him to wait right here, unless..."

"Unless what?" Marcus urged her on.

"Unless he heard something," she said, "then I told him he should run. Do you think that spy person came here?"

"I hope not," said Miles, as he started to make his way around the dams, "if he was here and the spy..."

"It's about time you guys got here." They all jumped at Cael's voice and turned to see him jumping down from a tall tree. "I figured the best place to hide was up." He pointed up at the tree he just descended from. Miles and Marcus sighed with relief when they saw him.

"Thank goodness you're all right," said Miles. Cael looked at the twins with the same apprehension that Whisper greeted them with a few days before. "Here, let me introduce

275

ourselves. I'm Miles and this is my brother Marcus." They approached Cael and they all exchanged handshakes. This set Cael at ease and he knew he could trust them. Whisper stayed back, hoping he would heed her warning and keep a respectful distance between them. He finished his hellos with the twins and then looked at Whisper. Her stomach fluttered with his gaze and she looked down. Their attraction was even stronger in person. He caught her eye movement and a small smile appeared on his face; obviously she still felt something for him.

'Stop it!' she thought. 'I can't let my emotions get in the way.' She pulled in her feelings and put on a determined exterior. He noticed the change in her body language and his smile faded.

"And you are Whisper," he said as he came forward and reached out his hand. "It's nice to finally meet you in the flesh."

She stared at his hand, not wanting to touch it, afraid of what would happen when she did. Being so close to him, she could smell his sweat and feel his heat and she could feel her determination waver. He looked down into her face and urged her on with his eyes.

"Afraid to take my hand?" he whispered. This brought her back to the present. How dare he goad her on.

"No!" She grabbed his hand and ignored the shock that ran up her arm. He chuckled at her and she glared back at him. "Remember what I said before," she warned him under her breath.

"Oh, I remember, but it looks like you're the one who's

having trouble with it." She turned red, not because she was embarrassed, but because she was furious at the smug look that now appeared on his face.

"Okay, now that we're finally all together, what are we going to do?" Cael asked as he turned to face the twins.

"We must find a safe place," said Marcus. "You have no idea of the danger that is in these woods right now."

"I know, I saw him," Cael said and they stared at him in disbelief. Who had he seen?

"Who?" asked Marcus.

"Just after I got here everything went quiet, even the squirrels stopped chattering. I knew something was wrong, so I figured the best place to hide was up. That's when I climbed that tree." He pointed at the tree he jumped down from. "It's a good thing I did too, because no sooner did I get up there than this man passed by underneath me and I got a very bad feeling about him."

"What did he look like?" asked Marcus.

"He wasn't much bigger than I was, really. He had dark hair and wore very dark clothing and he was carrying something in his hand. It looked like some sort of axe and that's when I figured he must be the one that chopped down the golden tree. He moved quickly and I could tell he was searching for something. He never even guessed I was up there because not once did he think to look up into the trees. He must not know much about the forest." Miles and Marcus looked at each other.

"It's him! You were right!" Marcus looked at his brother.

"Who?" Whisper was still in the dark about who this man was and she didn't like it.

"We must get away from these woods; find a place where no one will think of looking for us," said Miles. "Then, Whisper, you must go back to Chrystalline and get Alannis. She can help us find a new portal."

"Alannis? Can't you find us a new portal on your own? Why do we need Alannis?" She asked, afraid to face them back at the fortress.

"I only know about the portals that lead *out* of Chrystalline and the closest one is about four thousand miles from here," said Marcus. "Alannis will be able to show us where the portal to Atlantis is and we can use that one. From there I can get us back to the fortress."

"Atlantis?" Cael looked at Marcus like he was insane. "You mean it really exists somewhere?"

"Yes, lots of things exist that you never knew about before," Whisper said. "Hopefully, we'll make it out of here so I can explain them all to you."

"I'd like that." She ignored his comment.

"Okay, I'll go back, but not until I'm sure that you guys are safely hidden somewhere." She turned to Cael for guidance. He knew this area. Hopefully, he knew where they could hide. "Where can we go to hide?"

"We can go into the city and hide out at my parent's house," he said. "As you know they died yesterday and no one will even think to look for me there." They all knew that Cael felt no sorrow over the death of his parents. Whisper had explained to him in their dream walk that they were just spies sent by Dougall but it was still weird to hear him talk so bluntly about the people who posed as his parents.

"Good, let's not waste anymore time." Marcus turned to go. "Whisper, take Cael's hand so that he can run faster. You guys lead the way and we'll follow. Don't look back." She looked at Cael awkwardly and he smiled and held out his hand. She rolled her eyes at the look of victory on his face.

"Come on," she grabbed him and dragged him to the front of the group, "let's go!"

They took off. It was amazing how fast a person could go when driven by fear. Whisper never thought much about her running capabilities. They were average at best. In fact, whenever she had gym class she never won any races, she never lost any either; she was average. By the surprised look on Cael's face as they ran through the trees, however, it was obvious he had never run so fast in all his life. By holding his hand, Whisper was able to push her energy through him and he was able to keep up, for a while. It was not long before the fact that his feet were moving quicker than his brain caught up with him, and she started to feel him slowing down. Eventually, he came to a stop and let go of Whisper's hand.

"I can't do this." He was out of breath now. "My feet don't move that fast. Can't we go just a little slower?" She looked at him and then put her hands on both his shoulders and looked into his eyes.

"We have to go before anyone discovers we're here," she said. "You can do this, I know you can." Miles and Marcus caught up to them.

"What's wrong?"

"We're going too fast, his feet can't keep up," she said as she let go of his shoulders and turned away from the angry look that was now on his face.

"Then carry him!" Miles said. She looked at him as if he were crazy.

"I can't carry him! Look how much bigger he is than me!" She was appalled by the thought of carrying this man through the woods and, for once, Cael looked like he agreed with her.

"Trust me, you can do it," Miles said.

"He's right, you're strength has been multiplied tenfold with your awakening and your training. Try it." She looked at Cael and shrugged her shoulders, then turned around so she could give him a piggy back.

"Come on, hop up," she urged.

"Now, wait just a minute. There's no way I'm letting a little girl like you carry me! I'll take my chances running," he said emphatically.

"Little girl! LITTLE GIRL!" Whisper was angry now. "I am not a little girl! If you want to run go right ahead, I'll try to go slow enough so the *little boy* can keep up." Cael found her little outburst amusing and the twins just looked at each other and threw up their arms in frustration.

"Whatever way you want to travel, let's just go!" they said.

They returned to running, Cael held Whisper's hand again. She knew he had trouble keeping up but she didn't want to slow down even a little. She was still too angry that he called her a little girl. They followed the river for two miles and eventually, came to a point where they would have to cross. It was getting dark and impossible to see what was on the other side.

"Do you think we should find a place to hide out for the night?" Cael asked. "I can't really see anything anymore and don't want to lose my bearings. I know this territory but not well enough to wander around in the dark. Besides, as soon as the animals settle down for the night, it will be too easy for anyone to hear us running through here." He was right but Whisper was not so sure they should stay somewhere out in the open either.

"Do you know where we are?" she asked him.

"Yeah, we're actually not too far from an abandoned cave I used to explore years ago," he said.

"How do you know it's still abandoned?" she asked.

"Because too many people have explored it over the years and the scent of humans has made any animal too scared to

281

use it. It's just up the side of that hill and in amongst the rocks." He looked at them anxiously, hoping they'd take his advice, he was getting tired.

"What do you think?" asked Marcus.

"I think he's right. We can still get to the city early in the morning, but right now, I'm finding it difficult to see anything around me. It would be easy for Dougall to ambush us," Miles said.

"What about this cave?" asked Whisper. "If so many people have explored it, doesn't that mean it would be easy to find?"

"Only in the daylight and only if you've heard of it before," Cael said. "You see, that's how I found out about it, word of mouth amongst the people that come up here all the time. The new set of *tourists*, the ones that come here with their lattes and organic tea, they've never heard of it." It sounded all right and Whisper looked to the twins for their opinion.

"It sounds perfect. Lead us to it young man." Cael led them up the small hill and back among more bushes. These ones had thorns and Whisper scratched her arms several times pushing them out of the way. They traipsed through the wet snow and tangled branches and sticks that had fallen to the ground over time and she wondered how Cael could possibly know where he was going out here, each clump of trees and bushes were starting to look the same to her. Finally, they came to what looked like a random pile of rocks. It was pushed against the bottom of a hill that eventually formed itself into a mountain. From down here at the bottom, though, it just looked like a pile of rocks.

"It's just through here." He scrambled up the loose rock and disappeared out of sight.

"Cael! Hold up, it's dark and we can't see you!" Whisper yelled quietly. Suddenly, a head popped up out of nowhere and she jumped back, nearly taking Miles back down the rocks they had just climbed up. Cael started laughing at her near tumble.

"I'm sorry." She could tell that he wasn't. "Come on, just jump down here and you'll be in the cave." He reached up to lift her down but she didn't want his hands touching her.

"I can do it," she protested.

"Suit yourself." He backed away and let them all come down on their own. It was hard to tell how big the cave was because it was pitch black and closed in.

"How do you know there are no animals in here?" she whispered.

"I don't," he said calmly, and then walked away from all of them. Whisper stood close to the opening, wanting to be able to make a quick escape if she had to. "You guys didn't happen to bring a flashlight with you did you? Or food by any chance?"

"As a matter of fact…" Miles reached into his pocket and pulled out a crystal. Whisper had never been so happy. He closed his eyes and within minutes the cave was lit up with a soft glow. Now that there was light, the cave didn't really look so bad. It was pretty big, with enough room for all of them to sit in a circle with their legs stretched out. It wasn't tall enough to stand up straight but there was enough room to crouch. It was sheltered from the elements so the ground was dry and clear of any debris. There were a few cobwebs here and there but, other than that, it was pretty empty and clean.

"What is that, a rock?" Cael moved closer to Miles so he could have a look.

"Sort of, it's called a crystal," explained Miles. "A gift from Alannis before we left."

"Take off your coat, brother, and unpack will you. I'm starved." Marcus sat back against the wall of the cave and waited. Whisper looked at Miles and wondered what the odd little man could have possibly put in his coat that could feed all of them. She watched him in stunned silence as he started to unload his pockets. He pulled out a loaf of bread, some meat wrapped in wax paper, cheese, a couple of tomatoes, a bottle of milk, some glasses, plates and a knife. He also had some extra water, some apples and some grapes.

"How did you fit all of that in your pockets?" she asked, not willing to believe he had squashed everything in there.

"Marcus is known as the key man and I am known as the packer." He smiled as he started getting everything ready to eat.

"Pretty handy, isn't he?" Marcus laughed.

"I'll say," said Cael, "give me some of that milk."

They sat there and ate almost everything Miles brought. They saved the apples and some of the milk for breakfast in the morning. It was delicious and it was nice to relax a little after such an exhausting day. After they ate, their attention turned back to the task at hand and Whisper knew she would have to leave to get Alannis. She was not looking forward to leaving the three men by themselves.

"Do you think we should scout the area to be sure that no one followed us?" she asked.

"I think we're pretty safe," said Miles. "But just to be on the safe side I'll go find some scouts to warn us if anyone is coming."

"Scouts? Who else did you sneak into your coat when we left?" She smiled at Miles as she wondered who he was talking about.

"Whisper, have you forgotten all the things you know?" She looked at him, now very confused. "What animal can see all? What animal can we speak with because we have spent centuries learning their language?"

'Of course!' she thought. 'How foolish of me to forget.'

"The birds!" she exclaimed.

"Birds, what are you talking about?" asked Cael.

"The birds of your world are also the birds of our world. They're able to fly back and forth between the two and many others as well. We've learned to communicate with them. They're very interesting creatures," she explained to him. "But what birds are out at night?"

"Owls!" Cael said with excitement.

"That's right, young man, owls and if it wasn't for the fact that Alannis was inside the fortress right now, I'd send one of them to fetch her. Give me a few moments and I will tell them to give a screech if they see or hear anyone approaching our hideout." With that Miles scrambled out the entrance and disappeared from view. They all sat in silence, waiting eagerly for him to come back.

"I'm afraid I have some bad news," he said upon his return.

"Is Dougall on his way?" asked Whisper.

"Well, sort of. Dougall *is* in the forest but, like us, he has stopped his search until morning. He is camped not far from the portal but, I'm afraid, he has caught our trail and will follow it as soon as the day breaks."

"What else do you have to tell us?" asked Marcus, sensing there was more bad news.

"We were right. The spy is by his side and ready to attack us when ordered to. I'm afraid you must make your way to Alannis as soon as possible, Whisper. We must find a new portal before Dougall can come for us. He's very fast and it will be hard to outrun him." Whisper got up and Miles reached out for her hand to help her through the entrance. Cael got up as well to see her out.

"But will you guys be all right without me?" She didn't really want to leave them but she knew she had to find Alannis. She was the only one who could go between worlds without a

286

portal.

"We'll be fine," said Cael. "Remember, I *am* a warrior." She smiled at his attempt of bravery in a situation he really knew nothing about. They walked down the rock pile to the flat ground at the bottom and then stopped as she got ready to go.

"Whisper, I want you to tell Alannis something when you see her." Marcus looked her straight in the eyes. "It will stress the urgency with which she must come. Tell her the Axeman is in the woods and has destroyed the portal." She looked at him, strangely and he urged her forward. She closed her eyes and in a few minutes she was back at the restaurant above the fortress.

Chapter 23

She flew through the elegant restaurant all the way to the back where the kitchen stood. Ignoring the strange looks of the people working back there, she ran to the stairs that would take her down to the basement and the freezers. She remembered which one led to the fortress and walked through to the back. She didn't know how to make the door to the hallway of the fortress appear so she just started pounding the wall, hoping Kisho was standing on the other side and could hear her.

"Miss Whisper?" He recognized her voice and let her in, surprised to see her coming from the restaurant alone.

"Kisho, have you seen Alannis?" she asked him, urgently.

"She's in the lounge, why? What happened?" She didn't have time to talk and pushed by him to get to the lounge.

"I'll explain later. Guard that door!!" She turned and ran to the lounge.

When she got there, she burst through the door and thrust herself into the large room that was so familiar to her now. They were all there, sitting at a table in the middle of the room. Alannis, Taro, Jiro and Aria were all sitting and laughing and talking as if there was nothing of any consequence going on outside these walls. She envied their ignorance and wished she didn't have to destroy it. At the back of the lounge Astra and Gelraen were busy reading their books. The two gnomes were playing some sort of card game and didn't even look up when she came in. When the door shut behind her, all their eyes looked in her direction. Their faces were painted with confusion as they noticed that she was alone and was obviously very shaken. Aria, of course, was the first to recover from her shock and got up from the table and ran over to her friend.

"Whisper!? What's wrong? Where is everyone else?" Whisper looked at her and saw her own panic echoed in Aria's eyes. It was then that the full impact of what happened in the Earth dimension hit her and she knew she had to sit down.

"I-I have to talk to Alannis." She stepped past Aria and headed to the table. Alannis stood up and waited for her to come to the table.

"Alannis, we have to talk." Whisper looked around the table and wondered if she should tell everyone what happened.

'What difference does it make?' she thought. 'They'll all know soon enough anyway.'

"Sit," Alannis said and pulled out a chair for her. Aria came up behind and pulled her chair over to one side so Whisper could fit in better. After she sat down, she took in a deep breath and proceeded to tell them everything that happened since they went through the portal to the Earth dimension.

"I knew something like this would happen," said Aria.

"You should have let me go with you." Whisper didn't think she meant to hurt her feelings with her remarks but she did nonetheless. She was right, though, Whisper was too inexperienced to think she could have done this all alone. Alannis noticed the look of shame on her face.

"The fault is not yours," she said, "it wouldn't have mattered who went with you, the result would have been the same." With Alannis' words Aria realized that what she said she hurt Whisper's feelings and looked away. "Now, tell me what I can do."

"Marcus told me that the closest portal back to Chrystalline is over four thousand miles away. It would be impossible for us to make it there before Dougall found us. He wants you to come back with me and show us where the closest portal to Atlantis is so that we can use that one instead. Is there one close to where they're hiding right now?"

"Yes, there is one, higher up in the mountains. Those particular mountains are very special and hold portals to many worlds. Marcus only knows of the ones that lead to Chrystalline; it's why we sent him with you." She got up from the table. "I must go to my room to retrieve some things for the journey then we will be on our way."

"We'll come with you." Taro joined his wife by her side. Alannis smiled at his devotion.

"My dear, you can't come, it would take you too long to cross through the portals to reach us." She kissed him on the cheek. "You must stay and finish recuperating; Cael will need you when he gets here." She started to walk to the door.

"Alannis?" Whisper got up from her chair and looked at the Atlantean with deep concern. "Marcus wanted me to tell you something."

"Yes?" She was looking at the girl; waiting to hear what Marcus could possibly tell her that would make things worse.

"He said to tell you; 'the Axeman is in the woods and it was he who destroyed the portal'." If Whisper wanted to she could have pushed Alannis over with one finger after she delivered Marcus' message. Alannis stood there, frozen like a stone statue. All the colour drained from her face and her eyes stared ahead at nothing.

"Alannis?" She walked over to her; wanting to snap her out of the stupefied state she was in. "Alannis?" She reached out and touched her arm. This seemed to do the trick and her eyes shifted to Whisper and tried to focus.

"We must hurry; there's no time to waste!!" She grasped Whisper's arms as she spoke with a look of terror on her face.

#

Aria heard the words but still she couldn't quite believe what Whisper said.

'The Axeman,' she thought, 'he's back!' She looked around the table and noticed that no one was paying any attention to her. She could easily slip out; pretend she was too sick to wait up here. After all she was very stressed out and emotional since Whisper left that afternoon. Since leaving the world of Soul-healing, no one ever questioned anything she did. They all left her alone, gave her space. At first she appreciated being left alone but now, it was becoming too painful to endure this burden all alone.

When she was assigned to watch over Whisper, she was happy to be around her friend again. Then she was put in charge of Whisper's awakening and could barely control her excitement. At last she would have her friend back. They could talk and she could finally unburden her sorrows on someone who would understand. But Whisper didn't come back the way she was supposed to. She had no memories of anything from her past and worst of all she didn't remember Aria or their friendship. It was hard to accept the amnesia that had a hold on her friend but she knew, eventually, everything would be okay and Whisper would remember something. Already a bond was starting to form between them.

Aria knew of the love that Whisper felt for Cael and was not surprised by it. She kept this knowledge to herself, though, knowing what the others would say if they found out. She planned to talk to her when she came back with him. She wanted to see how the two of them acted around each other, but that would have to wait.

The Axeman was back and everything had changed. She must slip away from the fortress and go to the woods. Somehow, she must make everything right. She waited until Alannis and

Whisper left and then she pretended she was sick and needed to go to her room. On her way she convinced Kisho that she was going to the restaurant to grab some food for everyone who was waiting for the warrior to return.

#

Dougall paced back and forth in front of the fire that was burning. The Axeman did a good job of keeping the flame high and the heat intense. The last thing he wanted was for his master to feel any cold. Dougall's rage was boiling all evening and anything to keep him relatively calm would serve the Axeman well. When Dougall came to the realization that he would not be able to continue his search in the dark he was livid. He yelled and cursed and destroyed whatever was in his path. Now, he had calmed down and seemed satisfied with just pacing. The Axeman figured it was as good a time as any to discuss strategy.

"Master, we must think about what we will do tomorrow," he started tentatively. Dougall stopped and stared at his loyal servant.

"What we will do?" he asked. "We will track those insolent beggars and bring them back with us. Is there any other option?" He continued pacing.

"I know that is our goal but we must strategize on how to achieve it." He wanted Dougall to realize how hard this task may be to accomplish.

"Strategize? What's to strategize?" Dougall's temper was starting to rise again. "We will go there and take the warrior and

293

the girl and leave!"

"That is what you want but think about who is there and who is here." He wanted to be clear on this next point. "They already have the warrior, who may or may not be coming into his own power by now. And they have the girl. You know what she is capable of."

"Yes, it's one of the reasons I want her." He stopped to listen to what the man was saying.

"They also have the tricksters, who can be taken care of quite easily if they were on their own, but when combined with the other two they could make things more difficult."

"Not a problem, we can do it." Dougall didn't see anything too hard to overcome.

"But, I was thinking," said the Axeman, "what if they get help?"

"Get help? How could they?" Dougall looked closely at his spy.

"The girl, she can travel without the use of a portal," he said. Dougall was always confused about who could travel where on this planet. "What if they decided to get help to find another way back?"

"Like who?" asked Dougall, now very attentive to what the man was telling him.

"They could bring the Atlantean. She could show them a way through to Atlantis." This concerned Dougall immensely because he knew how clever this woman could be and if she were to somehow bring others from Atlantis their fight would be very hard indeed.

"Do you know if any such portal exists?" Dougall asked.

"Oh, I know they exist but the question is where?" said the Axeman. "When the Atlanteans came to the Earth dimension they were excited to bring the people here back to their world to teach them. When they discovered their lust for power and their greed for riches, the Atlanteans became cautious and placed their portals in very secret places. Only a handful of men throughout time have found them and of those only one has ever been able to figure out how to use it and he has been dead for several centuries now."

"Are you telling me that you don't know where this portal to Atlantis is or even if there is one around here at all?" Dougall started to boil up again.

"I'm telling you that there's a good possibility that the girl has gone to get the Atlantean and they will head for the portal as soon as the sun starts to show its face in the morning," he said. "And I am also telling you that I have no idea which way they'll be headed." Dougall began pacing again, this time thinking of a way to stop the group of misguided souls from leaving this world.

"What can we do?" he asked.

"We have time, I could get reinforcements," the Axeman suggested.

"Bayha will be back from the Abyss shortly. He can join

us," Dougall said.

"Bayha is good if his prey is tied up and helpless to fight his torturous ways. As for fighting, just *one* of the tricksters would be able to bring him down. Let me get a couple of good fighters, ones that will be able to cripple all their defences." Dougall saw no other way.

"Okay, go, but be quick. We don't need them to get any kind of a head start."

Chapter 24

Whisper returned with Alannis shortly after two o'clock in the morning. It was cold and dark but there was a sliver of a moon so, she could just barely make out where she was going. As they approached the cave she heard the far away screech of an owl and knew they were still on watch duty. She looked up as he came swooping down and assured him that Alannis was a friend and meant no harm. Satisfied, he returned to his perch high up in a spruce tree to continue his watch.

"You've recruited some help, I see," Alannis said with a smile.

"It was Miles' idea and a pretty good one at that. They've been very helpful with informing us on Dougall's position." Just as Whisper finished her sentence, Miles poked his head out of the cave and smiled when he saw the two of them.

"You are here! Good. The others are asleep and I have information that I must share with you." He pulled himself out of the cave entrance and came to meet them down on the ground. He greeted Alannis with a warm embrace and shook Whisper's hand to welcome her back.

"I have been talking with the owls. They have been flying over Dougall's camp all night to keep an eye on him," he said, "and they have come back with some disturbing information."

"What is it?" Whisper asked, wondering what else could have gone wrong.

"It seems the Axeman has left the camp."

"What? Why would he do that?" asked Alannis.

"Is there any possible way he could know where the portal to Atlantis is?" Miles looked at Alannis anxiously waiting for her answer.

"No, there is no way he could know where it is. We hid our portals well. There isn't even a lot of Atlanteans who know where they are." She started to think about any other reason the Axeman would leave. "Did the owls see where he was going?"

"No. I do have another guess about where he could have gone, though, and I hope that I am wrong," he said. They both stared at him, waiting to hear his guess. "I think he assumed we would send Whisper to get you and has convinced Dougall that they need reinforcements. My guess is that he went to get help." Whisper looked at the grave look on Alannis' face as she considered what Miles just said and could tell that she agreed with him. Whisper wondered what kind of 'reinforcements' he would get.

"What you say makes sense. What plans have you considered?" she asked.

"How far is it to the portal?" he asked.

"It is far, over twenty miles and through some rough terrain. It will be hard for us to make it in one day." It was what

298

Miles feared. There was only one thing they could do.

"We must not wait until morning, we have to go now and make as much progress as we can before Dougall can pick up our trail." Alannis nodded in agreement.

"Yes, that would be the best." They started to head back to the cave.

"Alannis?" Whisper had thought of something that hadn't been asked yet. "Which way is the portal?"

"West." It was what she feared. They would have to backtrack and head in the direction of where Dougall had set up his camp.

When they got in the cave, Marcus was already awake and Cael was just opening his eyes. He sat up quickly when he realized Whisper had returned safely with Alannis. She caught his smile and turned her head away quickly before he saw her blush. He chuckled to himself at her sudden shyness and asked to be introduced to Alannis. Miles introduced them and they nodded their heads to each other in greeting. He explained the situation and they all agreed that they should leave as soon as possible. They ate up the apples and drank the rest of the milk and Miles put his jacket back on and returned the crystal to his pocket. Then the five of them left the sanctuary of the cave.

They decided they would cross the river and follow it west as far as they could. Keeping to the underbrush and avoiding the snow as much as possible, they tried hard not to leave any evidence of their presence. They made an attempt to climb the trees and jump from branch to branch, trying to wipe out any trail for Dougall to follow, but this way of traveling didn't work well for Cael. He could climb the trees, no problem, but when it came to making a leap from one tree to another he just didn't have the ability to do it, so they ended up running on the ground most of the way.

When they were close to the turn off for the beaver dams, they sent an owl ahead to check on Dougall. The bird came back with news that the Axeman had not returned and that Dougall was eating a rabbit he caught and roasted on the fire. He had no idea the group was so close to him. Content with their safety, they resumed their trek.

They kept following the river for a few more miles until it started to wind its way up the mountain. By then, the rocks became too steep and jagged for them to take the chance of following it. Alannis suggested they cross back to the other side and start to climb up. The portal would be at the top of the peak shaped like a pyramid, which was just over the small hill they were on now.

Climbing the hill was easy but now that they were up a little higher and were starting their ascent up the mountain it became harder to climb. They came to a section of loose shale and had a hard time keeping their grip. Whisper was worried that, with every loose piece of shale that slid out from under her feet and down to the bottom, the probability of Dougall hearing them increased. She wasn't the only one that thought this either.

Their pace seemed to have slowed down and she could tell that they were all trying to avoid making the rocks fall.

Halfway up they came to a plateau where they could sit and rest and have a drink of water. They'd been going for about four hours and the sun was now rising in the sky. They could see for quite a distance around them and hoped they'd be able to see Dougall if he was following them. The owls retired for the day but not before Miles could seek out a new ally to help them. He chose to speak to a few crows, a noisy bird but one that was not afraid to get in close to the enemy and return quickly with information.

While they rested, the crows were sent out to check on Dougall's camp. They came back with the news they were dreading to hear. The Axeman returned and brought a couple of people with him. One man was tall and thin with a face like a skeleton. He had dark eyes and sallow cheeks with teeth that looked like bones jutting out from his mouth. He wore a dark suit and the crows didn't like the way he looked at them as they flew by.

"The Scarecrow," said Marcus. "The man looks quite feeble but his power is deadly. He has the ability to turn his enemy to ice and then shatter them into a million pieces."

"What?" Whisper looked at him with a sense of fear.

'How the hell could anyone beat that?' she thought.

"He can be defeated though, just stay out of the glare of his eyes," said Miles. That sounded easier said than done. "If you can do that; he is weak and can be taken down easily." Alannis reached into the bag she packed before leaving the fortress. She pulled out five small crystals, each about the size of a marble.

"Astra was right to tell me to pack these. Keep them close to you and, if the Scarecrow happens to try and freeze you, throw them on the ground and a wall of fire will rise up in front of you. It won't last long, but long enough for you to get away from him," she said.

"Or long enough to attack him," said Cael, looking at the tiny crystal and turning it over in his fingers.

The other man was the opposite of the Scarecrow. He was of average height but built like a rock. His skin was dark like ebony and he wore the clothes of the ancient tribes of Africa. His laugh was diabolical and his face was one that many people knew well in this world. He had haunted the minds of people in the Earth dimension for thousands of years and was known by many names. The crows were afraid of this man and stayed far away from him.

"The Darkman; I was afraid of this," said Marcus.

"Why, who is the Darkman?" asked Whisper.

"He's an evil entity who plays games with the people here in the Earth dimension. He jumps out of the shadows and screams in the dark then laughs at his helpless victims."

"But what powers does he have?" asked Cael.

"He can enter your mind and fill your thoughts with terror and then, once you have become paralyzed with fear, he can rip you apart limb from limb with his bare hands. He's strong and hard to fight," Marcus finished.

"What can we do to stop him?" Whisper asked.

"Our minds are more advanced than the people of the Earth dimension. We can close our thoughts to him and block ourselves from his mind attacks. If we can do that, it will come down to a physical battle and he's not as powerful against one who is properly trained. Our biggest worry will be to keep him away from Cael. His mind can still be tampered with and once the Darkman has him under his control, I'm not so sure he will stop from tearing him apart even if Dougall commands him to." Whisper swallowed hard and hoped her fighting skills would be good enough to protect Cael. She looked over at him to see how he was reacting to all this information and was surprised to see him standing and stretching out his arms, looking as if he was preparing to fight. He almost looked excited by the prospect of a battle and she was surprised by this. Then she remembered who he was and realized that maybe the warrior inside was coming to life after all and a shiver ran down her spine. Then he stopped his warm up exercises and cocked his head towards the twins.

"What about this Axeman? How do we defeat him?" he asked. She was wondering this as well and looked over to them for their answer.

"We don't!" Alannis said. "The Axeman has been around forever. He's been well trained and fights better than anyone I've ever seen. Every part of him is lethal and he can use that axe like it's another limb. It's a part of him."

"Have you fought him before?" Whisper asked. Alannis looked at her with a cold stare.

"I have come face to face with him before but we did not fight," she said with sadness to her voice. "The best way to fight the Axeman is to run and pray he doesn't catch you!"

"He must have a weakness, every man has a weakness," Cael urged.

"Not the Axeman," said Alannis. "And I wouldn't stick around to try and find it either." The crows also told them that a big, monstrous looking man stumbled into camp just as they were leaving. From the description they gave, the twins started to laugh.

"Bayha! That useless slob! I can defeat him with my eyes closed," said Miles, getting his laughter under control.

"Who is Bayha?" Whisper asked.

"He is Dougall's pet monster," snickered Marcus. "He does whatever Dougall tells him to, which is usually torturing helpless victims Dougall has caught somehow. He's so fat and can barely move. His only power is his hideousness. He will be easy to take care of."

"Provided we have to fight," said Miles. "We could still make it to the portal before any of this becomes relevant. Alannis, how much further do we have to go?"

"To the top," she looked up to the peak, "perhaps another three or four hours."

"Then we should go," said Marcus. They all got up and stretched out their legs.

"Wait a minute," Whisper said. "We've talked about everyone else except Dougall. How do we fight Dougall?"

"Dougall won't fight," Alannis said with a smile. "Dougall usually sits back and lets his henchmen do his fighting for him. If it looks like he's going to lose he runs away and if it looks like he's going to win he comes in at the end, all glory and thunder, and finishes off his victims. He's really all bark and no bite. His biggest fear is getting himself hurt. He puts on a scary show and throws his powers about recklessly, destroying buildings, crushing objects and killing weak beings but when it comes to actual combat, he prefers the sidelines."

"But could he do damage if he wanted to?" Whisper asked.

"I suppose so but Dougall will leave if he senses that any part of him could be damaged. He usually backs away with a grand display of his abilities and vows to return again someday. He is ultimately a coward and it's been his greatest downfall over time."

#

The Axeman knelt down by the river and touched the footprint that marked the mud there. They left camp at sunrise and followed the trail of the little group all the way to the cave and now back down to the river. There was an extra set of footprints down there, confirming what he told Dougall last

305

night. They had retrieved the Atlantean and must be on their way to the portal now. He stood up and looked at his master, who looked a little dishevelled this morning after a night in the woods. It was a good thing there was no mirror around or he would cringe at his appearance, image being so important to him.

"They must have crossed the river here," he told Dougall.

"Well, let's go then." They all made their way across; Dougall, the Axeman and the Darkman jumping across in one leap while Bayha and the Scarecrow slowly crossed through the frigid waters. The Axeman was already growing tired of Bayha and wished Dougall would send him back. He was only slowing them down with his massive bulk and his constant whining. They should leave him behind and let the bears devour him.

"Here are their tracks." The Darkman picked up their trail amongst the bushes up from the riverbank. They started to follow it and realized the group had double backed sometime through the morning. The Axeman growled with frustration when they passed by the portal he destroyed yesterday.

'They were here,' he thought, 'sometime during the morning, they were right here. If only we had known we could have captured them instead of taking this blasted journey through the bush.'

"It seems we could have cut our time in half had we discovered this trail when we headed out," said Dougall, the closeness of their passing not going unnoticed by him.

"Yes," said the Axeman, not wanting to ignite his

master's temper, "but who would have guessed that they would have to come back this way."

"Perhaps one who knew of the portals in this area?" The insult was not lost on him. Being that he was raised in this world, Dougall expected him to know everything about it and when he didn't Dougall was not afraid to let him know how disappointed he was despite what the Axeman had done for him over the years. He brushed off the insult and continued on his way.

Soon they got to the place where Whisper and her group started their climb up the hill towards the mountain peak. The Axeman looked up and recognized the significance of the shape.

'Of course, the pyramid mountain,' he thought, 'the portal must be at the top.' There was no way they could beat them up from this side of the mountain. They were probably already halfway up by now. They could race to the other side and make their ascent from there. He was quick and strong and he knew that Dougall could do it and so too could the Darkman, but Bayha and the Scarecrow would never be able to make it. He could carry the Scarecrow but he refused to even try to lift Bayha. He approached Dougall with his plan.

"Master, I think I know where they're headed," he said.

"Where is that?" Dougall was trying to get some rocks out of his shoe.

"Up there to the mountain peak." The Axeman pointed up to the mountain. "But there is no way we can beat them to the top if we climb from here."

"What can we do then?"

"We must go to the other side and scramble to the top as fast as we can." Dougall looked at him doubtfully. "We can do it I know we can. It would be a mere few jumps for you and the Darkman and I would not be far behind."

"And what of the Scarecrow and Bayha?" he asked.

"I can carry the Scarecrow on my back he weighs but nothing," said the Axeman. "But I cannot carry Bayha, we must leave him here."

"Yes, he has become somewhat of a hindrance, hasn't he?" Dougall looked at the pathetically huge man.

"Yes, master." The Axeman could sense that Dougall was ready to cut his ties with the monster.

"Very well, Bayha!" The big man waddled over to him, trying hard not to lose his balance. "Your fat has become a hindrance and I cannot make allowances for you anymore." Bayha looked at Dougall, too stunned to know what to say. Dougall looked over to the Darkman.

"Come over here and practice your fighting technique. I want to see if you've improved since I last saw you." The Darkman smiled at the idea of showing off his strength to Dougall. Bayha, on the other hand, started to whimper with fear. "Stop crying! How is the Darkman ever going to know if he has scared you himself if you are already cowering away?"

Bayha tried to stop his shaking but it was too hard to do,

he knew his life was coming to an end. The Darkman didn't care; freezing their minds was just a boring means to his real enjoyment anyway. Maybe, if there was some fight in this man, he could have even more fun with him. He closed the gap between them in one leap and looked Bayha in the eyes and smiled.

"Don't worry, it won't hurt…much." He reached down and grabbed the massive arm that hung limply at Bayha's side and started to pull. His screams filled the woods and silenced all the animals. Soon the river filled with blood and pieces of Bayha could be found all over waiting to be carried away by all the different beasts that live in the forest. The group of men had already gone to the other side and were headed up the mountain by the time the crows flew back to report what they had seen.

Chapter 25

A chill ran through Whisper when she heard the terrifying scream from below. They left their resting place just an hour before and did not get very far. The slope of the mountain rose to a sharp incline and it was getting harder to find the proper footholds. Just another thirty feet or so and they would be past the difficult part of the climb but that scream froze them all in place.

"What was that?" Whisper asked to no one in particular.

"Nothing, just keep climbing." She could tell by the tone of Alannis' voice that she was spooked by the scream as well. There was a greater sense of urgency in her as she coaxed them on. Whisper was getting tired of all the rock. Her legs were sore and her hands were starting to blister. She wished they could jump up this wall of rock but they couldn't. Cael couldn't make it and he was too heavy for anyone to carry. She looked over to him, worried that the climb was getting to him but he was having no trouble at all scaling it!

'What did Taro teach him, anyway,' she thought, 'how to be a spider? Look at the way he climbs!!'

Cael *was* having an easy time; in fact, this was one of his favourite mountains to climb. He climbed to the top at least once every year since he was sixteen. He'd never been up this early in the spring, however, and it was the reason he never suggested they go around to the other side. This side of the mountain got the majority of the hot sun meaning that most of the snow had melted by now. The other side was not so lucky. The snow would still be deep there and probably very loose. It would be ready to come down in an avalanche if even slightly disturbed. Even that scream would have been enough to bring it all crashing down. For now, he was happy to do what Alannis said and keep climbing.

After another fifteen minutes they were finally past the steep rock. There was another plateau here, a lot smaller than the last one, but still, there was enough room to sit and have a drink. Whisper sat back against a rock and studied the sores forming on her hands. Cael sat beside her and she could start to feel the electricity between them. She started to get up but he reached out and held her back.

"Don't go," he said, and then he whispered so no one could hear. "I promise I'll behave myself. I just feel better when I'm close to you."

"As you should." Marcus surprised them; they didn't know he was paying attention to them. "Whisper is your Soul-healer and it is her job to put your mind at ease. You should spend *more* time around her, it would suit you well."

"Aye, aye, I will take your advice to heart." Cael saluted him then turned and smiled at Whisper and shrugged his shoulders. "Nothing you can do. We both have orders to follow!" She rolled her eyes and shook her head.

They were suddenly bombarded by a group of crows. They were flapping their wings and cawing in such a frenzy that nobody could understand what they were saying.

"Okay, okay, please calm down!" said Miles, trying to decipher their words. "Now, slowly, very slowly, tell us what happened." Whisper leaned over and spoke softly in Cael's ear, translating what the crows were saying.

They related the horrific scene of what the Darkman did to Bayha. There was no arguing between them at all; it just seemed as if Dougall had become tired of the large man and disposed of him. The crows had never seen an act so vicious and unprovoked before and they were scared for the group of people they were spying for. There was no telling what other atrocities these creatures were capable of. Miles thanked them for their concern and asked where the men were now. He was pretty sure that they still had a good two hours on them. The crows told them that Dougall and his men had gone to the other side to try and climb up that way. They also said that they were fast and would make up ground on us quickly. When Whisper told this to Cael he started to laugh and they all looked at him as if he were mad.

"What's so funny?" she asked, starting to get annoyed at his devil-may-care attitude.

"Well, I didn't want to tell you guys this but, I've climbed this mountain before, a few times actually," he said.

'That's why he was quick up that last bit of rock!' thought

312

Whisper.

"Cael, why didn't you tell us this?" asked Alannis. "You could have shown us a better way to go."

"You picked the best way, trust me," he said as he got to his feet. "Had we been making this climb in the late summer then, yeah, I would have suggested we go to the other side. But, at this time of year, this way is the fastest and the safest."

"What do you mean the safest?" asked Alannis.

"The other side, the one they're apparently climbing up, is commonly referred to as 'Avalanche Alley' at this time of year. You see, the snow gets packed in there pretty good, doesn't even melt entirely until late July, but that doesn't mean the sun doesn't warm it up causing it to become very loose. Any sound, or movement, usually causes it to come down fast. There are usually several avalanches there every spring. It's why hikers avoid that area completely until summer," he finished.

"Are you saying that they have a good shot at being buried if they go up that way?" Whisper asked and Cael looked at her and nodded. "Cool!"

"That may be," said Marcus, "but we are talking about men that can punch a hole right through the side of this mountain if they wanted. I'm afraid a few feet of snow won't stop them." Cael looked down, his brief moment of happiness gone.

"No, but it will slow them down," said Alannis. "Do you know how much longer it's going to take us to get to the top?"

"Probably about another hour," Cael said, "and it's all

easy from here on up; just a steep hill, no need to use our hands anymore. It's funny, you know, I always thought this mountain looked an awful lot like a pyramid. Do you think that, maybe, aliens left it here?" Cael laughed at his absurd idea.

"Not aliens," said Alannis under her breath as she started climbing once more.

#

Aria thought carefully before she transported herself to the Earth dimension. 'Now, where would the people of Atlantis put a portal?' she thought as she studied the topography of the area on Cael's computer in his apartment. She looked at almost every mountain, lake and special land anomaly around before the definition of a particular mountain caught her eye. It was not a very tall mountain and it was described as being in the shape of a pyramid. She clicked on its image and immediately knew that this was it. The Atlanteans had a thing for pyramids and tried to hide a lot of their inventions in them, thinking that someday, they could come and share them with the people. This mountain must have been a real pyramid at one time but had since been overgrown with trees and grass and rock. It probably sat, untouched, for thousands of years. She quickly got the location from the website and prepared to transport herself there via Chrystalline; it would be so much easier if she could just mind-port here. She only hoped she could make it before anything horrible could happen.

When she got there, she noticed that the top of this

mountain pyramid was flat and very large. Snow piled up deep in some places and it was so cold. Other spots had no snow at all and you could see new grass trying to poke its way through to the sunlight that shone down on it. Aria looked around for anything that could be the portal. There were trees up here and huge rocks that looked out of place, any one of them could be it. She began to walk around so she could search better when she felt a sudden vibration under her feet. She ran over to the edge where she knew the noise came from. When she looked down she saw a huge cloud of white smoke and wondered what had made such a huge explosion. When it started to clear, she realized that there was no explosion, no fire, and no smoke. The white cloud was a huge slab of snow that had fallen from the mountain, burying everything in its path.

She was about to turn away and continue her search when something black caught the corner of her eye. Something was moving down there, trying to claw its way out of the snow. Her heart sank as she thought that; maybe, it was Whisper and the rest of her friends. She started over the edge to go down and help them when a figure burst through the snow and let out a loud evil growl. She froze as she realized she was wrong. It wasn't her friends at all. She scrambled back up to the top and frantically resumed looking for the portal.

'Where is it?' She screamed to herself. 'And where are they? Have I missed them? Did they already use the portal?' She raced to the other side to see if she could spot anything. There they were! They were about a hundred feet away and looking tired and out of breath. There wasn't much time and it was going to be very close to see who would get there first. She had to be ready to do her part. She ran to one of the trees and jumped to one of the top branches. Her time would come; she just had to be patient.

#

The sound of the avalanche had reaffirmed to them that Dougall was definitely on the other side. They knew the snow would not hold Dougall and his men back for long and they would have to hurry to reach the top. Alannis had the keys to the portal in her bag and reached inside to put her hand on them. She wanted to be ready to use them as soon as they got there. Whisper stuck close to Cael, convincing herself that she needed to protect him but she knew this wasn't the whole truth. She was getting a little apprehensive and, for some reason, having Cael near her made her feel safer.

Miles and Marcus were leading the way and just as they were about to climb up over the edge a crow flew at them and screeched a loud warning. Dougall had arrived on the other side. The snow didn't slow them down as much as they thought it would. Cael came closer to Whisper and squeezed her hand. She jumped and looked at him with a trace of fear in her eyes. He smiled his casual grin and leaned over to whisper in her ear.

"Don't worry, we're going to win. I have a lot of catching up to do with you." He reached over and pushed her hair away from her eyes and then stroked her neck. Whisper's fear melted away and she looked up at him. His face was very serious and then he nodded and smiled again.

'Who is this guy!?' she thought. Something about him made her feel stronger and more alive than she had ever felt before.

"Let's go!" He let go of her hand and headed up the hill.

#

They all came over the crest of the mountain together as a group. They were ready for whatever was waiting for them. Whisper's fear was gone and her body tingled with anticipation. She had the crystal in her hand in case the Scarecrow tried to freeze her and she had her mind ready for whatever fear the Darkman would try to throw at her. She was prepared for anything and held her head up proudly.

There was nothing there. Whisper saw some trees and rocks and a few piles of snow here and there but, other than that, nothing. The sun decided to hide behind a cloud causing a darkness to fall over everything. Could it be that the crows were wrong? That wasn't likely, they were right about everything so far. Whisper looked to Cael and noticed something strange about his face. He looked confused and she detected a bit of fear in his eyes.

"No!" she said as she reached out with her mind and entered his thoughts.

'Get out of here! You have no control over this mind, he

is mine!' Whisper fought the Darkman as if he were standing right in front of her. It was a mental battle that no one outside could see but one that she knew she had to win. She threw her thoughts into Cael's head and tried to bring him back.

'Don't listen to him Cael! Focus on me. You are stronger than he is and can keep him away. Just think about me!'

Cael started to focus on Whisper, turning his eyes in her direction. She kept trying to block out the Darkman and started to feel it working. The Darkman was getting weaker. Cael's eyes cleared and he smiled at Whisper and she knew he had control of his mind again.

"Thanks," he said. This all happened in a matter of minutes and still Whisper saw no one.

"Are you all right?" Alannis asked, keeping her eyes on the field in front of them.

"Yeah, Whisper dove in and blocked that SOB," Cael said. "But where is he? Where are any of them?" It was a question they all wanted an answer to.

"Look out!!" cried Marcus and then he threw his crystal in front of Alannis. The Scarecrow came out from behind a rock and tried to freeze her.

"They're sending the Scarecrow and the Darkman out first," he said. "It's because they are expendable. Dougall wants to know what kind of damage can be done before he has to fight." Just then, Miles ran around to face Cael and put his finger to his lips to keep him quiet. Marcus saw what his brother was doing and ran the other way to stand in front of Alannis, leaving Whisper in the middle, unprotected. She looked at the two of them and tried to figure out what they were doing.

The Scarecrow saw his opportunity to catch Whisper and started to walk her way. Miles held up his crystal and urged Cael to do the same. Alannis handed hers to Marcus and they waited until the Scarecrow held his gaze long enough to send a beam of ice at Whisper. All of a sudden they all threw their crystals at the same time, creating a semi circle of fire around the tall thin man. There was so much heat from the flames that his ice immediately turned to water. He tried to back away but it was too late. Miles and Marcus came at him from either side so quickly that nobody saw them until they were right at the Scarecrow's feet. While the flames were still hot and the Scarecrow could only produce water, they jumped him. Whisper could barely see through the wall of fire but she could hear blows landing, bones cracking and flesh being torn. She prayed the two odd men she had come to admire were okay.

There was hardly any time to recover from the attack of the Scarecrow when an evil laughter arose from the trees to their right, next to where Alannis was standing. As she turned, a dark figure sprang out at her, but she was quicker. She jumped in the air and let the Darkman pass underneath her. He forced his body to stop and looked back at her, anger spreading across his face.

"Not very accurate are you, Darkman?" She smiled at him tauntingly. He howled with rage and came at her again. This time she jumped up and to the left, propelling herself sideways and came down with a fierce kick to the back of his head. He went down in shock and anger, cursing loudly. Nobody had ever done that to him before. Alannis stood there, waiting for him to get back up. She looked so elegant in her long flowing white robe and her beautiful white hair and at that moment Whisper saw the strength that was inside her and knew that the Darkman didn't stand a chance. Alannis winked at her and smiled then turned on the Darkman as he tried to get up from the ground.

With both the Scarecrow and the Darkman being taken care of, Cael and Whisper stepped forward in search of Dougall and the Axeman. They knew the two powerful men would be theirs to fight alone. Whisper kept close to Cael and looked everywhere but could not see where they were. Then the sun emerged from behind the clouds and out of the corner of her eye, Whisper caught a gleam of metal. It was too late. The Axeman came out of nowhere and brought his fist down hard on Cael's back. She started towards him but something jumped in front of her, blocking her way.

"Not today, Thadeus. Today you are mine!" It was Aria!

'Where the hell did she come from,' Whisper asked herself, 'and what was she doing here?'

"Aria?" The Axeman stopped his assault on Cael and stared at the woman in front of him. "What are you doing here?" He stood up and a look of calm came over his face.

"Thadeus, you may have thrown away *your* life. But you

will not do the same to Cael." She reached her hand out and an invisible force pushed the Axeman back. Cael started to come to and Whisper rushed to his side. He shook his head to clear away the fogginess from the blow. He looked up and saw Aria with her hand outstretched and keeping the Axeman away from them.

"Who is that!?" he asked.

"That's Aria," Whisper told him while she helped him up, "my best friend."

"I know her!" he said, with a look of surprise on his face. "She's been coming to me as a vision ever since I was a little boy. I thought she was a ghost. She's saved my life a few times." Whisper looked from Cael to Aria, wondering how much more about her friend she didn't know about.

"Aria," said the Axeman, "don't do this. You know it doesn't have to be this way."

"Yes, it does!" Aria's eyes started to fill with tears. "You left me! You chose the wrong side!"

"No, it is you that left me," he pleaded with her. "I wanted to be with you. You were supposed to heal me!"

"And you were supposed to be Gwynn's warrior!! Faithful to only him!!" she yelled. "But I saw your dark side. I knew you would turn on us. My love couldn't keep you..." She was crying now and her hold on him was starting to weaken.

"I begged you to come with me. Dougall would have let you and we could have been together forever." He felt his opportunity approaching and steadied himself for it.

"No, Thadeus. Dougall will never let you live forever," she said. "Don't you see? He's using you and won't hesitate to get rid of you once he sees how powerful you can be." She was exhausted now and her grip on Thadeus had almost completely disappeared. It was the moment he was waiting for and he jumped in the air and came down with his axe slicing sideways in the air. It all happened so fast and yet, at the same time, it felt like time stood still. Whisper saw the axe come through the air and started towards the two of them.

"Noooo!!" she screamed as Aria fell to the ground, blood flowing from the wound in her chest that the axe had made. Whisper threw her hand up, her palm facing the Axeman and thrust every bit of energy she could gather at him. A blinding, bright light came out of her hand and rushed towards the man standing in front of her. His face contorted in fear and he dropped the axe and tried to turn and run. But it was too late, Whisper's light hit him like a steel rod in his chest and she pinned him to an invisible wall. His back arched, his arms fell limp at his sides, his body totally under her control. She knew she had him beat and lifted her hand up. Slowly, his body rose up in the air and he turned his face to Whisper. He looked into her eyes and her mind picked up his thoughts.

'Thank you,' was all she heard and then his body exploded into a million pieces.

#

Dougall watched the foolish woman come down from the

tree and try to stop his Axeman from capturing his victims. Then he laughed as she fell to the ground, but then Whisper jumped to her rescue leaving Cael all alone…leaving Cael all alone!!! This was his opportunity! He may lose one warrior but he would claim another! In a flash he was across the field and had Cael in his arms. Just one more leap and they would be gone from this place.

Cael didn't know what hit him at first, and then he felt himself flying through the air. He looked up and saw the face of a man. A man that looked young and boyish, not really evil at all. Could this be Dougall? The man that controlled all the evil that was in the Universe. Could this really be him? He looked at the hands that were grasping him around his waist, trying to carry him away. He reached his free hand over and tried to break the hold. When his flesh touched Dougall's flesh he felt the true essence of the being holding him. He was pure evil and Cael felt a surge of energy rise up within him. He struggled and broke free of Dougall's grasp and then he fell, rolling on the ground and springing to his feet to take a defensive posture taught to him by Taro. Dougall slowly floated down from the sky and stared at him.

"Come now, let's not make this difficult," he said with an air of arrogance.

"I will *not* go with you," Cael said, preparing himself for an attack.

"Why not?" Dougall whined like a spoiled child.

"Together we can rule the Universe. You can even keep your little tramp if you want," he said pointing over towards Whisper.

"She is not a tramp!" Cael yelled with anger.

"Whatever you say," he said. "You both can come nonetheless."

"I will never fight for you and I will never come with you," Cael said.

"Then you will die!!" Dougall said, as a sinister look appeared on his face and he started to come at Cael. He held his hands high above his head and then flicked his fingers at him. Bolts of a blue electric light came streaming out and Cael dove to the ground and rolled back and forth, avoiding each strand of deadly light. Dougall's frustration at missing his victim ignited his anger and he began to throw his arms about carelessly, hitting trees and boulders with every misguided twitch of a finger. Cael jumped back to his feet and waited for the evil man to get closer. Dougall saw that Cael was much too quick for his attack and decided to try a different approach.

As Cael waited patiently for his opportunity to spring, Dougall rose up in the air and hovered just above his head. Cael looked up and wondered what kind of attack he could possibly launch from there. Then Dougall began to spin himself faster and faster and Cael could feel himself being sucked up into some sort of vortex. He got higher and higher until he was face to face with Dougall. He saw the man grin an evil grin and then he felt the pain of a solid blow to his stomach. Dougall roared with laughter

324

as Cael fell to the ground, hunched over and grabbing his stomach. Dougall came down from above and stood over him.

"We will fight hand to hand now," he said.

'Yeah, now that you've already knocked me down, you coward!' thought Cael.

Dougall lifted his leg and kicked Cael hard. He could feel his ribs break and rolled to his back, his face wincing in pain. Then Dougall came down hard with his knee to his groin and Cael got up on all fours and screamed in agony.

'This is it,' he thought, 'this is how I'm going to die and I didn't even get in a good punch. What kind of warrior am I?' He started to think of Whisper and how disappointed she would be in him for giving up so easily. He remembered what she looked like when she came to him in his dream, the concern on her face when he met her by the portal, or the glances she gave him in the cave and he remembered the feel of her hand while they ran. Then something strange started to overcome him, memories filled his mind that were not of this life. He saw himself with Whisper in places he knew he had never been and yet they were there, together, in battle, fighting side by side. He saw himself holding her tightly and kissing her and knowing that he never wanted to let her go. He knew, then, who he was and that Whisper had always been with him, had always guided him through his battles. She was part of him and he would not fail her now.

Dougall lifted his foot again, this time aiming for Cael's

325

head. Cael waited and when the foot was about to make contact, he reached up and grabbed it and twisted it with all his strength. Dougall fell to the ground hard; landing on his back then rolled over onto his stomach and tried to get up. Cael jumped on top of him and wrapped his arms around his neck. He pulled Dougall's head back with one hand and squeezed hard with the other, stopping the breath that was trying desperately to get out. Dougall was panicking now and rose to his feet with Cael clinging to his back. He spun around in circles trying to dislodge him but the boy hung on tight. He backed up towards a rock and slammed himself into it and Cael let out a gasp of air as he released his grip.

Dougall turned to face his opponent, out of breath and rubbing his neck. The boyish face was gone, replaced by a grotesque image of sweat and anger and he rushed at the warrior. Cael welcomed the attack and just as he was about to get tackled to the ground he grabbed his arm and twisted it backwards, flipping Dougall in the air and smashing the bones in his arm at the same time. Once he was on the ground, Cael jumped on top and brought his fist back ready to punch. Dougall put up his good arm to defend himself.

"Please don't!" he pleaded. "Don't touch my face!" Cael laughed.

Vanity, it's everywhere lately,' he thought, as he brought his fist down hard into Dougall's face. His nose exploded in pain, the bone shattering, then darkness came and Dougall was out cold. Cael got up off of his opponent, knowing that he wouldn't be going anywhere for awhile. He looked around the field to see what damage had been done.

#

The twins were straightening out their suits and congratulating themselves on a job well done. The Scarecrow lay at their feet all twisted and broken. It may have taken the two of them, but there would be no more ice coming from the man again.

Alannis was just finishing her battle with the Darkman. He never had a chance, really, with her experience and knowledge; the fight was strictly one-sided. She was not a cruel woman and so she didn't let the Darkman suffer. When the end came, it came quickly as she twisted his neck and heard the snap that indicated his life had come to an end. Then Cael's eyes sought out the Axeman.

Chapter 26

Whisper disposed of the Axeman swiftly but he was not her main concern. She knew Dougall was battling with Cael and she knew, somehow, that Cael would be okay. Her thoughts were focused on Aria. After the Axeman exploded, she ran back to her friend lying on the ground. Her wound was bleeding so much.

"Aria?" she said as she grabbed her friend's hand and held it. Aria opened her eyes and turned her head towards Whisper.

"Whisper, are you okay?" Still, her concern was for Whisper.

"Aria, why did you come?" Whisper looked at the weakness in Aria's eyes and felt tears sneaking down her face.

"I had to...I...had unfinished business," Aria said as she coughed.

"I heard you. Why didn't you tell me that you were his Soul-healer?" Aria turned her head from Whisper in shame.

"Because, I failed!" she cried out. "He was one of Gwynn's warriors and my job was to bring him back but I failed."

"No," Whisper said, "you did your job. It was he that chose to go to Dougall, there was nothing you could have done about it." Aria turned back to her.

"I think…I know that now," she said, and then a smile came across her face. "I loved him, you know." Whisper squeezed her hand and held it to her face, tears flowing freely down her cheeks now.

"I know," Whisper said. They were so much alike and she never realized it until now.

"Just like you love Cael." Whisper sobbed at her words as she looked at her friend's dying face. "Thadeus didn't love me back but Cael loves you. I have seen it and now I can feel it."

"Aria…" Whisper wanted to help her, make her pain go away.

"I've been reading your mind since you got to the fortress. Don't deny your love for him." She was starting to speak so quietly now, Whisper could barely hear her.

"But, it's wrong to love him; I'm his Soul-healer," Whisper said, finally able to confide in someone.

"No…it's not," she cried out and Whisper brushed back her friend's hair and tried to calm her. "Look at Alannis and Taro. She was once his Soul-healer."

"What…?" Whisper looked at her, confused. The thought had never occurred to her that Alannis was Taro's Soul-healer. "You mean…?"

"Yes." Aria started to cough uncontrollably and Whisper knew it wouldn't be long now.

"Aria, please don't talk, save your strength." She stroked

her forehead. "We'll take you through the portal to Atlantis. They have crystals that can heal you there."

"It's okay, I know my fate." Her eyes closed and Whisper felt panic fill her body.

"Aria!!??" Aria opened her eyes and smiled.

"You and Cael were meant to be together from the beginning," she whispered.

"How do you know this?" asked Whisper.

"Because you have saved him many times before. It's why his soul keeps calling for you. You're meant to be joined together and nothing can tear you apart." Her body began to shake and Whisper held on tightly to her hand. The others started to gather around them now and Whisper looked up to them, seeking their help with her eyes.

"Can we take her to Atlantis?" Whisper pleaded with Alannis. The Atlantean shook her head no and Whisper felt deep despair take hold of her.

"Whisper…?" She leaned forward so she could hear Aria's words. "I wish you could remember how much you were my best friend." She smiled and Whisper's heart ached to remember anything of their life together. Aria turned her eyes to the sky above and released her last breath. Whisper lifted Aria's head and cradled it in her arms, crying as she had never cried before.

After what seemed an eternity, Cael put his hand on Whisper's shoulder and she turned to him. His face showed compassion and love and she accepted his hand to pull her up. He took her in his arms, despite his broken ribs, and she let him hold her tight. She was not afraid of her feelings for him anymore and she buried her face in his chest and cried.

The others stood guard over Dougall, who was still knocked out, and debated on what to do with him. Cael and Whisper walked over to join the conversation. It seemed half of them wanted to kill him right then and there while the other half wanted to keep him prisoner, locked away forever, with no chance of escape. They stood there, arguing loudly, for what seemed a very long time. None of them noticed Dougall's eyes start to flutter open and his body start to adjust itself.

"What is to become of Dougall is not for you to decide." The voice came from behind them and they jumped at the sound of it. When they turned to it, they were almost blinded by the bright light that surrounded the figure of a man standing close to where Aria's body was. He was tall and handsome and looked very kind. His hair was golden brown and his eyes were the color of the sky. His face was smooth and soft and he smiled at them warmly. He wore a simple outfit, blue jeans and a white sweater.

"Gwynn?" Cael took a step forward.

"Ah, my mighty warrior, it is so good to see you again." He reached out his hand in welcome. Cael took it and fell into an embrace with his creator.

"Why are you here?" asked Cael. "We've already won the battle."

"I know," Gwynn said. "I have been watching. You are all very good fighters." He nodded his head in acknowledgement of their skills. "I am proud to have you on my side."

"Thanks." They all kind of mumbled it together. They were a little shocked that he was standing there, in front of them.

"I came to clean up," he said, looking around at the destruction of Dougall and his men. "I see I have a lot to do."

"But what will you do with them?" Whisper asked.

"Well, those two gentlemen over there," he pointed to where the bodies of the Scarecrow and the Darkman lay, "can be put in a special place where their souls can be washed clean of my brother's evil influences." He reached out his hands and the two bodies rose in the air. They turned into a bright light then suddenly vanished into thin air. They all looked on in awe.

"I'm afraid there is no hope for Thadeus," he looked over to Whisper, "Whisper, you are a powerful Soul-healer, the best I have ever seen." Her face turned red and Cael looked at her and smiled proudly.

"As for Dougall…"

"Yes, brother, what are your plans for me?" Nobody even heard him get up but there he stood, nursing his broken arm.

"I think I will send you back home where you belong and block your passage to this planet," Gwynn said.

"*You*, block me!" Dougall laughed at this. "Never in a million years."

"Yes, that sounds about right," Gwynn said as he raised

his arms again, "a million years before you can come back here." Dougall's smile faded as he realized Gwynn was quite serious.

"No, don't do…." Before he could get the last bit out he was gone. Everyone looked at each other surprised and relieved. Whisper smiled and turned to Gwynn to thank him.

"Where is Aria?" she asked as she noticed her friend's body was no longer lying on the ground.

"She will come with me," Gwynn said, very sober now.

"But I thought that if a Soul-healer died here they were gone for good?" she asked.

"Yes, they are gone from your realm, but they can live with me in mine," he said. "I have sent her to a place where she will never feel pain again. She has been a brave warrior and I will reward her for that. Take solace in the fact that she will never want for anything again." Whisper felt tears come to her eyes again but, this time, they were tears of happiness.

"Thank you," she said to him and he nodded to her.

"Cael, you must come with me." He put his arm around Cael and the two of them walked away from the group. Whisper wondered what they were talking about and waited impatiently for them to come back. When they did, Cael came over to her and stood by her side. She couldn't read the expression on his face and he was trying hard not to look at her directly. He was swinging his arms back and forth, testing his ribs, obviously healed by Gwynn's touch.

"Now, I have one more question to ask you?" Everyone looked at him, waiting to hear his question. "Do you still want to use the portal to Atlantis or shall I return you all to Chrystalline right now?"

"Speaking on behalf of everyone here," Alannis said, "I think we would all like to go back to Chrystalline as soon as possible." With that, Gwynn waved his arms and the top of the mountain shaped like a pyramid disappeared.

Chapter 27

Within the blink of an eye they all arrived in the restaurant above the fortress. Cael looked around in shock, having never travelled like that before. Whisper took his hand, trying to reassure him there was nothing to be afraid of. Still, he checked to see if all his parts were still there. Whisper laughed at him and he looked at her angrily. She hurt his feelings with her laughter and apologized for her insensitivity.

The restaurant still held the same buzz of activity it did on the first day that Aria brought Whisper there for lunch. That was the day Whisper found out who she was. She remembered the look on Aria's face as she joked about having to bring her through her awakening *again*. Well, she wouldn't have to reawaken Whisper anymore. She closed her eyes to fight back tears that were starting in the corner of her eyes. Cael sensed Whisper's sadness and put his hand in hers and squeezed it. She looked at him and saw how concerned he was. She smiled, feeling a bit better.

"Why don't you tell me where I am?" he asked, trying to get her mind on something else.

"Okay," she said, "this is a restaurant."

"Yeah, I kind of gathered that. Why would Gwynn send us here?" he asked, looking around at the different dining rooms that branched off the main hallway. "Do we get a free dinner or something?"

"No," Whisper laughed, "come on; wait 'til you see what lies beneath this place!"

"I'll take over from here, if you don't mind." Marcus jumped to the front of the line, happy to be back on familiar ground. They let him take the lead and followed him down the stairs. When they got to the door guarded by Kisho, Cael let out a long whistle.

"Wow!" he said, looking down the long, stone hallway. "This is amazing!"

"Yeah, I thought so too when I first saw it," Whisper said, excited by Cael's enthusiasm. Kisho was happy to see them back safely.

"Y-you're back!" he said, as he started hugging everyone. "What happened? Tell me everything!"

"We will!" exclaimed Alannis. "But first, let's get everyone together. I only want to tell this story once."

"What about the door?" Kisho asked, not wanting to abandon his post.

"Don't worry; it should be okay for now," Alannis reassured him. "Are they all in the lounge?"

"Everyone, except Aria," he said. "I think she's still down in her room. Should I go get her?"

"No!" Whisper said abruptly, and then realized how rude she sounded. "That'll be fine, just leave it." He looked at her questioningly then shrugged and they all headed for the lounge.

When they got there, Kisho pulled the door open for them. Whisper could just see a little of the room from over his shoulder. Cael couldn't see anything because he was positioned directly behind the tall guard. Jiro and Taro were talking with Astra and Gelraen who, amazingly enough, were not reading any books. The two gnomes were also sitting there, quietly listening to the conversation.

"Look who I found!" Kisho said with a huge smile on his face. Everyone at the table looked up at the returning group and immediately got to their feet.

"It's about time you guys came back!" Taro said as he started towards them, and then his tone turned serious. He looked into Alannis' face. "I'm so glad you made it back safely." She smiled back at him appreciatively, dreading the moment she would have to tell everyone about Aria. "Now, where is my warrior, also safe, I presume?"

Cael turned to Whisper and raised an eyebrow, could it be? She smiled and nodded, then moved aside so he could come out from behind Kisho's back. When he saw his old friend standing before him he was consumed with joyful disbelief.

"Taro!?!" He couldn't believe his eyes. It was him, his master, with no bullet holes, no blood, nothing. "I don't believe it! How are you...? Why did you...? Where did you...? What....?" He couldn't talk; no words could ever express what he was feeling.

"I told you, brother, you can understand him way better than I ever could." Jiro came forward then and clapped Taro on the back. That was it!! Cael could not believe that both of his teachers were standing here in front of him.

"Jiro! You too?" Then a thought occurred to him and he turned and looked back at the rest of them. "Wait a minute, am I dead? Is this heaven?" They all laughed at this.

"No, Cael," Whisper said, "this is the Chrystalline dimension; my home. Let me introduce you to Alannis' husband." She pointed to Taro and Cael was shocked, yet again, as he looked from Alannis to Taro.

"You're married?!" he asked his friend as he gave him a big hug. "Man, you sure know how to keep secrets from me!" He looked at Taro suspiciously. "I have a few questions for you, my friend, and I would appreciate some honest answers. First, how the hell did you survive? Second, when did you get married? And, third, why didn't you tell me Jiro was your brother?" Taro looked at his student and figured he did owe the boy some sort of explanation.

"Okay, let's see," he said, "first, Gwynn, second, a long time ago and third, because." Cael tilted his head, waiting, and then started to protest for more information. Taro held up his hand to stop him. "Those are my answers; the details can come after you tell us everything that happened today. We've all been sitting here waiting patiently for your return." Alannis came to her husband's side and kissed him, she was glad to be back with him.

"Didn't Astra and Gelraen tell you what would happen?" She smiled and winked at the two Mirai women.

"We knew that your fate had not yet been decided and so kept silent," Astra said happily.

"I see," said Alannis. "Then I suppose we should all sit down and we'll tell you what happened."

"That's what I just said," laughed Taro. He squeezed his wife around her waist and kissed her once again. Their display of affection was starting to annoy the twins.

"All right, all right," said Marcus, stepping in between them and waving his hands, "let's get some more chairs and we'll get on with our story." They all headed to the big round table in the center of the room.

"First things first," announced Alannis, "I need a coffee!" They laughed as she headed to the back of the room to satisfy her addiction.

Once everyone was seated and Alannis had her precious coffee, Whisper sat back and let the others tell the tale. Cael sat back with her. Having just met everyone, he was more interested in watching the way they all interacted than contributing to the conversation. As the day's events were retold, everyone listened intently. They applauded the twins for their fine work with the Scarecrow and Taro seemed fascinated with the fact that Alannis disposed of the Darkman so easily.

"It was nothing, really," she said. "He was so arrogant

and didn't believe he could be defeated. He worked off the fear of others and when he saw that I had no fear of him and was stronger than him; well let's just say his death came quick."

"But, still," said Taro, "his fighting skills have been renowned throughout the Earth dimension and many people have lived in fear of him for so long. I'm very proud of your victory." Alannis actually blushed at her husband's praise.

The discussion went on and Whisper listened to them talk about the woods and the cave. They talked about Bayha and his sad execution and how hard the climb up the mountain was. They raved about how the owls and crows helped spy on Dougall and his men. The gnomes nodded their approval that Miles had the foresight to ask for their help. Finally, the part Whisper was dreading came up. They wanted to know about the Axeman which brought the conversation to Aria and the room fell silent for a few minutes. Painfully, Alannis related the way that she died and the bravery she showed. Silence filled the room as they remembered Aria and her heroic ending.

"I can't believe she still felt the guilt for Thadeus' betrayal," said Jiro, looking down into his cup and shaking his head.

"She carried around a lot that we didn't know," said Alannis. "It's a shame she felt she could not come to any of us and talk about it."

"I think she was waiting for me," Whisper said, talking for the first time since they got back. Everyone turned to her and waited for her to say more.

"What do you mean?" Alannis asked.

"Well, I think she was waiting for me to get my memory back, to reignite our friendship, then she could share everything she was feeling with me like old times," she said. "But that didn't happen." She looked at the others with the pain of her friend's death still on her face. "Could someone please tell me about Aria and Thadeus? I'm afraid I still don't remember anything." Everyone looked at each other uncomfortably and then Alannis finally cleared her throat and started.

"Aria was, like you and I, a Soul-healer. She was a good one too and saved many souls before she was pulled by Thadeus. It happened over two thousand years ago in the Earth dimension. Thadeus was a soldier in the Roman army and ran into trouble with their ruler, Caesar. Because he was really a hidden warrior of Gwynn, his fighting skills were unparalleled and Caesar recognized this and was impressed. He tested Thadeus time and again, sending him to the hardest battles and pitting him against the enemy's strongest fighters and every time, Thadeus would win. Satisfied with his abilities, Caesar invited him to his palace and offered him a job. He wanted the young warrior to play the role of assassin, but not just any assassin. He was to disguise himself and enter the cities that Caesar wanted to conquer. Once he was there, he was to visit their governors and the commanders of their armies and kill them and their entire families, including their wives and children, making it easier for Caesar's armies.

"Thadeus refused, it was against the principles that Gwynn had instilled in his warriors when they were created. But Caesar was insistent. He gave Thadeus everything he wanted; a house, jewels, money and the promise of any woman that caught his eye. Still, Thadeus held strong. Caesar became frustrated and tried another tactic. He started to torture Thadeus' family, killing his mother and imprisoning his father. Finally, Thadeus gave in and took the job. He was given a weapon to carry out his diabolical deeds, one that made him well known amongst his enemies."

"The axe?" Whisper offered.

"Yes, that's right. He had the reputation of being quite lethal with it. In fact, it was rumoured that he could kill three people with just one swipe of his axe. That's how he got the name 'Axeman'. He did his job well and started to enjoy the riches that Caesar bestowed upon him and, slowly, his principles started to fade away. Then, one day, he was sent to a home of a family he didn't know. This was nothing new, but he didn't expect the man of the house to be so kind and generous.

"This man was a governor who was blind from birth, an ailment that would have left most men jobless and beggars in the street. But the man refused to accept his fate and spent his whole life working hard, trying to make his life count. He went to school and studied, eventually becoming a governor but he never forgot where he came from. The poor and the sick became his passion and he did everything he could to help them. He had a beautiful wife and two small girls and Thadeus' heart, which had grown cold since his employ with Caesar, started to soften when he met him. He hesitated to kill him.

"Caesar was livid and threatened to take everything away from Thadeus if he didn't execute the man and his family. Thadeus sank into an inner battle with his soul that finally pulled Aria to him. Her presence became a breath of fresh air for him and slowly the two of them fell in love with each other. Ignoring the warnings of everyone here, Aria moved to the Earth dimension so she could be with the man she loved. They were happy together and Aria kept up her training while she was there. Caesar, however, was furious.

"He plotted to kill Aria so he could get his executioner back. Thadeus got word of this plot so he took Aria and fled to the countryside. Caesar was relentless and eventually cornered them on a farm outside of Rome. He tied up Thadeus and tortured Aria. He wanted to kill her slowly so Thadeus would understand that deserting his post meant consequences. Aria didn't fight back for fear that they would kill Thadeus if she did. What Caesar didn't count on, however, was you, Whisper."

"Me?" Whisper was surprised to hear her name. What could she have done to help Aria?

"Yes," Alannis continued, "all this time you were keeping an eye on your best friend, ready to help her if you had to. Your opportunity came when Caesar's men tied Aria up and started beating her. You couldn't stand it anymore and went to the Earth dimension and brought Aria back here. She was badly injured and spent many months recovering."

"I don't remember anything," Whisper said quietly.

"Her absence sent Thadeus into turmoil," Alannis continued. "He called for Aria again and again but she never came. He was lost and empty and agreed to return to Caesars employ. His despair, however, was heard by another. Dougall had been searching for Gwynn's warriors throughout time and when he heard about Thadeus he raced to the Earth dimension. It was easy to convince Caesar's assassin to come work with him. He offered just as many riches as Caesar did plus much more. He could give him powers beyond his imagination and a promise to live forever and help rule the Universe as Dougall's right hand man. Thadeus was happy to agree and go with Dougall, except for one thing.

"At around the time that Dougall was courting Thadeus, Aria recovered from her injuries. She was anxious to return to the man she loved, to get back what she lost. When she returned, however, she discovered that Dougall's influence was strong. She began to think that she might not be able to convince Thadeus to stay with her. Their love had faded during her absence. Aria knew the rules of being a Soul-healer; she could not force him to choose her over Dougall. He had to make up his own mind.

"Thadeus wanted it all. He asked Dougall if Aria could come with him and Dougall agreed. But Aria would never work for Dougall even if it meant losing Thadeus. Thadeus made up his mind; he would leave with Dougall. The offer was too good to turn down. He knew he would lose Aria but he didn't care anymore. He turned his back on his warrior side and joined Dougall, taking his axe, the only part of his life on this planet, with him." Whisper couldn't imagine a warrior turning his back on Gwynn. She looked at Cael and silently thanked him for being faithful to Gwynn.

"Aria was devastated," Alannis said. "Not only did she fail to save a soul, she lost her only love in the process. Her heart was broken and when she came back from the Forest of Dreams it was still in ruins. She could not be consoled, not even by you, her dearest friend. It was decided that she would never have to save a soul again. It would be too much to ask of her and it would totally destroy her if she ever failed again. We couldn't take that chance. She became a teacher and a watcher. She nursed the Soul-healers that were coming close to their awakenings and she taught them how to use their new found abilities. She immersed herself into her new role and it helped ease the pain of losing Thadeus, at least we thought it did."

"I guess, with my awakening she was hoping to resume our friendship but I came through too fast and couldn't remember anything about her." Cael squeezed her hand, knowing how horrible she felt. "I guess when she heard that the Axeman was in the forest, she saw her chance to make up for her past mistakes." She sighed as she felt frustrated by the whole thing. "I just wish she would have realized sooner that it was not her fault

345

that Thadeus went with Dougall. It was his decision alone. He knew what he did was wrong but he couldn't help himself. Our souls are so complicated, more than Dougall or Gwynn ever wanted when they made us."

"How right you are young Whisper," said Jiro. They continued talking for a while and then Marcus piped up and declared that he was starving. They all agreed and decided that they would go up to the restaurant and order everything on the menu. When everyone got up to leave Cael put his hand on Whisper's arm and spoke quietly to her.

"Is there somewhere we can go to talk?" he asked.

"Y-yes, we can…" she started. Alannis leaned over and placed something in her hand.

"Take this and take your time." She smiled and walked out with the others. Whisper looked in her hand and saw the wooden key to the training room.

Chapter 28

Whisper opened the door to the room that she practiced her fighting skills in not so long ago. It looked like a forest then; Jiro made it feel so real. Now when they walked inside, however, it looked like an old smelly gym.

'Why would Alannis give me the key to this room?' she thought. 'Didn't she say the Celestial Room was her favourite?'

"This is nice," said Cael, sarcastically. "It makes me feel like I should go and get Mr. Yam…Taro to come and give me a judo lesson."

"It didn't look like this when I was here before," said Whisper. Cael looked at her like she was joking. "Honestly, it had trees and grass and birds were flying around. It was really pretty…" Then she remembered what Jiro had said:

"The eyes can take all the logic from your brain and convince you something is one thing when it is really something else." She had to take the logic away from their brains and convince them that this room was really something else. She closed her eyes and concentrated. Within minutes the room transformed. It was now the place where the little stick houses sat in the woods. Cael looked around, not wanting to believe what he was seeing.

"Did we go back to Earth?" he asked.

"No, I just made this place look a little better, that's all."

347

"How'd you do that?"

"Magic," she laughed, "do you like it?"

"Yeah, but why did you pick this place?" He was now wandering in and out of the few trees, picking up loose sticks and throwing them in the pond.

"I didn't," she said, following behind him. "I just searched your memory for a place that made *you* happy and this came up."

"You did all this for me?" He turned and faced her now. Suddenly she was embarrassed. Maybe she was being too presumptuous. She looked down at her hands and let her hair fall over her face to hide her eyes.

"Yes," she whispered.

"It's great, thank you." He picked up another stick and turned it over in his hands.

"How long have you been a Soul-healer?" he asked as he tossed the stick high up in a tree, trying to hit a pinecone. A bird chattered noisily at being disturbed and then flew away.

"Forever, I guess," she said, putting her hands in her pockets and leaning against a tree.

"You guess? You mean you don't know?"

"Well, no." She was starting to feel like he was mocking her. "How long have you been a warrior?"

"Touché! Very clever." He laughed and cocked his head sideways. He looked very appealing like this. "Why do you look so annoyed when you're with me?"

"Annoyed? You think I look annoyed?" She couldn't believe he would think that. Annoyed was the last thing she felt.

"Yeah, you're always looking away, fidgeting with your hands." She tried to laugh his accusations away. "Did that kiss really offend you? I'm sorry if it did. It was a dream and I was caught up in the moment. I thought you liked it, but maybe I was wrong. I mean, you've been trying to avoid me ever since and you seem angry with me. If that's the case just tell me and I'll never mention it again." He looked at her with intense blue eyes.

'Oh, how can I tell him that I'm petrified by how he makes me feel inside?' she asked herself. 'That I've never been kissed like that before and I'm scared of where it will go.'

"No, I'm not annoyed," she told him. "I was just trying to focus on the mission."

"The mission," he paused, "is that what I am to you?"

"N-no, I mean, you were but that's not the only reason I helped you."

'I'm such an idiot,' she chastised herself. 'I don't even make sense when I talk!'

"It isn't?" He came over to the tree she was leaning on and stood next to her. He reached over and started to peel away some of the bark. He was so close to her that she could hear his heart beat and she felt herself tremble inside. "Why else did you help me?"

"Tell me something," she said, scooting away from the tree and avoiding his question. He turned to her and smiled.

349

"What?"

"Why did you tell me we had a lot of catching up to do?"

"Oh, that. Just words said in the anticipation of impending doom." He brushed it off with a shrug of his shoulders.

"Strange words to say to a person you just met."

"I suppose." He walked over to her again. "When you said you can't remember anything did you really mean it?"

"Yes I did. Why do you ask?" she looked at him and this time it was he who trembled inside.

"Just wondering. I've always found amnesia fascinating. How can a mind forget everything that has ever happened to them? I don't get it. Surely something would come along to trigger some kind of memory; a sound, a smell or perhaps even a touch." He looked away and she could tell he was trying to tell her something.

"No, so far nothing has done that for me." She walked over to a huge boulder and leaned against it.

"Tell me, when we were climbing that mountain did you notice the moss growing on the side of the rock?" he asked, coming to face her again.

"Moss? No, I can't say I did." She looked at him, confused by his question.

"I did, it was a beautiful deep green and so soft to the touch." He reached out and delicately let his finger slide along Whisper's arm. Her whole body froze and she quickly bent her head down so her hair would cover her face and he wouldn't see her blush.

"Why do you do that?" he asked, reaching up and pushing her hair back off her face.

"I-I don't know." She felt her breath caught in her chest and was afraid if she didn't let it out she would faint.

"You shouldn't hide. You're so beautiful and I want to look at you." He trailed his fingers across her forehead and down the side of her face.

"I-I don't like people to see me, I like to hide." She looked into his eyes like a scared little girl. If he only knew how his touch made her feel.

"Well, you don't have to hide around me." He stood up straight again. "Now, about this moss…?"

"Yes?" She shook her head, the question bringing her out of the trance he had put her in.

"Well, when we were on that mountain and I saw that moss and I knew we would be fighting soon, a memory came back to me." She looked at him, totally confused by what he was trying to say.

"Yes?" she urged him on.

"A memory of you and me." He focused his eyes back on Whisper.

"Really?" She didn't know what he was talking about.

"Yes, we were preparing for another fight in another time and we were together." Her eyebrows came together as she looked at him questioningly. He cocked his head and let his eyes study her reaction to his next statement. "I don't just mean side by side in battle together, I mean together, as lovers."

'WHAT?' she screamed to herself. 'What was he talking about, lovers?' Her head automatically fell forward, her hair falling over her face once again. He reached over and put his hand under her chin and lifted her head up to look in her eyes.

"I told you, you shouldn't do that." He smiled and she took a big gulp of nothing and smiled back.

"I-I'm sorry." she apologized and bit her lower lip.

"You don't have this memory?" he asked again, still holding up her chin.

"No." she whispered.

"That's too bad because if you did you would remember how much I love you!" He leaned in closer and pressed his lips to hers. She could feel his arms slide around her waist and pull her body into his. She reached up and ran her hands across the back of his neck. His heart was beating fast and she could feel *his* body tremble now. She felt an intense heat in her stomach and knew that everything that was happening was meant to be. She was a part of him and he was a part of her. It was much better than the kiss they had shared in the dream walk. She held nothing back now. She knew that it wasn't wrong to love him and that nobody would be angry about it. They held their kiss for what seemed like an eternity and when they finally parted, her eyes were still closed. He laughed and slowly her eyelids fluttered open.

"Nothing?" he softly asked.

"W-what?" She couldn't think straight yet.

"No memory of our life together?" He searched her eyes, looking for some sort of answer.

"No, I'm sorry." She wished she could remember *something*. He smiled and leaned in to kiss her again.

"Oh, well, I guess we're going to have to keep trying and maybe *something* will jolt your memory." They kissed again, this time closer and longer.

#

They were walking now, hand in hand and Whisper was completely giddy. She giggled at his every word and practically skipped up the path. He told her about growing up and how he was always picked on and she told him about her school and her friends. It was nice and they felt comfortable together. They walked around the ponds hand in hand, listening to the birds and feeling the warm sun on their faces.

"Can we sit for a bit?" she asked.

"Sure." They picked a spot just up the bank of the pond. The grass was thicker here and, more importantly, it was dry. "What do you want to talk about?"

"How'd you know I wanted to talk?"

"I can see it in your eyes." He took her hand and she moved closer to him so she could rest her head on his shoulder.

"Cael, when do you think you'll have to go back?" She

didn't want to ask him this. She didn't want to know, but it had to be brought up. Someone from the Earth dimension had never come to Chrystalline before and she knew he wouldn't be able to stay here. He was, after all, still a Flatliner and his body would age and eventually die. Whisper's would not.

"Why do you ask that?" He lifted her head up to face him.

"Because, I know you can't stay here forever and I just wanted to know how much time we would have together." she told him.

"We could have years, I'm told." He sounded like he was joking with her.

"Oh, yeah, who told you that?" she asked, trying not to be too frustrated with how lightly he was taking the situation.

"A friend." He looked over her head at the pond. "Whisper, do you want me to stay?"

"Of course!" she said, facing him.

"Then I will." He got up and started walking to the door.

"Wait! Where are you going? What do you mean?" She ran to catch up with him.

"I'm hungry aren't you?" He wasn't taking any of it seriously. She grabbed his arm and pulled him back to her.

"What do you mean, you'll stay? Why are you so casual about it?" She was starting to feel panicked. "Nobody from the Earth dimension has ever come to Chrystalline. I don't think you understand what that means."

"Didn't I tell you?" He looked at her like a mischievous child.

"Tell me what?" she asked.

"Remember, up on the mountain, when Gwynn took me aside?" She nodded; she remembered that. "He told me he didn't want us to be apart anymore so he made it possible for me to live here forever with you."

"WHAT!?!?" She couldn't believe it. "But how?"

"He said he would let me stay here as a Cross-over…" She was so happy. She had him here with her forever. She jumped into his arms and kissed him over and over again.

"Oh, Cael!" He pulled her away from him and looked her in the eye.

"…provided," There was the catch? "that I go to school with you and learn everything about this planet and all its different dimensions." She laughed out loud.

'We can go to school together and I can help him with everything. Oh, wait until I introduce him to Elsie, Odella and Nascha they'll flip,' she thought as they walked arm and arm to the door, totally lost in their own happiness.

"Hey," she said, "do you know how to dance?"

EPILOGUE

The slow drip kept a constant pace. It was a part of the background noise, a sound not even noticed until it was gone, which was unlikely to happen anytime soon. The whole place was damp and bitterly cold. The stone walls were starting to crumble under years of neglect and the floors were covered with a thick layer of dirt and muck.

Jezebel sat in her cell with her legs pulled up to her chest and her arms wrapped tightly around them. She was rocking back and forth, watching Rob sleep and wondering how he could look so peaceful in a hell hole like this. They'd been down there for a couple of weeks now but it felt much longer. Without the sun, the line between day and night was erased and the days became impossible to count. She had all the time in the world to think and try to figure out what went wrong. She was so sure the girl was somewhere in those woods but she was wrong to trust the warrior. He tricked her, she knew that now, and she had been an easy victim. If only she had worked harder on mind reading when she was younger, maybe this wouldn't have happened.

When Dougall met her in the parking lot, she knew she was in trouble. Still, she clung to the belief that he really did love her. She felt deep in her heart that she was different than all his other conquests. She was special and she would be back with him again, someday. After all, he didn't kill her; he just sent her here instead. She looked around and shook her head, a half-smile on her face. She didn't like the way he did it, though.

Bayha had always scared her. With his ugly face and his huge body that reeked of sweat and urine, he gave her nightmares. When he grabbed her to drag her and Rob off to this pit, he had taken liberty and placed his hands intimately around her waist. She wanted to vomit at the memory of it. He laughed when he locked the door to the cell and got close to her face so she could almost taste his putrid breath and vowed he'd be back to 'visit' her soon. She shivered at the thought.

There had to be something she could do before he returned. She would rather die than have him touch her again. She got up from the hard wooden bench she was sitting on and began to pace back and forth. She paused at the slot where food was passed through and looked at the two slices of mouldy bread and two cups of watered down tea. How did they expect them to survive on this garbage? She needed more than this, something with sustenance. A cockroach crawled to the plate, apparently attracted by her meal. She reached down and grabbed it between her fingers. Without thinking, she put it in her mouth and bit down hard. There was a loud crunching sound as she chewed and the bitter juice ran down her throat. All of a sudden she stopped chewing and ran to the corner and spit up the bug, retching to get every last bit out of her body. Was this what she was reduced to? Eating bugs just to survive? No, not her. She turned her head to look at Rob again and straightened out her skirt. She could not live like this nor could she wait for Dougall to come and get her. She needed to get out. She needed to get out and find that wretched girl and her boyfriend and repay them for what they did to her.

"Robbie!" She walked over to his sleeping form and swatted him on the back. He rolled over and looked at her through cloudy eyes. "Robbie, get up. We have work to do!"